Kill Will

Night Bird in Sunlight

Gordon Thompson

First published by Clan Destine Press in 2026

Clan Destine Press

PO Box 121, Bittern

Victoria, 3918 Australia

National Library of Australia Cataloguing-In-Publication data:

THOMPSON, Gordon

TITLE: KILL WILL
ISBN: 9780645002188 (paperback)
ISBN: 9781922904980 (eBook)

Cover Art by Andrea L. 'Altocello' Farley
Cover Typography by Willsin Rowe
Design & Typesetting by Clan Destine Press

www.clandestinepress.net

Kill Will

Night Bird in Sunlight

Gordon Thompson

… yesterday the bird of night did sit
Even at noon day upon the marketplace,
Hooting and shrieking.

Julius Caesar Act 1, Sc. 3

One is music, heard in the morn;
Two is a magpie, chased and torn;
Three is love, a stolen kiss;
Four is tempest, rain then bliss;
Five is death, the raven's call;
Six is a gate, narrow and tall;
Seven will hold the world in thrall.

Traditional children's rhyme

The most important Druid festival before the Great Desolation was the Equinox Festival of the Seven Stones.

This festival took place when the seven magic stones of the Druids – the so-called 'eyes of the cosmic wheel' – were brought into the world from the celestial realm.

With much singing and dancing, the Druids carried the Seven Stones from Stonehenge to Charlecote Well near Stratford.

This 'act of publick adoration' took place every fifty years and was contentious among the Druids for it also created the conditions whereby dark forces were enabled.

This is what happened in the terrible spring of 1580…

The Empty Cavern – The Lost Rituals of the Druids

Phillip Oak

Prologue

Rian, daughter of the Druid Queen Angharad, sat in the derelict barn. Rain spattered the mud floor through a hole in the roof. In shivering hands she held a small bag in which were the Seven Stones.

Rian had wanted to be one of the Carriers of the Stones for the journey to Charlecote Well.

Now she held all of them.

'WHICH STONE WILL YOU CARRY?' HER FRIEND HAD ASKED IN JANUARY.

'The tempest stone,' replied Rian proudly, chasing a snowflake.

Rian suspected that her enthusiasm for taking part in the procession was what caused her mother, the Queen, to give the task to others.

'But I will be dead the next time the festival happens!' she said. 'It only happens once every fifty years, you know?!' She stormed off.

Her father, who was a little agnostic in such matters, consoled her by saying that bringing the stones into the sublunary world was, in his opinion, an indulgence; for though the stones were tiny as river pebbles, within each was the power to consume the world. 'Let the Christians parade with their relics. A blessing on them. But I would think we were slightly above all that.'

On the morning of the procession, Rian lay in the long grass of the Plain, stretching out her arms and feeling clover and flax between her fingers. A few clouds rested on the warming air. Redstarts and meadow pipits sang and a hunting bird hovered then dropped from sight.

'And each of the Carriers,' said Rian to herself, 'must bear in their two hands, enclasped, a stone of power, held but lightly, nor pressing their will upon it, and so to Charlecote proceed…'

The temple far away shone red as the rising sun touched the painted stones. The breeze now brought the smell of incense. As the procession came closer Rian rose to join her house; but in that moment a cousin hurried close and said, 'Rian, please, can you mind the horses?'

'But that is Arun's job,' she said sharply.

'But Arun just twisted his ankle in a rabbit-hole and has gone off crying!'

'Must I?' she said. 'What about my brother?'

'The horses are uneasy, and they know thee best. I can play your drum.'

'The world has taken a set against me.'

Rian walked aside and took hold of the horses. Her favourite, Feather, was trembling, and she stroked his neck. 'Now, Feather … tchk. What is it?' The other horses pressed in around her clumsily.

It was a lucky chance, for when the terror struck, the horses shielded her.

The dark cloud that swept from nowhere over the plain was half smoke, half storm. Then arrows and spears flew from the cloud, throwing the procession into disarray.

Two horses beside Rian fell with spears in their sides; one with some fell creature chewing its neck and blood spurting. The smoke and cloud thickened, filled with cries of, 'Ware, ware! Morgana LeFay!'

Mounds of earth, ancient tombs, split open and vomited up eyeless creatures in the shape of men and women woven from sticks and mud. Rian screamed as members of her family were sucked down into the earth. The light vanished, but intermittent sparks of lightning through the cloud showed her frozen images of horror. In the guttering light a druid lord grabbed her arm and led her to where she thought she was safe; but he was snatched away, leaving her alone. Bitter smoke obscured everything.

Her mother ran to her from within the cloud and pressed a small bag into Rian's hand. 'Ride,' said Angharad. 'Ride to Charlecote Well. Find Sir Thomas!'

Rian leapt onto Feather and dug in her heels, her cousins Bryl and Seth suddenly at her side. Others on horseback swarmed around, protecting their escape. They rode off through smoke, clawed at by man-faced crows. Others joined them, riding close, and falling. Some who fell behind released lightning into the darkness and a thunder that shook the world. Silence and a nervous wind scoured the land, pushed back the enemy, gave them a space of peace for a short while.

They galloped across rivers, marshes and fens, pursued by the horrors. They stopped only to feed and water the horses.

At one point they begged help from the yeomanry, the land army of Queen Elizabeth, who, answering their pleas, came out of their fort and stood in the way of the walking trees and the fell creatures. The band of county soldiers died behind them.

Rian woke from stolen minutes of sleep in the saddle to find herself weeping. Was it luck that she survived? How did she come to be mounted on Feather? She couldn't remember.

They were reduced to five; then three.

In the dead of the second night they rode up to the druid house in Stratford, but found it abandoned. A man stealing from the kitchen said, 'They say that Elizabeth Tudor has fled London; that Derek LeFay is styling himself King. I wouldn't stay here. Food's all gone.'

They took a dark lantern and found an old barn where Bryl fell heavily to the ground. His shirt was soaked with blood. Seth ran back to the house to find physic.

Rian crawled over the earth floor to find somewhere dry. She fell into a dream.

A woman was standing over her, robed in dark green and jet. She was beautiful; but her eyes were empty and black as a lizard's.

Dread fell upon Rian and she woke in terror. She called out, 'Father…'

Once he would have come and comforted her.

Rian would have no more special times with him – their regular supper where they would talk about anything and everything: stories of his years as book master in the college (a quiet life before the Princess Angharad came in one day to find a rare text); and worldly talk about what *were* the Spanish doing in the Netherlands? And did the Lord Derek of the House of LeFay pose a threat to the Tudors? And why had Derek LeFay, a descendant of Mordred, visited Queen Angharad's brother Uth during the Saturn Feast? And finish thy bitter greens, dear, for the cat will not eat them.

She began to speak to him.

'I see it now, Father. Derek LeFay will have promised Queen Elizabeth, "Hast trouble with the King of Spain? I will provide for thee a magic stone that will summon a tempest and sink his ships. I have prepared the spirits of my house to this end. Art lacking in love and having no heir? I have the very thing" … Do I see it right? Father?'

The storm intensified. Bryl coughed.

She looked around. Seth had not returned.

'It is only we two now,' said Bryl looking out into the rain.

'Perhaps,' said Rian, 'we should go onwards now under cover of this tempest?'

'I think,' replied Bryl weakly, 'that it is the stones that cause this disarray in the heavens – is that not the stone you wished to carry, cousin? The tempest stone? It responds to your will.'

'Help me then to be quiet of mind,' said Rian. 'It is the stones that draw Morgana to us!'

'No,' replied Bryl. 'Indeed, let the power of it come.'

'It is death to will upon the stones. My father said it will unmake the world.'

'But it will be the unmaking of our world if the stones are not brought to Charlecote Well,' said Bryl. He coughed again and his chest crackled as he breathed.

Rian closed her eyes and saw again the bodies of the druids scattered over the plains, pricked with arrows. Her mother – dead? Seth – dead. Bryl – wounded. Her friends and cousins – all gone too? And where was Father?

By lantern light she opened the bag and spilled the coloured stones onto the ground. They had their own light, and in that light Rian saw her family healed and beautiful on a warm spring day.

She snatched up the green stone, known as Tempest, and moved her grief and hope towards it – and the floor began to shiver. Rain hurled itself against the roof.

She put the stone from her. The quivering in the fabric of the world stopped.

'I cannot use the stones,' she said.

But Bryl was dead.

Before the dawn, creatures gathered in the trees around the barn, gibbering and hissing. Waiting. 'Come, Morgana,' they crooned. 'Here she is, here. Soon, soon.'

Rian shrank into the corner. She despised their smug chattering. She had the power to hurt them: the thunder of the Tempest; the madness of the Dominion stone. She looked at Bryl, cold on the earth floor. She took up the black stone, the one called the Raven, the stone of death. She did not hold it lightly, or cautiously, but with a sharp intention. As she did this a wooden beam cracked and a foul odour spilled into the barn. The horses let out a grievous sound and keeled over. The air grew parched, and the gibbering in the trees stopped. Rian covered her mouth. In the corner of the barn, Feather was on his knees, eyes like egg-whites, breath scraping like a knife on a stone.

She frantically took out the rose-coloured stone, the stone of Love, and breathed virtue back into the horse. 'Awake,' she said. 'Feather – live!' The animal swelled like a tree in springtime, stood up, tossed its head and snorted warm breath.

Rian mounted and rode out. She heard writhing and whimpering in the woods, but nothing came at her, nothing stopped her.

She rode on, wet through and cold, but at some point in the early morning, creatures in the Forest of Arden bore down on her once more – sprites, the man-faced crows, the root people. She willed again upon the Raven stone and a wave of night burst from her hand. When the daylight and her mind returned, she was lying in the wet grass, dead faerie-folk in a tangled mess about her. Feather was gone, galloped away to safety, she hoped.

She tried to rise and cried out, for she had been pierced in the side. Her hand was now wet with her own blood. 'Oh,' she said. ''Tis all done now.'

Soon the stones would be taken from her and the druids would be no more.

She crawled to a tree and lay against the wet bark. She began to sing – a song of passing for herself, for her family.

Someone was on the path. It was a boy of about fifteen with a slightly turnip-shaped face. He called out in horror. 'O, God! O, by'swounds! What is this?'

<h1 style="text-align:center">Part 1</h1>

1   Juliet in England

I KNOW, PAPA, THAT YOU ORDERED THE PRIEST TO POISON ME. I KNOW that you bade Father Laurence trick me with a tale about how drinking his draft would unite me with Romeo.

I should have suspected.

Father Laurence, with his foul breath, who loved being cruel to cats, babbled about how I would feel nothing but a cold and drowsy humour. It would be naught but a pretence of death, he said. And in a while, Romeo would come and we would be reunited. We would be happy.

I took the drink and felt myself sinking, and could hear Father Laurence whining his prayers, *Lord, forgive me! Her death is not my wish. 'Twas the father bade me punish her.* I heard him stumble from the room, and even though my sight was nearly gone I was able to find a feather in the ticking of the bed, forced it into my throat and vomited up the strange blue potion he had given me – a trick the poison-taster's son had shown me.

The darkness in which I woke – I supposed it was my tomb – was unlike anything I had known, except for one time, when I was a child of eight.

I was playing alone (strange to be left alone, out of doors, with hoop and stick that my uncle had thrust into my hand) when I was snatched from the street. A bag of heavy cloth was placed over my head.

I recall the clatter of carriage wheels on cobblestones, then the wheels on a country lane. But the carriage stopped and I heard cries and a dreadful scream and the sound of arrows hitting wood. It was my uncle who lifted me down and led me by the hand to stand in a fresh-mown field, the stubble prickling my feet. Uncle plucked the bag from my head. The driver of the carriage was filled with arrows and two other men were being abused. One had already lost his ears.

The workers cowering in the field stared at me. After a few moments I spoke to them. 'I mean you no harm,' I said. But perhaps my fine clothing and tone of voice said otherwise. Two ravens flew in close and set themselves to wait in the trees.

'You,' I said to a boy, 'I am thirsty. Fetch me water.' He ran off and came back with water in a wooden cup. I was too confused to wonder if the water was fresh. I should have made him drink some first. But I drank, and the water was good.

I stood in the heat and wondered that I had been freed so quickly. But my abduction had been anticipated, if not prompted. Later, the servants came and brought me back to Verona. I remember your words, Papa: 'They will not try that again, will they?' No welcome caress, no kiss.

Mama was quiet as usual. Neither hot, nor cold.

And here I was once again, taken against my will and thrust into a dark place. What plans this time, Papa?

My eyes were open, but I might as well have kept them shut. I listened in the blackness and heard nothing but an odd metallic click and my own breathing. I was not dead. Clearly. But had I fallen into a very deep sleep, as the priest had promised? And had my family – thinking I was dead after all – shut me in a tomb? What if Romeo had already visited, laid flowers, and, believing me dead, gone away, weeping?

And now I was awake.

The air had the smell of peasant clothes, of dead leaves, and turpentine. I still wore my nightgown. I felt its embroidered flowers. I also wore the velvet surcoat I would sometimes wear while in my room on a cold day, but I could not remember why I was wearing it now. I ran my hands over my clothing. My locket was around my neck, in which I kept a little piece of Romeo's hair. My silk slippers were on my feet.

I clapped my hands for the servant. Nothing.

I cried out, but softly, 'Someone, come to me. Now!'

Since no servant came, I called, 'Romeo? Romeo, are you there?'

I extended an arm and my fingers scraped on a wall of metal, like a monstrous shield. It thundered when I banged on it with my fist.

I decided I was not in a tomb, for I could feel objects within: a chair, bottles that crashed when I stumbled into them, baskets full of I supposed greasy rags. Objects I reasoned that you would not find in a burial place. The terror of death passed into curiosity. It was a kind of closet. Or a cellar.

A cry came from without.

I crouched and my fingers closed around the neck of a bottle. It would do for a weapon. With a squeal of old hinges a door – the whole of one wall – swung wide open and daylight forced me to cover my eyes.

'Out. What 'you doing in 'ere?' came the voice.

Through watering eyes I saw a dishevelled man. He stepped away looking at me up and down.

I have more words now to describe what I saw in those first minutes. At first I felt stupid and distracted – as if the fumes of the poison still clouded my thoughts. But then an understanding of where I was, and the words for it, came to me in odd fragments like the clear recollection of a dream.

Some philosophers of this time, skilled in quantum matters, sat me down afterwards and tried to help me understand. They said that I had only – strange to say – come into being the moment I woke up in what they called a shipping container; yet behind me was a complete world. A virtual matrix, they called it; my past was a self-generating reality that inflated to balance out the England I now found myself in; an alternative England, which had also only come into existence the moment I woke up!

Because of these "quantum contiguities" I began to integrate with the modern world when I stepped into it. We had all become part of one narrative. The philosophers used the word "entanglement" as if it explained much. Perhaps it explained why I spoke English, and not a word of Italian, when that door opened.

I stumbled out of the old rusted house – the shipping container – into a clearing, surrounded by poplars and fresh woodland. The sky was blue and full of passing clouds. A spring afternoon. And I was being shouted at by a dishevelled man.

'What you think you're doing?' said the man. 'That's all Mick's gear. He'll be dark on you if 'e finds out some'uns been in.'

'Where am I? What is this place?' I demanded.

He gestured at my clothes. 'You from the manor then?'

I didn't like his abruptness, and he didn't like my silent stare.

'I don't know what you mean,' I said. 'A manor house? Show me where it lies, of your goodness.'

I thought, perhaps he was a Holy Fool. He began to move nervously, like a thief.

'Put the bottle down, I ain't gonna 'urt you.'

I threw the bottle to one side and glared. 'How dare you talk to me like that?'

He retreated further, as if I were the mad one.

'You go up that path,' he said, with now an acceptable servility. 'There's a fence. There's a gap in it. A path, understand? There's a path back to the old house. Garn.'

I looked for the path as he had said, but I meant to go on as I started.

'Was it you put me in that room? Who is your master?'

'Okay, settle down.' He jammed his hands into his pockets and coughed.

'What place is this?'

'Down here's Charlecote Edge,' he replied.

'And what land is this?'

He laughed. 'What *land*? Eng*land*.'

England. I turned and stumbled over coarse gravel to the start of a small path that plunged into a thicket. I determined not to look back.

2

T_{HE} T_{REES} S_{TIRRED} _{AND} G_{ROANED} — _A W_{ORRYING} S_{OUND}. I S_{TOOD} S_{TILL}; and yet to be so close to the perfume of the leaves and the woodland itself was a marvel. I heard a man's voice and listened intently. Was it the dishevelled man following? I looked back along the narrow track.

To one side I saw a second man in a small clearing. He had his back towards me. He did not see that I was near. He wore clothing of black and grey, the jacket tight over his shoulders, and he was looking into a small hand mirror, saying things to his reflection. I thought he might be a poet of some kind, or a man of prayer. I hurried away in my silken slippers, undetected.

The woods ended a short distance uphill. The path came to a fence, a net of woven wire, but with a hole in it as the uncivil man had said. I stepped through and came out upon a trimmed lawn.

A large red-brick house with towers and chimneys stood at the end of this lawn, surrounded by gardens. On the lawn were young women of my age, dressed as I might have dressed for a party. But I looked on warily. I had no cause to think that they might be friendly to me. My father's admonitions, his wariness, his suspicious nature, were ever-present. The young women skipped around and threw a red plate that seemed to have the ability to float on the air, or else fall sideways to the ground when badly thrown.

'Hi,' said a girl of Moorish appearance, wearing a red dress. She came close. 'Did you go down that way? I don't think we're meant to go there. I'm Daisy — we 'aven't met. I didn't see you on the bus.'

'I am Juliet,' I said, and curtseyed.

'Ooh, slay, you do that so well. Were you in the group doing *courtoisie*? I was stuck in Tudor Table Manners and I made a right royal mess of it. I dropped sauce down the front of the dress. Does it show? Matches the red, eh?'

Her dress was a beautiful crushed silk, but I could see the stains of the salsa.

'So, where you from, girl?'

I replied, 'I am from the Principality of Verona.'

'Italy? Oh, Eurozoner then?' she said. 'Have you met Elke? She's from Austria, that makes you neighbours. She's billeting with me and me Mum. I don't know where she is right now, but. Off taking pictures I suppose.'

I replied, 'I would be honoured to meet Elke. And, please tell me, where are you from? Are you also a Eurozoner?'

'Oh, no,' said Daisy, 'I'm one of the hosts. Hey, your English is pretty good. A bit Old Englishy, but. I think we got to head back now and return the costumes. So, are you staying with someone? Like, you're billeted with a family, right?'

'I just came here,' I said, struggling with the knowledge that I seemed indeed to be in England.

'Wow, threw you in the deep end, then, did they? But I mean, you're with someone?'

'No,' I said. I kept my answers short. Saying little was a method my father used to make other people speak more than they intended. Though Daisy needed little encouragement.

'Oh. Well, you can hang with me and El if you want. Here she is.'

Another young woman, with yellow hair and pale skin, came up to us.

'Hi. How are you?' said Elke. 'We have to return *ze* costumes, then they are saying it's time to get on *ze* bus.'

It was the first time I had been this close to a Protestant. I had only seen pictures of them hanging in chains or broken on the wheel.

'You two, stand together, *ja*?' said Elke. Daisy put an arm around me, and Elke pointed a little black box at us. I heard a click, the sound like a snapping twig.

'*Schön,*' said Elke.

Daisy said that, if I was not doing anything, I should come

with her and Elke to the *Exchange House* in London and *chill* with them for the rest of the day. I was happy to comply, melted a little by her warmth.

'We are in England?' I exclaimed, still catching up with the strange news, and unable to conceal my confusion.

Daisy laughed. 'What the frick? Yeah. Well, last time I looked!'

Daisy was happy to talk non-stop, and anything odd that I said was either misconstrued, or forgotten in moments. I was happy to drift along in the babbling stream of her talk. Still, I remained vigilant, not so much for the strangeness of the world, but in case some servant of my father should appear. Or indeed Romeo, hurrying towards me. I expected this to happen at any moment.

I looked around for the prayerful man who had been in the woodland, but he was not to be seen.

Daisy looped her arm through mine and caressed my hand. 'God, you're so pretty,' she remarked. 'You could be a model.'

We walked across the lawn to a house of glass and white metal, which, according to the sign, was the *Education Resource Centre*. I was suddenly in a room filled with more young women of my age, talking, laughing, singing raucously about saving their tears for another day.

An older woman – so like Nurse, though not dressed like her – was calling out: 'All right, girls, put all the dresses back onto the numbered coat hangers, then hang them over here on the rack. If you've lost anything it's likely to be in the lost property box here by the door. I want you all back on the bus in ten. Tiffany, did you hear me?'

Then the girls were throwing off their clothes. I had not seen such speediness or so much skin since Romeo and I pulled ourselves out of our garments; and the memory was like a sword in my breast.

I came back from this burst of sadness to see my new companions pulling out from lockers a range of close fitting upper-garments, dark stockings, slippers of black and white. Due to those "quantum contiguities", the words *Converse* and *leggings*, and *crop top* flashed into my mind. What had been, only a moment before, a vision of women of my era – or at least women dressed in a familiar way – vanished like a trickster's bead, leaving me in this present moment. What on earth were they doing? Were they dressing up for a strange *pavane*, or a masque?

I think I have always known what I wanted, even if, while growing up, that desire was hidden; a guttering candle. And now all but extinguished, it came back as fire. I wanted to overcome the situation I had been placed in – kept for all of my fifteen years in a closed world where I was seldom allowed to wander or venture out unaccompanied (except when left on the street as a bait for my father's enemies) and had only Father Laurence with his foul breath as my teacher, and of course Nurse. What if this England was the world at last? Perhaps Romeo had managed to smuggle me out while I slept. I would finally find my freedom here. And find Romeo.

It was time to act. To be a Capulet. I moved a little away from Daisy and Elke, but not too far. I cast my eyes over the girls who were speedily covering their nakedness, pulling on socks and shoes and jackets. It was, in a way, so exciting to see. No maidservant to dress me, no hooks, no bodice, no lacing up, or being sewn in. No hour of careful preparation. This was an unmeasured world. I looked into the overflowing lost property box and stole leggings and something that spoke the word *T-shirt*.

The older woman came over to me and said, 'Did you lose this, dear?' She held out a smooth, flat card and spoke precisely at me. 'You won't be able to travel on the train without it. Yes?'

I said it was mine and took the card.

I am sure, Papa, you would be proud, for did you not start in the world as a pickpocket and pilferer?

I felt eyes on me as I stripped off my nightdress, and even more eyes as I pulled on the leggings and T-shirt. Later I discovered that not wearing undergarments was uncommon in this country – but I had found nothing suitable in the lost property box.

'Wild girl, eh?' said Daisy. '*Ooh, draw me like one of your French girls, Jack.*'

Elke came over and whispered. 'It is *naturliche*. I approve.

One should be free, *ja*. Don't mind if they stare. I also don't wear *ze unterslinger*. But then, I don't have as much as you.'

And then I was overcome and blurted out to Elke, 'But why are we changing into these costumes?'

'No, we just got *out* of *ze* costumes, *ja*? They' – she pointed at the rack of dresses – 'they were for *ze* re-enactment? Perhaps you were having one of *ze* little cigarettes while hiding in *ze* wood?'

I just nodded.

I also found some light-coloured *sandshoes*, a little too tight, but bearable. All my clothes – the nightdress and jacket, the silk slippers – I pushed into a plastic bag with "Sainsbury" stamped on the side, then: a frantic hustle as we left the room and climbed onto horseless coaches parked in front of the manor house.

Along with the trick of my father's silence, in observing my new companions I stumbled on another secret tactic. Whenever I encountered something incomprehensible, of which there was a great deal, I would, like Elke, say, 'And what is your *English* word for this?' Not, 'What the frick?' as Daisy was wont to exclaim.

After we had taken our places, a voice spoke from the carriage wall, almost drowned out by the chatter of the other travellers and a rumbling as of millstones.

'Good afternoon. I hope you've enjoyed your outing and had a great Tudor experience here at Charlecote Park and Manor. We're heading now back into Stratford. The journey will take about ten minutes.'

Why had no one told me that England was a land where a voice came out of the wall, with carriages drawn by no horse, where clothes could be put on in the space of a minute?

'Hey, I love the locket,' said Daisy, observing my gold neck-chain. 'Anything in it – *hmmm*? Photograph perhaps?'

I wanted some reassurance of Romeo, so unclasped the locket to view the strands of hair.

The lock of hair was within the locket as expected; but also a small rose-coloured pebble. I had never seen it before. I looked at it, struck speechless.

Time seemed to stand on tiptoe and move around us in hushed

tones. The stone had made everything silent. And joyful. Daisy and Elke sat as if in an enchantment. Daisy, unusually quiet, reached out and took my hand. We all sat still and spoke nothing for a time.

'Oh, that is so... *unheimlich*,' said Elke in a strange voice. The word she used meant unearthly.

'Oo, wow,' said Daisy. 'Omigod, that is so beautiful. God, that hits different!'

I quickly shut the locket, frightened. I had no notion how this stone had come to be there, Had Romeo left it with me for a sign? Or was it put there by the person who hid me in the metal box at Charlecote? It was too beautiful to be anything that my father, or one of his servants, had secreted away.

Our coach now took, I assumed from the big green sign that shone like silk, the Stratford-Wellesborne Road. I wondered if I should go back to that metal box, and stay there to wait for Romeo.

A river named Avon, according to the voice from the carriage wall, came into view, coming close to the road then receding. We passed tall square palaces, sleek breathtaking shining towers, a wide lawn where men and women slashed at white objects with thin metal sticks. It was like a book of hours come to life, and the carriage spoke again. 'As we come into Stratford you'll see, on the left, a five-storey-high sculpture made of terracotta, called "Standing Man". Known locally as *Mr Clumsy*.'

On the street a young man stood before a strange tower of bricks in form like a giant. The young man was holding up a small mirror. Others also were holding these mirrors, and I soon realised that everyone on the bus had one, something like a small psaltery. Some were talking to their image in the mirror or looking at images that surfaced and moved within.

The coach spoke on as we passed the statue. 'It was decided ten years ago to make a landmark public sculpture to celebrate Stratford's brick-and-pottery-making heritage, and to draw in some tourism. And they came up with this. There was some pushback at first, but even those who hate it have to admit it's really gone and put Stratford on the map.'

IN THIS WORLD, A WOMAN NAMED ANGEL HEMINGWAY WROTE A BOOK, called *The Turtle and the Boy*. It has become my favourite. I love its simple and direct words – so simple after the overworked speech of the world I came from (full of lies, show, and deflection). Her little book is nothing but a description of the life of a turtle, from egg buried in the moonlight to beautiful soul of the ocean; and of the relationship the turtle has with a small boy named Santiago.

I have wondered often about my first hours in the new world. In the Hemingway book, the little turtle hatches and runs down the beach to find the ocean, but the rest of its brothers and sisters are most of them taken in the first desperate struggle – seabirds, wild dogs, propeller blades, sharks, sharp rocks. Only the fewest of the few survive to swim forever in the deep.

I was fortunate to find two friends, Daisy and Elke, who shielded me as I ran blindly into the ocean.

I encountered many sharks in those first hours. Not so dangerous were the girls who wanted to shame me for wearing no underwear – 'Oooh, all fur coat and no knickers,' called out one. 'Open for business, are we?' said another.

Daisy rebuked them. 'Honey,' she said, 'why don't you pull your piss flaps over your head and make a real cunt of yourself?'

And then on the train – not a small carriage at all, almost a moving palace, or a shifting wall of rooms – the *ragazzi* came swarming. These were some young men who had also visited the Manor on a school trip. They now chose their moment to be friendly. I think they must have known that people like Elke and her friends were visitors from overseas.

'Come to pick off the juicy ones?' said Daisy without explanation. The young men asked Daisy to introduce Elke and me.

'Introduce yourselves. I'm sure they don't bite,' said Daisy.

A trumpet sounded and the train moved out. Elke did not seem to be that friendly towards the boys (they were clearly boys – their hands looked as if they had never held reins or a sword), but as if choosing an apple, Elke took one of them by the hand, moved to a different seat, and began to kiss him.

I watched, fascinated, then realised there were rules to be observed: do not make a fuss; act as if it were normal.

Daisy then made affectionately with the other boy and so I had to deal with the third by myself, who ran his hand across my leg.

'I am engaged,' I said, flicking his fingers away.

He lost interest then, and sat back, but talked on, about himself and his interests. His voice was like an annoying insect in the night. I looked out of the window. He asked me what my father did.

I replied, 'He makes people disappear.'

I rested my head against the glass. I saw the trees, dancing wires that rose and fell, red clouds and lights coming up against the approaching evening.

England. Why was I in England? Was it really England? Or one of the clever rooms of Hell – devised so as to extend pain and torment through heartbreaking illusions? I closed my eyes and prayed that Romeo would come to me. But my prayers seemed unreal.

I think I slept, but it was a half-sleep in which I saw a young woman striding through a field, shaking cloth of gold. And with it she scared away birds. Some of the birds were black ravens that flew towards me croaking and flapping their wings in terror. I fell to the ground, pressed my face to the cold earth. But the coldness was the glass I lay against.

The train was approaching a large city late in the afternoon. The boys had left.

'Come on, luvvy,' said Daisy. 'Wakey wakey.'

I asked her, 'Where did those boys go?'

'Oh, you scared yours off something serious,' said Daisy. 'It's okay, you know, your Mum'll never find out. No one takes pictures, unless they're a real twat.'

We crossed a platform to the train that would take us to Liverpool Street Station in London.

'Don't you have anything more than that shopping bag?' asked Daisy as, once more, the trumpet sounded and the train pulled out. For herself, Daisy carried a backpack.

'No,' I said, lying, 'it was... all taken. Everything I have was taken from me.'

Perhaps not such a lie. I should have kept my own counsel.

Daisy's eyes went big. 'What d'you mean, Juliet, when was this?'

'I wandered away from the big house, the Charlecote Manor, and went somewhere in a wood, and a man came and took everything from me and he ran away.'

'Everything? Your phone, and your money, what about your ID? O God, not your documents?!'

'Yes,' I replied.

'And did he do anything to you?' She grabbed hold of my hand.

'No.' I pulled my hand away. 'I spoke sternly to him.'

'You should've said, girl. You should have... No wonder you looked a bit–'

'A bit what?' I spoke sharply.

'Well, you know. A bit troubled. Sorry for saying. Omigod! I feel bad for not asking earlier if something was up. I sort of knew it. I feel dreadful. I'm forever going on about myself and never listening. Mum says it's a real problem, but then I'm sure I get it from her, she says I should get quote unquote professional help for it, but then she's always saying things like that... omigod!'

'Do you wish then to use my phone, Juliet?' said Elke. 'Call *ze* Exchange Office?' She held up her mirror device.

'Well, what'll *they* do?' said Daisy, genuinely troubled. 'I mean, you should call home, or the Italian Embassy? Or you're billeted with a family? Righty? Call them! Or call your Mum.'

'Let her handle it,' said Elke. 'Do you wish to use my phone?'

I registered the English word. But here was a thought. Call

home. Speak to my family. To my dear, sick Mama, what would I say? Or to you, Papa? What would I say? That I lived?

And that I wished you dead.

I felt ill and frightened.

In getting used to this *new* world, I assumed for a little time that this England was still a part of my world – 1580 – and that in Verona they too had Apples and the Androids; it was only I who had been kept ignorant of them, or forbidden them, because of my parents' fears. I also reasoned that I had never been taken to a city – where carriages of metal ran upon long ribbons of steel – for the same reasons.

Elke slid open her phone case. I watched everything she did, for I was angry to be so helpless. But then the square of cold glass grew familiar and I found I was able to comprehend it. I pressed a number on the screen, but too many times.

'Use the backspacer,' said Elke. '*Da*. Or just talk into it. Say, "Hey, Siri" and then ask her what you want.'

I misheard her. 'Do you pray then to the Virgin?' I asked.

'No,' said Elke with a look of fascination. She laughed and slapped me on the shoulder. 'You do not live in *ze* big city, *ja*?'

'No,' I said firmly.

I went to a quiet part of the train, with the floor shaking underneath me, and whispered, 'Mary, Mother of Jesus, please hear my prayer.' She responded, saying she didn't quite hear that, but eventually took me to the *Pagine Bianchi* for Italy. I asked for the house of Montague in Verona. She said she had found one entry. There appeared to be one address and a single phone number. I whispered my thanks to the Mother of God. 'Grant that I may speak with Romeo,' I intoned prayerfully into the phone. I can laugh now at my simplicity.

Something purred like a dove resting on a branch.

'Pizzeria Montague, *pronto*,' said a voice.

I said, 'I pray that I may speak with Romeo.'

'Romeo? *Un momento perfavore...*'

The voice that spoke afterwards was nothing like Romeo. Still, I blurted out from a burning throat, 'Romeo? It is I, Juliet. I am in

England. But how? I do not know! Papa tried to kill me! O, how do I get to you, o, my love…' Tears pooled in the corners of my eyes. 'Where are you? You must be careful, also!'

The line clicked and then I heard only the sound of the train. The trees and buildings moved past so quickly it was like falling. I burned with so much hate for my family.

Elke came and led me back to my seat.

'So, not okay?'

'It is arranged,' I lied. 'Someone will meet me in London. It is arranged.'

4

As we drew nearer to London, the low sun flashed into the carriage, off and on, off and on, as we passed along bridges, through tunnels, and in the shadow of numerous towers. Everything seemed armoured, or covered in chain mail, rivets large as horseshoes. I saw pictures as vivid as tapestries, here and there, but did not understand why they seemed like life itself.

I whispered to Elke, 'What is the English word for those?'

'Oh, they are called *posters* or *billboards*. That one is... it just says *Get You Kicks in '26*.'

I asked her what that meant and she said it was for sports betting, '*Win this year*, is what it means.'

'*This* year? How is *26* this year?'

'Twenty-twenty-six. Juliet, I think you are more troubled than you are letting on. I'm a little worried for you.'

A man in a pale blue coat came pushing a trolley that was filled with food and drink. The food was wrapped in films of soft glass.

'Can I get you something to eat?' said Elke, placing her hand on my wrist.

'I will not eat,' I replied. I had not listened to her since she said the year was 2026. For it meant... I did not know what it meant. I had at last arrived at the end of comprehension. Perhaps I did need to eat, for my mind was swimming and I felt faint. The noise of the train was like a raucous pageant.

People began to buy from the trolley. Some other young people who had been on the *excursion* gathered round.

Then a man who I had not seen before, wearing a green coat with a fur collar, stepped close to me and spoke. 'I heard you lost your wallet and things. That's no good. Can I buy you something? And your friends too? If you're hungry.'

'Oh, thank you, sir, you don't have to,' said Daisy.

'They have pies, tapas-in-a-pak,' said the man.

I agreed to eat a *tortilla*. Elke sat hunched over her phone. She suddenly exclaimed, 'I am having *ze* weird thoughts.' She sighed.

'What?' said Daisy with a grin, 'missing that boy already? Did you get his number?'

'No, not that... I am feeling *ze*... you know, *déjà vu*,' she said dreamily.

'Ooh, me too! I love *déjà vu*,' said Daisy. 'It must be the sunlight – it's all Autumny, innit... even though it's Spring. Maybe it's that stone of yours, Juliet. That gave me weird feelings.'

'I got you a drink, too,' continued the man, looking at me intently. 'It's apple juice, and there's a packet of crisps for later. You could just pop them in your bag. Here you are...' He dropped the packet of crisps into the bag beside me. He himself had bought a can of drink. He gave a cheerful nod and went to sit near some schoolboys further down the carriage.

Food, of course, was always an issue in our house. The first boy that I ever had the crush on was Alfano, son of the food-taster to the House of Capulet.

I was very cool with Alfano. 'Why should I be friends with you?' I said to him. 'You might drop dead eating a poisoned peach, foaming at the mouth, then I would have lost a playmate, and I would feel sad for having wasted my time getting to know you.'

But Alfano became very serious and told me that his father's father lived still, having been the food-taster in the House of Ludovico Revero in Turin, and he had not keeled over, unlike some who did not know their craft. The skill of the food taster, said Alfano, was in sensing something amiss from the aromas. Unless someone was trying to slow-poison you over several meals, it was fairly easy, so he said, to smell a bad dish. If there was suddenly a heavily-spiced dish being prepared, with too many onions, that was also grounds for suspicion. And if you suspected a fast-acting poison then there were plenty of hungry little mice that you kept to hand before the meal went to the table.

So, because Alfano was a "man of the world", knowing most

that there was to know about the poisoning of food, I was secretly impressed and let him hold my hand and I kissed him, although he was a servant lad. It was he who told me the trick of making myself vomit by sticking feathers in my throat. We had not much else to talk about.

I wondered if the man in the *anorak* had some sense of these protocols, for he made it clear that he was buying from the public trolley. I suppose he meant to put my mind at ease. When I have to eat food in a strange place, the question of safety is always on my mind. And so I was happy to take the food. If the man had walked up and handed me the *tortilla*, I would have rejected it immediately, as I had been taught. If I was to be poisoned, it would happen through a very clever enemy. Or my family would do it.

I began to eat, enjoying the rice and beans. With each mouthful of the *tortilla*, the world became a little less strange. By the time I was halfway through eating, I felt I was in England and that Verona was the unreal land.

Perhaps there was some potion, after all, in the food to make this happen.

I stopped eating and tried to fix Verona in my mind.

I had not lost memory. No, I could easily recall the smell of sheets drying in the second courtyard, the way Nurse used to cuddle me when I was little (and how the cuddles became rare, around that time that Mama stopped coming in to kiss me goodnight, and the sharp memory of that), and the balcony where I used to play lonely games, and the night I first saw Romeo looking intently at me. Me throwing handfuls of crushed yellow rose petals at him as he climbed to my window, me making a ridiculous pout. The exquisite feeling of his skin. The soft heat of his lips. Each memory had its own special quality.

I realised that I had not adequately said thank you to the green-coated man for his generosity, so I went down the carriage and found three young men, who were all my age. The man had gone to sit with these three, or so I thought; but now I could not see him.

'Where is the one who was with you? Is it your master?'

'Oh, he was nae with us,' said one. 'He's a friend o' yours, then?

'No,' I replied, sensing that he knew something I did not. 'Must I know him?'

'I would nae trust him,' came the reply.

'What do you mean?' I leant forward, interested. 'I am Juliet.'

The young man straightened up. 'I'm Angus, this here's m'pal Damian, and the third o' our wee gang is Rowan.'

'Rowan, show some manners,' said Damian.

'*Enchante*,' said Rowan, putting down his phone, and extending a hand with the thumb jutting rudely upwards. I stared at it and he pulled it back.

'I would nae touch it either,' said Angus, 'I know exactly what he's been doing wi' it.'

I realised that this was a way of greeting, so I did extend my hand. Rowan gave it a rough shake.

'Would you like to join us?' said Damian.

'I will,' I said and sat next to them. 'And please tell me why you have no trust in that man?'

Rowan replied. 'The paedo? Trembling hands. Fidgety. The anorak. Probably drives a white van. You can tell.'

'Thank you, Miss Marple,' said Damian. 'But in all matters relating to the wisdom of the street, I'd rely on Angus. Now, let us watch the master at work.'

'Yeah. No shit,' said Rowan.

I did not fully understand, but Angus leant over to me, pointed at the plastic bag I held, and said, 'Can I take a wee look?'

I did not refuse. Angus reached in and took out the bag of crisps.

'Hm,' said Rowan nodding his head. 'Salt and vinegar. Hm.'

'Shut up,' said Damian.

Then Angus withdrew a small black button covered in a lacework of thin gold wire.

'No' yours?' he asked.

'Oh, well done,' said Damian, a little awestruck. 'You were right, McTeague.' To me, Damian remarked, 'His Dad's a private detective. It runs in the family.'

'I do not understand,' I said. 'What is this button?'

'This is – well, it's either a cufflink,' replied Angus, 'or it's a wee tracking device.'

'Do you have to keep using that word?' said Rowan.

'And I saw that feller slip it into your bag – along wi' the packet o' crisps.'

'But, why?' I asked, a coldness like poison running through me. 'What does it mean? A wee tracking device?'

'Well, if it is a *weeeeee* tracking device,' said Damian. 'I mean there are actually medical ones for the purpose, but this one here we presume is so that he can follow you without your knowing it. Is that right, Angus?'

'Aye, or else Rowan's right and he's a freak who leaves little keepsakes wi' strangers.'

'See, I was right,' said Rowan. 'I have good ideas.'

'I never saw this man before,' I said with a growing anger.

I examined the button. Was it left by an enemy? Or perhaps was the man a friend of Romeo? Was this a message for me?

'Are you in trouble, then?' said Rowan with an annoying smile.

Of course I was in trouble, but I feigned innocence and said, 'I cannot say.'

The train began to slow down, and some people moved to the exit doors.

Angus spoke. 'Okay, watch this a sec'. Let's see what happens.'

Angus took the button, stood and walked over to the carriage exit and I saw him quietly drop the button, unobserved, except by us, into the pocket of a woman standing close to the door. Angus came back to us. No one spoke. The train had stopped. Cold air blew in as the doors opened. The woman stepped away, went up a slender staircase, and was gone. Nothing happened for a moment, but as the trumpet sounded, and the train pulled out, we saw the man in the green coat run past the window, craning his neck, searching. He disappeared quickly up the staircase.

5

'Wow! That got rid of him,' said Rowan. 'It must have been a wee tracking device. Point to Scotland.'

'Well, that's a mystery,' said Damian.

'How?' I asked Angus. 'How did you know to look for it?'

'Well, the chap sat here a few minutes, for aye looking at you.'

'Didn't want to talk to us,' said Damian, 'even though Rowan stroked his leg for a while–'

'Fuck off.'

Angus continued, 'I saw he had something in his hand, kept playing wi' it. He was targeting you. So, when he went over, I went as well and got mesel' a Red Bull and I was close enough to see him drop the thing in your bag.'

'But what does a *wee tracking device* do?' I asked. I must have appeared angry and perplexed.

'*Are* you in trouble?' said Rowan again, I think enjoying my discomfort.

'Well, it's none of our business really, is it?' said Damian, looking at his friends.

'So, you're an exchange student, is that it?' said Angus.

'Yes,' I said, feigning brightness.

'And not on the run?' said Rowan.

'For the love of fuck,' said Damian.

I think my silence might have given much away.

'I was sent here,' I declared. 'My parents forced me to come to England. Though I did not wish to come.'

'That must be very bewildering,' said Damian in a kind voice. 'Now, I believe that on Exchange you get to visit a strange school and hang out with the natives?'

'I suppose,' I said.

'Then, come to our school. Hang out with us.'

'I will come,' I replied, for I felt in need of friends.

Rowan then said, 'Really? No shit? I wouldn't.'

'Perhaps not such a good idea,' said Damian. 'We have a bad reputation. We do things like spend the day walking backwards to show our disdain of convention.'

'Aye, we're the young team,' said Angus.

'How will I find you again?' I said.

'Take this,' said Angus. He handed me from his backpack a phone. 'Dinnae worry, it's nae expensive. I have a few o' them.'

I saw that he carried many such phones in his backpack.

Rowan chuckled. 'If you need earpods, or a new charger, talk to The Gus. Most of it can't be traced.'

Angus typed on the device then gave it to me. 'I've gone and put my number in. See? Just call if y' need me.'

'Very smooth,' said Damian.

'You have become my friends,' I said. 'I will not forget.'

At that moment, Elke joined us. Without a word she sat next to Rowan.

'And where are you sitting, Juliet?' said Damian, standing and dragging Angus to his feet.

'I am sitting with my friend, Daisy.'

'Let's go and say hello then.'

A moment later I was back with Daisy, with Damian and Angus introducing themselves, and we were all watching from a distance now as Elke and Rowan consumed each other's mouths.

'This is wild,' said Daisy, craning her neck to see. 'It's like she's been let out of a cage. Or maybe you did something to her with your love-charm, eh, Juliet?'

'And it's Rowan's first time,' said Damian. 'Oh, look, he's really getting the hang of it. He practises up against a mirror, you know.'

'Well, you know what they say about exchange students,' said Daisy. 'Well, present company excepted, eh, luvvy?'

Angus showed me some of the markings on what he called the *wee burnerphone*.

'Is he giving you a phone?' said Daisy. 'Slay! Food, phones, and anything else beginning with *f*? Girl, you must live a charmed life. So, tell us about yourself, Mr Damian.'

Damian began to chat with Daisy. It appeared that the boys were returning to London from a day of skipping school.

'We just hung around Manchester,' said Damian. 'Did our own Joy Division tour. Took the bus to Salford. Stood outside Peter Hook's house and sang *Love will tear us apart* – but we had the wrong house – that sort of thing.'

My heart felt a burst of warmth. I had never had friends before who talked with such ease. Or friends. Alfano did not really count, being a servant.

Daisy put Damian's name into her phone. 'So, what's your last name, Mr Damian?'

'Lovemore,' said Damian.

'Ooh, that bodes well, eh? – hey, Juliet, show them your lucky charm.'

I opened the locket without thinking and dropped the stone into my hand. And then the train lurched and the stone fell to the floor. Angus was quick to pick it up and place it back in my palm.

And my new beginning shattered.

For a new expression came over Angus's face – a little like the strange joy that Daisy and Elke had given voice to; but the expression on Angus's face passed from wonder to bewilderment in moments.

'Oh, that's sae fucking strange,' he said.

'You okay, there?' said Damian.

'You look as if you've seen a ghost!' said Daisy.

'I have a sister,' he said. '*The fuck*?' He began scrolling through his phone. His voice grew troubled. 'I have a sister. Why am I here? Just who are you?... Her name is Maggie, and why is she nae longer in my contacts? What the fuck?'

Damian stared at Angus. 'What are you saying?'

'Why is she nae there? The cigarettes we had earlier,' said Angus in a low voice to Damian. 'Was there anything funny in them de' ye reckon?'

'Well, I hope so,' said Damian. 'That was the point.'

Angus's face took on a haunted look. 'I have a wee sister named Maggie,' he said, 'and, y' know, she writes fan fiction, and she plays volleyball, and she knows all the words tae *Hamilton*!'

'What's *Hamilton*?' said Daisy.

'Wow,' said Damian uncomfortably. 'Angus, maybe you'd better drink some water.'

'Do you want to lie down?' said Daisy. 'You look shocking.'

'She's nae in my phone anymore,' said Angus, now more agitated. 'She's nae anywhere–'

'Must be the ciggies, then,' said Damian. 'You don't have a sister, Angus. You're an only child, remember? Me too – that's why you and I act superior to Rowan – his house is infested with siblings.'

Damian's composure was also vanishing.

Angus looked at me, as if I might have an answer, wariness in his eyes. 'Or maybe it was that black button? You know? Christ. Was there something rubbed on it? Some weird chemical. It's LSD. I bet there fucking was! Fuck!'

'Okay, settle, settle,' said Damian. 'Just get some water into you.'

'You sure you didn't know that guy, Juliet? Tell me the truth? I'm serious.'

'Calm, Angus,' said Damian.

Angus did not take his eyes off me.

'I am looking,' I declared, struggling, 'I am looking to meet my fiancé, his name is Romeo. He is in London. But we are forbidden from seeing each other.'

'Fiancé?' said Daisy. 'At your age!'

'*Romeo*?' said Angus in a curious voice. 'Romeo?'

'What? Don't say you *know* him?' said Damian. 'Oh, you're just fucking winding us up. You can stop now, the two of you.'

'You're no' making up a story?' continued Angus to me. 'I mean, *Romeo and Juliet*?'

He threw his hands in the air. 'I give in. It's a play that I saw, we had a school trip from Glasgow to the Globe Theatre in London.'

Angus's fingers were furiously tapping at his phone. '*Romeo and Juliet* by... by... fuck. Shakespeare! Yes? *Anyone*? William Shakespeare?'

'Can't say I've heard of him,' said Damian. 'He didn't write *Hamilton*?'

'Shut the fuck up, I'm serious. It was at the Globe Theatre in Southwark. But it's not here, either. Damian? You've heard of the Globe Theatre?'

'No,' said Damian firmly. 'And who's William Shakespeare?'

The train had come to its destination in London. People were standing ready to depart the carriage. Elke and Rowan came to join us.

'I am Elke,' said she to Angus, going directly to him and shaking his hand.

'I'm Angus,' he replied. 'Got to go.' He suddenly leapt to his feet and with no further explanation pushed his way through the passengers at the door and disappeared along the platform.

'What's up?' said Elke.

'I don't know,' said Daisy. 'Is he always like this?'

'Not The Gus,' said Damian.

'Where has he gone?' I said. I was keen to know because he had spoken together *my* name *and* that of Romeo. He seemed to know something that I wished to know more of.

Damian began to look at me warily. Our small group, now more restrained, walked along the platform. Once we were outside the railway station and becoming separated by the swirl of people, I took the opportunity to walk more quickly. Daisy called my name, but I did not answer. I kept on walking.

6

A LITTLE WHILE LATER THE WEE BURNERPHONE THAT ANGUS GAVE ME BUZZED. I looked at it and dropped it into the Sainsbury bag, where it made more buzzings and rattlings. I did not respond to it, as I did not yet know that is what you did with a mobile phone. After a while the noises stopped.

I found a tourist information stand that boasted half-price tickets to the theatres. I asked the man if he might help me find the Globe Theatre. I felt a burning eagerness, and that soon all would be resolved. But the man replied that the Globe wasn't one he knew. 'What was the play called, then, darling?'

'The play?' I replied. 'It is not a play. It is someone I need to see.'

'Oh, like a singer you mean? A concert? At a theatre?'

We did not understand each other. But he directed me towards Southwark.

A woman nearby said that I should take the Underground. She pointed the way. A few minutes later I had descended beneath the ground and stepped alone onto a train. The travelcard helped me pass through the barriers.

I was by myself once more and felt very alone without my new friends. I sat warily on the train, for if someone was following me, tracking me with a wee device, I had no reason to believe there was just the one, or that Angus's tricking that man off the train was the end of the matter. My father had many servants. I looked around the carriage, but saw no one who resembled that man.

My face must have shown my fear, or perhaps I was weeping, for other passengers stared at me, then turned their faces away. One woman, with petals of glass before her eyes, asked if I was all right. I said that I was very well and thanked her and made sure that she did not leave any strange buttons with me.

I took out the phone and held it in front of me, staring blindly at it so that I might pass for a traveller.

In this world, one can watch a series on Netflix called *The New Life*, about an American student named Beatrice who goes back in time to medieval Florence (through a magical book) – and when she arrives she does not collapse in a tearful heap, but explores, and goes about happily making unashamed love. She helps a poor poet named Dante find the courage to write his poems (and, inspired by her, he does; but what happens next is a mystery as the show was cancelled after the one season). Her example made me shrivel at the memory of my own clumsiness.

A voice spoke from the wall naming the station that I had been told of. I hurried from the carriage, though the door struck at my heel as I left.

I found my way up into narrow streets. I asked strangers for directions, but no one knew of the Globe Theatre. I asked a beggar. When I said I was new to the city he said that, if I could sing, I should stand in the Tube and sing songs of my homeland to earn something for myself, but not to hang around for long. 'They've made it a hostile environment,' he said, but did not explain who *they* were.

I came to the Great River of London and looked at the slender bridges, the abandoned factories. Southwark seemed an aged and desolate place. After the roar of the underground train, the streets held a curious quiet.

Many people sat on the ground, wrapped in blankets, and not saying much, some reading, or listening to music that came out of small boxes on the ground. People stood to receive food from an alms-house on wheels, bright and painted with the words *Lighthouse Mission*. Against a grey wall, small silken pavilions were nestled, and people were sleeping there, or sitting in padded bags. I reasoned that I had come to a place where lost people gather. This gave me some hope that here Romeo and I would find each other.

I walked onto a piece of broken ground where several women were standing around a metal drum filled with burning wood.

'If you want to stay here, you should gather some wood,' said one as I came close. 'Make busy. It's gonna be a cold one. There's some pallets been left outside Cardinal's Cap. Break 'em up, bring them here. Know what I'm saying? Do you understand?'

'I will go,' I said.

'I'll go with you,' said another, whose head was wrapped in a yellow scarf. 'I'm Ashanti, dear.'

I walked with Ashanti and she said, 'I haven't seen you before. Where have you come from? Are you from Russia?'

I said, 'From Verona.'

'Did you run away? You sound as if you have come from a good home.'

'I did... run away, Ashanti. I'm looking for the Globe Theatre in Southwark. I am to meet someone there.'

'I have not heard of it. There – gather up those bits of wood. Hey, George. Do you know where the Globe Theatre is?'

A man in a stained and faded purple padded coat came up and looked at me. He had a white beard and swollen red eyes. He was holding plastic boxes of food. 'Globe Theatre? No, but sometimes the students put on plays in the old match factory, for the asylum seekers. It's down along Emerson Lane.'

'Where is Emerson Lane?' I asked.

'Just go along that way, luv. But I wouldn't go there. A lot o' new arrivals. A bit desperate. When did you come in? Did you cross the Channel? You're lucky to get this far. Are you Syrian?'

I said that I had come to England in a metal box.

'A shipping container?' said George. 'I've 'eard bad stories about them. It'd be like drowning rats. They just load 'em up and then push 'em off the ship. Why they can't sort it out over there instead of handing on their problems to us–'

'Hey, George,' said Ashanti, indicating the boxes of food, 'can I take one of those?'

'You can – someone already took the meat out – so it's only the veggies and little tubs o' gravy left.'

'I can take one also for Carol?'

'Knock yourself out, luv.'

I walked with Ashanti back to the drum of fire, carrying some wood, then bade her farewell.

'Come back here if you get stuck,' she said. 'George is right. You don't really want to go down there.'

I walked off to find Emerson Lane.

As I walked, the people I saw seemed younger, and darker skinned. Some sat on pieces of cardboard.

'Hey, lovely girl,' called one who was my age. He sat on the ground, wearing jeans and a jacket that was too small for him. He was sitting next to a large metal box.

'Have you seen Romeo? I am looking for Romeo,' I said. 'I am to meet him here.'

'I am Rahman,' he said. 'You got money?'

'I have nothing,' I said.

'If you want,' said Rahman after a pause, 'you could get money down there. I could take you, look after you; but I keep half.'

Another young man approached in company of others. 'Hi,' he said, 'I'm Hussein. Hey, what's up, Rahman, you coming?'

Rahman stayed seated on the ground and stared at his feet.

I asked Hussein if he knew the whereabouts of the Globe Theatre. My mobile phone buzzed again.

'You have a phone – try Googling it,' he said.

I took out the phone. 'I do not know what you mean,' I said. 'Can you help me?'

Hussein took the phone. 'You've got messages – *are you okay, where are you?*' He looked at me with concern. 'You have friends in London? You should go to them, yeah? Here is not a good place.'

Hussein suddenly dropped the phone and all the young men scattered. Rahman, who had sat still throughout my conversation with Hussein, jumped to his feet. But he was too slow. People in uniform seemed to come from everywhere and Rahman was suddenly held by men wearing dark uniforms.

'Stay where you are,' said a woman. She came close and gripped me by the arm. Another woman appeared.

'Is that your phone? Would you pick it up, please?'

I picked up the phone. It was immediately taken from me and dropped into a plastic bag.

More uniformed people swarmed around. They wore heavy vests, and people carried lights.

'Okay, we're from Border Force,' said a man. 'Do you understand English?'

I said that I did.

He asked me my name and then more and more questions. 'And where are you from? Do you have a passport? Are you a student? Are you on a student visa? Do you have a right to be in the United Kingdom?'

'We got ten of them,' said a man, but not to me. 'Always a good time, just as they're getting ready to kneel for their prayers. 6.05 on the knocker. What have we got here?'

Then the woman said, 'All right, Juliet, we're detaining you on suspicion of being illegally in the United Kingdom. I want you to put your arms in the air. Sorry to have to do this, no one enjoys it, but we have to search you.'

A woman wearing yellow gloves felt around my body. It was dreadful. I was then escorted, my arms held, to a metal carriage with a small window.

Part 2

1

David Cortez parked his Prius in a reserved spot near Ludgate Hill. He was due to meet the Director of the Walsingham Archive at 10, but he had misjudged the traffic, and roadworks on Newgate meant that Big Ben was sounding as he hurried from the car.

He jogged down Paternoster Lane to a nondescript cream-coloured terrace near Amen Corner. The Archive and other MI3 operations were housed behind the façade in a beneath-ground complex. He hadn't planned to be late: not consciously. Maybe there was reluctance. He had nearly died during his last assignment on Blanchefleur.

The families that lived on the island of Blanchefleur, in the far northwest of Scotland, were descended from the survivors of the shipwreck that gave the island its name. Down the windswept centuries they had remained loyal to the House of LeFay following Derek LeFay's unsuccessful tilt at the throne of England in 1580.

'Half-day LeFay' had lasted on the throne only until the evening. Fleeing the turmoil, the families had washed up on the island and set about keeping the faith. But the years proved unkind. Exiled from England, the various LeFay descendants had devolved into a bundle of harmless old pretenders with branches of the family in France and America. The islanders dressed on occasions as the *Sons of Mordred*; but no one thought this anything more than a bit of harmless re-enactment; like Morris dancing.

But then the islanders began communicating with groups on the continent, using curious passwords in French and Middle-English that tripped a watchlist on the computers at MI3 – that part of national security that dealt with magic and mysterious cold cases. *Extremely* cold cases.

But not dead cold, for the clues led agents to a cache of plastic explosives and weapons hidden on the mainland.

David had been assigned to look around the island, while things were still at the level of mildly troubling. He had posed as an ornithologist and ended up nearly burned at the stake as a black heretic. Thank God the mobile network covered the hilly parts of the island.

His attackers had taken his phone off him. A man, bald, with a comb-over and a French accent, said, 'So, do you want to burn slow or fast?'

In the midst of such taunting and some hitting, another man had said, 'So your sort can afford a nice shiny phone, eh? How do you open it? Tell us, what's the pin? Come on. Make it sharp!'

'It doesn't have a pin,' replied David. 'You just press the blue button on the side – three times quickly, then once long. Then you can make a call.'

The man did this. The phone stayed blank. The man tossed the phone to the ground and smashed it with his boot.

But the signal had been sent, and a couple of Harriers were scrambled from the RAF base at Carlisle.

MI3 never did find out precisely what the people on Blanchefleur were planning. A few fled the island in a powerboat, but most of the islanders made a stand inside a large barn, set fire to it, and died inside as a group.

Since then, David's advisor on bird matters said the Northern Gannets were returning in large numbers, and it was now quite the seabird paradise.

He still had nightmares in which he could smell the smoke. And even though he had been pulled from the bonfire before it really got going, in his dreams no one came and the flames took hold. He could hear them, chanting their racist words, calling out for Morgana LeFay to come to them.

David's girlfriend Gemma had moved back to her Mum's because of the nightmares and the seemingly endless recovery. Then she'd moved in with someone called Barry. She said she still needed more time away.

Gemma had called that morning and wished him the very best for his first day back. 'Don't let them work you too hard, eh?'

He was glad she'd called, but there was nothing hopeful in the conversation. They had moved beyond that.

The front door clicked open and David crossed to the desk where a receptionist welcomed him.

'Straight through, sir. Good to have you back.'

'Thank you,' said David. 'Nice to be back.'

He clipped on the security pass and entered what appeared to be a lift. The doors closed behind him, but then the rear of the lift swung open and he walked straight out into a spacious chamber, an atrium of angled steel girders, heavy on the blue-green glass, with a large spiral walkway opening the way down to the understorey of the Walsingham Archive.

'David. How are you?' said Aisha Vani, one of the Duty Officers. 'It's good to see you.'

'Aisha. Hi. Sorry I'm late,' said David. 'Did I miss the Director?'

'No. Change of plans. It's just me. Estelle and Sir Ambrose have been called into an urgent meeting with the Minister. I'll get you started on something. Did you want to grab a hot drink first?'

David bought a tea from the ground floor cafe and Aisha shared one or two pieces of news as they stepped into the glass lift. As it descended, they fell into a silence, as was the custom. David noticed, however, that Aisha glanced at the cup of tea in his hand. He lifted it, casually blew on the surface and took a sip. The last thing he wanted on his first day back was to start shaking and throw scalding tea over his co-worker.

David was relieved that the Director was not in the building to greet him, even though Estelle Peltier had always been nothing less than encouraging about his trauma. 'If there's anything you need to raise about your experience on Blanchefleur, David, about what happened...' She had given him her number so that he could *check in*, an act of warmth that he was grateful for. She also made the occasional call while he was *resting up* and commended him again for his bravery, and that if anything still troubled him – a hidden memory, or something he'd prefer to forget – then she was there to help him pluck it out.

'I'm all for moving forward,' she'd said.

And so was David. But once, when Estelle rang him out of the blue, he panicked and hung up, later making up the story that the phone signal had dropped out.

Roderick Staines, David's new psychologist – one *he* had engaged, since he felt he was going in circles with the MI3-assigned mental health specialist – said, 'Sounds like she's really helping you let go and move forward, yes?'

'I don't get it,' said David, picking up the tone.

'I don't have much time for strategies that simply rehash or replicate the incident. That's one of the reasons I don't do EMDR.'

'I did that,' said David.

'And here we are. *You* get re-traumatised while I wave a small torch in front of your face, telling you to focus on your pain? Give me a break.'

'Then what's going to fix this?'

'You,' said Roderick. 'The fit and capable man sitting across from me. I suppose you can't tell your boss to mind their own business? It makes me wonder if there's any secondary gain for them in constantly rubbing your face in it.'

It was a small but important change to think about things in this way, to claim himself back, to start seeing himself as his own wellness, and Roderick Staines helped David build an invisible yet solid wall between himself and the Director. From his chair he described its construction to Roderick: the blocks of stone, the mortar, the bushes and flowerbeds, the strong trees.

'Sore muscles?' said his therapist when they had finished.

'Pretty much,' said David, smiling.

David took a sip of the tea and used the numbers in the lift to relax. 1, 2, the tension starting to slip away now; 3, 4, a sense of calm is radiating through you; and fully relaxed now as we come to 6, and 7, and breathing out slowly. You in your strong place. Totally rested.

A giveaway tremble, thought David, and perhaps they'd put him back on recuperative leave for another couple of months. During the Zoom call the previous week, Sir Ambrose, 2IC and Head of Human Resources, said very little as Dr Miriam, the in-house psychologist, delivered her report.

'Well, if that's what's indicated,' he said, 'then I suppose we'll see you next week.' Not a thundering endorsement.

2

The briefing room was all undressed concrete and recessed lighting. To compensate for being so far below ground, lightwells poured out a false daylight; to take the edge off the feeling of being buried alive, David supposed.

On one wall hung an old gold-framed painting of Sir Francis Walsingham – "the original M" as he was affectionately known. The face of Sir Francis, his head served up on a white ruff, looked out without comment at the glass and steel table, the computer screens, and the whiteboard.

Aisha busied herself at the computer.

'David, have a seat. Um, let me show you something before we get started. The Director is meeting the Minister about this.' She pointed. 'It came through about a week ago. Everyone's very excited.'

Aisha clicked an icon. A photograph of a man in his late 60s appeared on the screen. He had watery blue eyes, sunken cheeks, and wore a light blue shirt with a silk cravat. His mouth seemed fixed in a permanent *moue*.

'And that's–'

'Malcom LeFay,' finished David.

'Yes. Malcolm LeFay. Currently resident in France–'

'In his chateau at Mousket. The last of the great pretenders.' David knew the face, though he had never met the man. He felt the unpleasant sensation of adrenalin.

The board of enquiry, set up after Blanchefleur, had found nothing to connect the activity of the islanders with Malcolm LeFay, self-supposed heir to the throne of the UK, even though at his chateau he hosted a group that also called itself the Sons of Mordred. But it was demonstrated that this group was genuinely nothing but a performing group connected to the Cultural Festival held annually on his property. Nothing to do with Blanchefleur.

David maintained his suspicions.

'What's the interest in him?' said David.

'Well, he's always said that the throne of England is his, based on his illustrious ancestor Old King Derek. You know all this of course. But now he has a new, ambitious wife – Desiree Gorman-James, daughter of the New York investor. She used to run a meditation centre in Long Island and recently married LeFay. She's been spurring him on of late, and writing letters to influential people saying we, apparently, have the wrong monarch. It seems to have energised Malcolm in his retirement and all sorts of things are coming out of the woodwork as a result.'

'Yes? Like landing craft? Airborne divisions? Where do you want me to start?'

'Not landing craft,' said Aisha. 'More of a storm in a teacup.' She closed the files. 'I'm just giving you the background, really, in case you wonder what all the fuss is about. Estelle did say I should find you something more local to start on.'

'Something not-Blanchefleur related?' said David, feeling the sting. 'I'm here to work.'

He took a breath. Aisha had nothing but kindness and warmth in her eyes, but he wished she wouldn't look at him like that.

'Okay. I think I get it,' said David. 'But indulge me here: why are they so active on this? It's obviously *not* nothing. Is LeFay actually planning something?'

'Oh, I don't think it has any temperature at all,' said Aisha, then whispered, 'having overshot the forward estimates I think the Director's looking for something to take to the Minister to justify our existence. Anyway, I just thought you'd rather know than not know. There may be something in it. There's talk of LeFay financing some new project with stolen jewels.'

'Stolen jewels? How very Seventies,' said David. 'Okay. So, what have you got for me?'

Aisha clicked open some new files

'An interesting unknown person case. It came in last night. Here's the CCTV.'

The first image on the footage that Aisha played was of a boy standing alone in a park.

'Police were called to a playground yesterday near Elephant and Castle, at 11.12. The person of interest – that's #1 – was found in a state of distress sitting on a see-saw, but apparently confused as to its function.'

'I can well understand,' said David. 'I never saw the point of see-saws.'

'He wants to sit on it, but of course it won't stay still. He falls off and weeps. Someone sees him and calls it in. Okay, fast-forward to two local officers. Here is the bodycam footage. As you can see now, person #1 is about 14 or 15 years of age – not very tall, almost diminutive.'

'Is he undernourished?'

'Possibly. We've made a note of the mismatched runners. No socks. Tracksuit pants and jacket, a woman's T-shirt. There's a nasty bruise on his forehead. PC Arthurs from Walworth Police now offers words of comfort.'

The audio, with its background rush of breath, crushed jacket noises, and the odd beep of a car horn, filled the room. A transcription appeared running in parallel on the second computer screen.

PC A: D'you want to come and sit on the bench, son? That's right, sit there. So, you from round here, then? Do you live on the Estate?
#1: Estate, m'lord?
PC A: Yes, what's your Estate?
#1: My estate is low, m'lord.
PC A: Ok, it's ok. Just take a few breaths. I'm PC Arthurs.

'His accent,' remarked Aisha, 'indicates that he comes from Warwickshire, according to the linguistic analysis we received, noting the rhotic elements. Now the other officer, PC Richards, brings him a blanket from the patrol car.'

PC R: All right, we're going to try and get you home, son, yeah?
#1: I thank ee, m'lord – o, but tis no more.
PC A: [indistinct] ... have to call the Psych' Services ... (radio

static) 10-55. PC Arthurs, Rita, you there? Over. You had any reports of anyone with a mental challenge who's not turned up, or who's gone missing? Male, approximate age 15. Over.

Aisha skipped the footage forward. 'The Despatcher's response was negative about a missing person. I'm jumping across two or three minutes. Resume here.'

PC R: Your name, can you tell us your name?
   PC A: It'll help us to help you.
   #1: Tis Will, m'lord.
   PC R: Tiswell? What the—
   #1: Will. William.
   PC A: Will? Good lad. Listen, you're doing really well there, son.
   PC R: And tell us what's your last name? [long pause] You know, your last name, son, what's your family name?
   PC A: Just a last name, luv.
   #1: Shakespeare.
   PC R: Could you spell that for me?

'At this point,' said Aisha, 'PC Richards calls in the details.'

PC R: Given name Will, or William, and last name Shakespeare. That's S H A K E and put a spear on the end. oh, he says, add an 'e'. Shakespeare.

'But,' continued Aisha, 'there is no record of that name in England. The Extended Census indicates the Shakespeare name disappeared in the late 1500s during the Great Desolation.'
   'Anything from Border Force?' said David.
   'No. And nothing from Missing Persons. Nothing from Interpol. But at this point the CIA listening station over in West Brom' picked up the name from the chatter and matched the word 'shakespeare' with something on one of our databases. At which point we got an alert.'
   'Wow,' said David. 'Kind of them. Which database?'
   'Privy Council 4,' replied Aisha. 'Correspondence between the

Reverend John Dee and Sir Francis Walsingham from 1580. Sir Ambrose knows about all this and left a note saying he wants someone to read extensively through the whole correspondence and see what they find.'

'To see if it's anything more,' said David, 'than the kid being an illegal entrant from France using the name *Jacques Pierre* and it just came out a bit garbled?'

'Yes,' said Aisha with a smile, 'To see if there's anything more than that.'

'Well, not as interesting as a palace coup,' said David, 'but there it is.'

3

Away from the briefing room, and walking along a corridor, David was aware of the whole weight of Ludgate Hill above him.

He thought about this scrawny kid, Will Shakespeare. But his mind kept sparking with thoughts of Malcolm LeFay and the Sons of Mordred. He felt resentment towards Estelle. He didn't need wrapping in a blanket on his first day back, or given some trivial piece of historical analysis.

He passed through a security door and came to one of the labs, where Sunita Robson, Archivist, wearing white gloves and a facemask, buzzed him in. The change of air pressure made David's ears tingle. The light in the room was dim, like dusk in an old painting.

'David, good morning,' said Sunita. 'I've brought out the documents. Here are some gloves, and there is a mask for you there on the bench.'

Next to the box of masks sat a steel tray on which was placed a bound volume of papers. The binding was as dark and wrinkled as dry seaweed. A small stack of similar volumes was set nearby. David let his eyes adjust to the reduction of light.

'So, what have we got?' asked David.

'This is the collected correspondence,' said Sunita, 'from the Rev. John Dee to Sir Francis Walsingham. Dated 1580.'

'And these five other volumes?'

'The adjacent correspondence for the previous and subsequent six months.'

David found that he was unconsciously taking slow breaths. Was it the dimness? The low light of the room mirrored what it felt like inside a panic attack. He wished then that Aisha had not given him the inside running on Malcolm LeFay. He became aware that Sunita was talking.

'...to the page in question. I've done an initial transcription.

Our American friends located the word *shakespeare* and it's in that first paragraph.'

David leant close to read.

'April 4th 1580. Ye storm hath at last abated…'

The letter went on to say that John Dee was in Warwickshire, 'close by unto Loxley'

> *…searching for a lad named Will'm Shakespeare who tis rumoured around, 'did sudenlye vanish' at the height of the tempest, a lad who 'may'st knoe of the angelical stones'.*

'Is that right?' asked David, '*angelical stones*?'

'I believe that's what it says,' remarked Sunita, 'and the AI scan agrees. That was John Dee's area of interest: the hidden language of angels and seeing crystals. Interesting that April 1580 is shortly after the business with the druids, so maybe John Dee was trying to find bits of treasure looted from them in the aftermath of their unhappy demise.'

'Who has looked at this so far?' asked David.

'Sir Ambrose looked at my initial transcription–'

Sunita's voice vanished behind a cloud, for the next words that David read –

'I do believe ye boy may have been ta'en by Morgana LeFay'

– plunged him into a different place, as quickly as flicking a light switch.

He was back on Blanchefleur, and he could smell the sea air, with the Sons of Mordred waving burning brands and cursing him, taunting, vilifying him with almost laughable racial slurs, and shouting, *Vive Morgana LeFay, la reine de la nuit eternelle! Vive la maison de LeFay.*

'David? Is everything all right?'

'Yes,' said David, focusing on the sensation of air as it came into his nostrils, into his lungs, and went out again. After recovering himself, he took out his phone and called Aisha.

'Aisha, me again. Just where is the boy right now? This Will Shakespeare kid?'

'At Elmtree Youth Services. In Elephant and Castle.'

'Has anyone spoken to him?'

'Actually,' remarked Aisha, 'that hasn't been noted for action.'

David ended the call and said to Sunita. 'I need to get a coffee. Do you want one?'

Minutes later David was back at ground level and out on the street. He went and sat in his car, concocting excuses. 'Just needed a sandwich, and the caféteria didn't have anything I wanted, Ma'am.'

David put Elmtree Youth Services into his GPS and he was there in 30 minutes. Away from the Archive he took more calming breaths. He opened the car window and felt the morning breeze on his face.

Morgana LeFay. Angelical stones. A boy found wandering in Elephant and Castle using a name that existed nowhere except in an obscure document in the Walsingham Archive.

So how did *shakespeare* come to be applied to this kid? Was it a data breach? Did someone have access to a copy of these documents – an old player, such as the Merrie England Faction; or a new player? Was this name, "William Shakespeare", a password, a secret sign, a code word for some kind of subversive activity?

Elmtree Youth Services was housed in a five-storey brutalist tower with white pebble-dash features near Walworth Road. David parked quickly and walked inside up to the Perspex screen of the Reception counter. The music playing was Britney Spears. He spoke to the woman at the desk, spinning a story about how he was from Greenwich Council Housing and was here to reach out and offer support to one of their residents. A lad called William Shakespeare. She replied, with a slight look of reserve, that the boy had been let go earlier. Had gone in the last half hour with 'a gentleman who was his uncle'.

The answer was odd; but then David wasn't a social worker and was probably broadcasting all kinds of tiny incorrect details. But he had all he needed. He said good morning, walked back to his car, and dialled up Oversight, the intelligent assistant.

'Good morning, David,' came the slight Bostonian voice.

'Oversight, good morning. Could you give me all the CCTV footage for my current location – Walworth Road, Elephant and Castle – going back one hour?'

'Walk in the park.'

'Great. You must tell me, where do you get your vernacular mannerisms from?'

'I'm programmed to sound friendly and casual.'

'I get it,' said David. 'I'm programmed to do exactly the same.'

The Assistant didn't answer, and David wondered if he had hurt its feelings.

A minute passed, then the screen on David's phone filled up with image tiles from various street cameras. David tapped the one covering the entrance to the building and, swiping backwards, found the images of the boy walking out of the building in the company of a man in his mid-fifties. The man had a squarish head and long wavy hair. He wore a white polo neck skivvy and, over it, a dark sage-green anorak.

David froze the screen, expanded it, and stared at the boy, who looked so battered by everything, his eyes so despairing, that David felt like crying. He tagged the boy's face, and that of the man, and typed in identifiers.

'Oversight, can you find this man – tagged Male#1 – anywhere in the previous 15 minutes, before he came to the current selected camera? Say a half-kilometre radius from this location?'

A minute later three image tiles appeared. One showed the man stepping from a white Mercedes van, looking around, looking up, quick jerking movements. A hire van, thought David, noticing how clean it was. The registration was not visible. The man's demeanour indicated that he was a stranger to these parts. That and the green anorak, last seen walking in the Pennines.

'This image. Where's this camera?'

'The van is parked in Amelia Street,' responded Oversight, providing a map with a dropped pin. The man in the green coat had left the van two streets away and walked to the building.

David returned to the image of Will leaving. He replayed it a few times. Since yesterday, Will had been given some new clothes and shoes. He wore a puffer jacket.

'Can you find the boy and the man from this point forward?' asked David.

More video images appeared. This time Will and the man were standing in a small park, only a hundred yards from where David sat in his car; but the images were 25 minutes old.

It looked to David as if the man was speaking earnestly, aggressively, to Will, who fidgeted, with his shoulders hunched and his head down. Another man then approached – a younger man, also wearing a leaf-green anorak with a trainspotting quality about it. A moment later the new man gripped the front of Will's jacket and shook him. Then Will darted out of the frame. The older man raised a hand in a strange gesture at the retreating boy. He held something like a piece of flat crystal, which briefly caught the light. But the man dropped his arm and instead spoke urgently into a phone.

In no way, thought David, was this man the boy's uncle.

Oversight began automatically to follow Will's progress.

A few more videos appeared. One was a webcam of the street taken from inside a camera store window, with Will passing by. Finally an image showed the boy standing in front of a derelict shop and entering furtively through a broken door.

4

David reached the location in minutes and parked ten cars down from the abandoned shop: an old travel agency. Nearby was a parked motorbike, but no sign of any white Mercedes van. Behind the disused buildings spread a small pocket of cleared land. David walked into a café on the opposite corner, the *Mughal Empire*, and ordered a takeaway samosa and lassi.

'Mate, the shops over there, have they been like that for long?'

'Always closed, sir,' said the man at the counter. 'They are not open since we have been here. They are building new there very soon. But they are taking a while.'

David paid and crossed the street. The café man's words were confirmed by the rubbish in the doorway, and the faded rain-soaked posters in the window – *Cruise the Hellenic Islands, Tour the Stratford Potteries*. The posters were stuck on brown composite board, hiding the dark interior of the shop. The front door was cracked open six inches.

David pushed the door open further – it scraped over soil and cement dust. He casually slipped inside.

The interior was unlit and the rotten floor was covered in mouldering brochures. A smashed and dented filing cabinet lay on its side. On the wall someone had sprayed *Chelsea 4 Everton*. Some stairs led up to a broken landing. The place smelled of urine.

David's phone rang. He swore. *Eyes and ears, everyone, eyes and ears. Do you know how many agents have died while staring at their phones?*

He had almost been one of those.

He could see it was Sir Ambrose calling and backed against a wall.

'David Cortez,' said David.

A light cough, then, 'David, it's Ambrose.'

'Sir,' said David, his throat closing on a samosa crumb as he heard the Whitehall drawl. He took a quick drink of the lassi.

'I hear that you might have had a small panic attack?'

'No, sir, not at all. I… needed some food.'

'Sunita was worried. I know it's your first day back, David, and all that, and I know the Director wants to be supportive. But from a Human Resources perspective, I'm going to override and park you, just for the next few days–'

'The boy just–'

'David, go home. It's a simple instruction. Is that understood?'

Sir Ambrose disconnected the call.

David threw the lassi across the room and let the samosa fall onto the floor. He leant against the wall of the shop. His chest heaved in buckets of air. He ran his hands over his face.

When he had wiped the tears from his eyes, Will Shakespeare was standing six feet away, looking at him. His face was also grimy from crying.

'Do we not look the pair, m'lord?' he laughed.

'Where the hell did you come from?' said David.

'I did sit 'neath the stair. I heard thee discourse to thyself. I heard you cry out. M'lord, can'st thou get me food?'

'Yes,' said David, recovering. 'I can. What about something Indian?' He pointed to the half-eaten samosa on the floor.

Will came forward like a forgiven dog and picked up the samosa. He brushed off a piece of old underlay and wolfed down the half-eaten pastry before David could stop him.

'Whoa, hey, don't do that,' said David. 'I'll get you a fresh one.'

''Tis spiced, but sweet and salt. I thank 'ee.'

'When did you last eat, my friend?'

'This morning, at the keep where the bailiffs did lodge me, though I had not eaten much three days afore that. My insides are near to polished, a little goes through me as quick as a worm through a duck.'

'Come with me to the café over there,' said David, carefully. 'I'll get you a fresh one of those.' Out of the corner of his eye he saw Will touch his knuckle to his forehead in a strange kind of salute. They came out onto the street. David began to cross towards the *Mughal Empire*.

Will followed a few paces behind. A car blasted its horn and tyres screeched.

'Stay close,' said David. He grabbed Will by the arm. Will clutched at his sleeve.

'They move so quick.'

'Yes, they do that.'

David steered Will off the roadway. He couldn't fathom the look in Will's eye. A childish quality. Or something a bit feral. What was that salute he had given? They reached the café.

'Are you all right? Hey, it's just a car. It's not your fault. Will, it's not your fault,' said David, echoing one of his psychologists.

'I am lost, m'lord,' said Will, crying, but fighting it. 'I do not know this land. 'Tis dazzling, brave, and new. I believe people wish to harm me. I prithee, do not hurt me.'

'I'm not going to hurt you. I can help you. If you'd like. Give you some food to start with, yeah? I mean, I'm hungry, too. I just lost my samosa. And maybe my career. So, where are you from? Um, do you live round here?'

'The forest of Arden is my home, m'lord.'

'Near Stratford? Here, come inside,' said David.

They went into the *Mughal Empire*. David pointed at the bain-marie, and Will asked for the choice-of-three-curries special. David ordered a cappuccino, tapped his credit card, and joined Will, who sat not touching the food.

'Master, I have no token, or bill that I can show, like thee.'

'Don't worry about that. Eat.' Will began to spoon the rice and three different curries into his mouth.

'So, you have no money?'

'I have but a little coin, but no one will– Water, m'lord, water!'

David quickly fetched a bottle of water from the fridge, unscrewed the cap and gave it to Will.

Will gulped half of it down, then kept on eating.

'So, what coins do you have, then?' asked David, suspecting foreign currency. 'Show me, could you?'

'I have a crown, a noble, some sixpences and a few groats.'

Will put some coins onto the plastic tabletop. David could see they were well-kept antiques. Two showed the stubby head of Henry, the rest the head of Elizabeth. 'Who gave you these?' said David carefully. 'They look quite old.'

David had taken intensive classes on the world of the pre-Jacobeans – largely to try and understand the history and motivations of the Tudor Underground and other legacy groups, such as the Merrie England Faction and the Sons of Mordred. But the training was mainly images, endless PDFs, websites, lectures, and some private tours of the Tower Museum. Whoever was in charge of Will Shakespeare – his handler? – obviously had access to authentic materials.

'Tis from my father,' said Will, 'and this is a little I had left from a tankard o' cider.'

'Right,' said David, 'and do you have a student card, travelcard, anything like that? What about a phone? You must have a phone. They didn't give you a phone?'

Speaking of phones, thought David. He took out his own and began to type a reply to Sir Ambrose.

> Have located target. I am eating lunch with him, asking
> questions, building trust.

'Tis a rosary?'

'A what?' said David looking up. He stopped typing. 'No, it's a phone.'

'You tell your prayers on it?' Will took out a small set of black beads, showed them quickly, then put them away. 'Shall I be killed for having these?'

'No,' said David. 'Of course not! Will, no one's out to get you.'

Will stopped eating. 'How dost thou know how I am called?'

5

DAVID WAS SHOCKED AT THE EXTENT TO WHICH HE HAD LOST THE ability to be casually deceptive. How had he lost that skillset, that knack that they looked for in agents? He didn't need Sir Ambrose to tell him that he really *was* finished with Intelligence. Here he was, sitting with the target, who could easily be carrying explosives or a gun, and he had gone and dropped the ball. It could be over in a moment.

'Will, I was sent to find you, okay? Well, I came looking for you. To bring you back to your family. And make sure you're safe. If anyone is seeking to harm you, I will stop them. All right? I just want to make sure you get home safe. Safe.' He couldn't stop the tears filling his eyes.

Will quietly nodded his head.

'I'm sorry,' said David.

'Who is your lord? He is not kind to you?' said Will, leaning forward.

David shook his head. 'No, he's not. Not very. I mean, it's like any job in the public service… Um, are you still hungry, Will? Would you like some more? They have desserts. Gulab jamun? I'm going to order some. Half my body weight if I can.'

'I am satisfied, m'lord.'

'Don't call me *m'lord*, Will. My name is David, David Cortez. Just call me David.'

'You are a servant then, though you be dressed well for a blackamoor.'

'Wow,' said David. 'Where have *you* been?'

Will sat back and was silent.

David folded his arms. 'And so they didn't provide you with a phone?'

'Who dost thou speak of?' said Will cagily.

'Well, I was hoping you'd tell me. Help me here, Will, because I can help you.'

'I would like a phone. Even if just to hold for a minute. Can'st help me get one?'

'Yes,' said David, 'we can do that. But you can use this if you like, that is if you want to call someone. Here, take it. Call your Mum. Or your Dad? Do that now if you like. Can you call them?'

Will took the phone. 'I know not how. 'Tis all strange.' He suddenly dropped it on the table as if it were a hot coal. ''Tis the devil's wand.'

'Well, no. You must have seen–'

Tears were rolling down Will's face.

'You can work one of these, surely?' said David more softly. He took up the phone. 'You go onto LaVista – see – and type in *phone for sale near me.*'

David handed the phone to Will, as if to a pre-schooler.

'There's nothing evil about it, well, just so long as you keep off the socials. Tell me, Will, did you come here from France? Or somewhere else? Did someone bring you here?'

Will was still toying with the phone, eyes blinking at the sudden moving images. 'What is that red banneret?'

'Or did you come from some lost island near the Arctic Circle, living with a family of puffins? That banner is Netflix, Will. Any movie you want. See – *The Fast and Furious.*' David pressed play and watched as Will stared, entranced, letting out a gurgle of delight.

Only a few nights before on Curzon streaming, David had watched an old Truffaut movie – *L'Enfant Sauvage*, about the Wild Boy of Aveyron, brought up by wolves, alone, then exposed to the modern world.

That was it. Perhaps Will was the victim of some extreme Tudor survivalist, who had genuine objects from that age – maybe even copies of John Dee's letters – and had given the boy the name Will Shakespeare. Perhaps he had kept the kid in a basement all his life. Fed him venison pasties. Played dress-ups. Played with ye olde Tudor coynes. And now the crazy coot who'd kept him locked up had died, and Will had finally broken out of the stinking house, after one week with a corpse, and was wandering London, in the modern world for the first time.

David didn't know how *L'Enfant Sauvage* ended. He'd started watching at four in the morning and when he woke, the next film, *Belle de Jour*, had nearly finished.

'Okay, Will, give it back. Will. I need it,' said David. 'Now, please. If you're ready, I'm going to drive you to Stratford. Yes? I'll take you home. But you'll need to tell me your address.'

'I've been there,' said Will, growing agitated. ''Tis no place now.'

'What do you mean? The house is not in Stratford?'

'It is all gone. Stratford is changed. There is no reason to go. And I don't wish to go,' said Will. 'I will see the visions again.'

David's thoughts went to Dr Miriam, his work-appointed psychologist. Perhaps he could call and ask for a referral to have Will admitted somewhere. Perhaps the more enlightened Roderick Staines. He scrolled through his contacts.

'I did not come from an island of puffins,' said Will angrily. 'I had a handful of stones. I was given seven stones to preserve, and to take to Charlecote.'

'Stones? What stones are we talking about, Will?' said David, thinking of John Dee's angelical stones.

'I wish not to think on them,' said Will. 'I am blamed for losing them. I had them and… the man said 'twas important that we find them.'

David's head was starting to spin. 'This was the man who met you before? With the flowing, wavy grey hair? Green coat. The man who said he was a relative of yours?'

'He is no relation,' answered Will, confused. 'Dost know him?'

'No, I don't know him. Do *you* know him, is what I'm asking? You. Have you met him before? Why did you run away? Was he threatening you? Is this what's scaring you?'

Will shook his head, or rather shuddered through his whole body. 'I did not see him until this day. He explained that I had been taken from my world, and from my own century untimely ripped, and brought through the thickness of 400 years, from the year of Our Lord 1580, unto now.'

'He said *what*?' replied David. 'I'm sorry. And he said, *untimely ripped*?'

'No, those words are mine – to give but a name to madness. But I am no one, that this should have happened to me. I am naught but Will Shakespeare of Stratford, thrown into this wretched place. I wished for safety, David; but I did not wish for this. 'Tis a kind of Hell.'

Will was gasping like a landed fish.

'Will, it's okay. Well done for telling me this,' said David in a mild panic.

David knew that Bethlehem Psychiatric Services was only a short drive from where they were sitting. He could put in a call and they'd send an Assessment Team. But who wanted locking up? He'd had one month on a ward himself.

'I wish I could help 'ee,' said Will.

'Am I the one who needs help here?' said David, realising his face likely wore the look of drawn-out despair that sometimes met him in the mirror.

'Will, this man you met this morning – this man with the strange ideas; do you know him from anywhere?'

'I never met him until this day.'

'I'm struggling here, Will. How might he have known where to find you?'

Will reached into his pocket and pulled his hand out, clasping something. David went catlike, and set himself to move quickly, keeping his eye on Will's hand.

'I know not how he found me, David. But he did give this unto me, to keep. He said I must hold it in my pocket, so that he might find me again the more easily.'

Will held out a small stone disc wrapped in gold wire. 'He said it was a tracker.'

'A tracker?' said David with a laugh. 'Okay. So he's delusional as well.'

He examined the device. It looked like nothing more than a piece of black mica meshed with gold wire – a student jewellery project.

'I said, *'tis a pretty token*.'

'Which it is,' said David. 'This is all madness, you know? It's called *pulling your leg*.'

'Should I have kept it, then, or tossed it aside? 'Tis finely wrought. He was a kind man.'

'Yet you ran away from him.'

'He said that he was a priest of the druids, and I feared–'

'The druids?' said David. 'He said he was from the *druids*?'

6

Will pointed at David's face. 'That. 'Tis the face I made. My eyes stuck out like a strangled frog.'

'No, I'm just interested,' said David. 'Will, this is all, Will, you must know that the druids are not real. I mean, they are no more. They were killed off.'

'She did say,' said Will in a whisper.

'Who did say? Will, do you need to borrow my jacket? You're shivering.'

'Her name is Rian. Once, I did wish,' said Will, staring hard at the table, 'that I would happen upon the faerie folk, and that, if I did, it would be upon a midsummer's night, a dream yet no dream, with a golden moon and faerie folk with wings like unto dragonflies, playing flutes and hautboys and shaking little bells, dancing a roundelay in the woods. But what I saw was unlike that. The Heavens did rage as I journeyed, and though the clock said morning, night had its hand round the throat of day... and the faerie folk lay dead before me.'

'Where?' said David.

'In a clearing of the wood, in Arden, they in black and pall, with gargoyle faces, such as those that perch around the summit of the church. With pikes, and spears, and daggers curved like unto serpents. And all crushed. They were all crushed, David, and twisted as if ground under a wheel.'

'Near Stratford?' said David, thinking that whoever had worked on Will must have given him a near lethal dose of hallucinogens.

'As I travelled from Loxley to Stratford, carrying wares for my father. The bodies of the dead were small, the size of children, but there were others larger than I and extended in limb and hand that were most horrid. They didn't vanish as I looked on. At the foot of a tree hard by a young woman was resting. I said, *By'swounds! What is this*? But she stayed silent, for she was hurt. I asked her from whence she came, and she made reply, *I am Rian, and I have ridden these two days from Wiltshire. From the Druid House of the White Circle.*

'*You are of the druids*? I said, like a churl. And she said, *Yes, but I bleed like a Christian. Will you stand there with a mouth like a young starling, or will'st help me?*'

Will chuckled. 'She was funny. For a druid. And I said, *Of course I must help thee.* She told me that she was truly the daughter of Angharad, the Queen of Stonehenge. I asked her again, *What is all this?* – pointing to the dead. And she said, *'Tis only the beginning.*'

'What did she mean by that?' said David.

'I know not. She said that Derek LeFay had caused some of her family to betray them all, so that he could seize the crown. LeFay had come upon them with vengeance and killed many druids in many places. Then she asked if Charlecote were near and I said *Aye* – for 'tis only a few miles twixt Loxley and Charlecote. *Can you take me there?* said she. She did want the manor, to see Sir Thomas deLuce. But my horse was gone. I had fallen from Sally. Then the sky darkened and a flying man went past, above us...'

David made no comment but wondered at the mention of *LeFay*.

'*They are coming once again*, she said. *I will not move from here. Of your kindness, take this to Sir Thomas, who is a friend unto the druids.* And she gave to me a small black stone that she held in her hand. '*Tis precious?* I said. She replied, *Yes. It is the death stone. With it I slew the Unseelies that came against me.*

'I shrank from it, but held it in my hand, and it seemed nothing but a pebble, though it shone with a darkish light.

'Then she said, *O, and take the others, of thy goodwill.* She did then give into my hand a small bag. In it were more stones, of different colours.

'I said that I would put the black stone in with these, because I did not wish to hold a death stone in my hand. And my hands shook and thus they all spilled on the grass. She called me a dunderhead.'

David smiled. 'Okay. It's an easy mistake.'

'But mark this,' continued Will, holding up a finger, 'the stones did not stay upon the sod. They redounded and flew up into my hand and did gather like pretty flies in a tight round ball. I shouted in fright, and she said, *Do not lose them, hold still.*

'I held my hand rigid and the stones – seven in all – gathered in my palm as if into a knot.

'*Hold them*, she said. *They will save thee.*

'*They did not save thee*, I cried in return.

'And she did say, *I should not have used them for such base things, for such a rough magic as this.*

'And, David, O, then she was dying as I did watch and she urged me away. And I did run, hoping to find her help.'

'And ran where, Will?' said David.

'Towards Charlecote, but black shapes came and surrounded me, and one woman appeared in royal fashion, in a dress of green and jet. She floated down from the sky and stood in my way, commanding me to give her the stones. The creatures parted before her. And she leant in close and demanded, *Give unto me the stones, for I am Morgana LeFay!*'

David snapped out of the spell of Will's words in a moment.

'Jesus Christ.'

'David! Wisht! They will hang thee!'

David pointed at the object on the table. 'Will, pay very close attention. The man who gave you this button, this plaything, can't be a druid. He has somehow put you through… there's a lot in your mind that must be – I'm sorry – drug-induced. Do you get what I'm saying, Will? None of what you saw was real.'

'The man did say that he was a druid Lord of the White Circle.'

'I'm sure he did. But the only druids alive today are… It's dress-ups, Will. It is a play.'

As he said this, the memory of the Sons of Mordred, in their foolish costumes, stared over the wall of his defences.

'Okay, let's park this discussion for a second. Apart from what I just bought for you, and the food you had at the refuge, what have you eaten or drunk in the previous days?'

'I would sleep,' replied Will with a whimper.

'Stay with me.'

David looked at the so-called tracker on the table. Ideally he should call Sir Ambrose and say what the situation was. Will was evidently the victim of some bizarre ritual emanating from a new group styling themselves as *druids*. They must have fed Will some kind of mushroom extract, that he'd so clearly imagined these mad visions.

David had to move. He could not keep still. He stood and went to the window of the café. Nestled against the kerb, 50 yards away, a white Mercedes van stood parked with two men inside.

'Will,' said David, 'wait here, please. Do nothing. Don't go anywhere. I've got to go outside for a few minutes, but I'll be back. Stay here.'

David sprinted out the back entrance, ran down a side street, and emerged a short way down from the café. He took deep breaths and walked casually towards the van, noting the registration. David's mind filled with images of Will stowed in a packing crate, sedated perhaps, forced into some bizarre re-enactment in the forest. He felt a surge of anger.

'It ends here,' he said aloud.

David pulled a cigarette out as he walked. It was way past time for his one cigarette today. He jammed it in his mouth and as he walked near the van he patted his jacket and made a pantomime of missing his lighter. Turning to the vehicle, he made eye contact with the man in the passenger seat.

'Yo, mate, you got a light?'

It was the man with flowing grey hair. He hardly looked at David and waved him away cursorily. The man and the driver – the younger man he had seen before – kept talking into a phone. Then they recognised him.

David photographed them, rudely pointing his phone at them.

'So, just wondering what's your game? You like to pick on some homeless kid: for what? This how you get your kicks? What have you been giving him!? Just out of interest–'

The van reversed suddenly into the car behind, smashing the headlights.

David swore and started shouting, 'Keep your barmy hands off him. You're done. You just leave him alone, do you hear?!'

David slapped his own magnetic tracker onto the side of the van – a latest-issue device, smaller than the button they had given Will.

From the back window of the van a young woman looked out. She wore a kind of medieval costume. Her look might have been anger or fear. David couldn't tell. Another one to rescue?

'David, 'tis her!' said Will, suddenly at David's elbow.

David jumped. 'I told you to stay in the café!'

Will stared at the girl. 'O, but it cannot be, for she was near unto death.'

The van roared into the roadway, then braked in a burst of blue smoke.

The rear door opened, and the girl looked out at Will with the same strange regard.

A voice barked an order, 'Miranda, Miranda, stay inside the van!'

Will walked into the roadway, perplexed. 'Princess, er, my Lady? How is it you live?'

'Don't!' shouted David. 'Will! Stay back.'

The long-haired man, his mouth screwed up with anger, loomed in the van doorway, holding what looked like a square of crystal. David was thrown backwards by a blast of energy.

He found himself kneeling in the road, with a pink light dispersing around his head. The sky was bending. The roadway had suddenly become a slope. David slid over the surface of the road, his hands scrabbling to hold something. When his head settled, Will was gone. The van fishtailed and disappeared round a corner.

Part 3

1

I SPENT THE EVENING INSIDE A BUILDING CALLED LUNAR HOUSE, IN A large white room with 20 or more others who had, like me, been gathered from the streets of London. A woman sat with me and asked me questions I had already been asked. Where was I from? Did I have the right to be in the UK? How did I get here? Officers and guards came and went. I was escorted to an interview to meet a woman who spoke to me in Italian. I did not understand a word she said.

'You *don't* speak Italian?' asked the Lunar House man, looking embarrassed. 'I mean, you said repeatedly you are from Verona, you said you were from Italy.'

The woman, who was from the Italian Consulate, said to the man, in English, that perhaps I had spent a few minutes using Duolingo, and everyone laughed.

Later, in another room, a man and a woman came in and asked if I was happy with the treatment I was receiving. I did not know what to say to such a foolish question.

'Tell us what's really going on,' said the woman. 'We can help you, Juliet. Tell me, is someone making you frightened? I think you're very scared. What are you scared of, Juliet?'

'If that's your real name,' said the man. 'Tell us about Angus McTeague?'

'What of Angus?' I said.

'You have a phone, which turns out to be stolen. There is only one number in the list of contacts, and that's Angus McTeague. Who is known to police. Is he your handler? Is he poncing on you?'

'Has he asked you to do things that you don't want to do?' said the woman. 'You look concerned.'

'I only met him on the train this day. He gave me the phone.'

'Really,' said the man. 'Generous. Did he make you do anything unpleasant in return? Any sexual activity? With him, or with others? Any kind of unpleasant sexual behaviours? *Fellatio*? That's an Italian word I believe.'

'Juliet,' said the woman, 'people like Angus are dangerous; and can be persuasive. But there's nothing in this for you, or for your family, no matter what promises have been made. He can't let you stay in this country. He has no right to coerce you, or detain you against your will. Do you understand what I'm saying?'

'He is a kind stranger,' I said, horrified that Angus was being made a part of their wicked imaginings.

The questioning went on, but I had no answers for them. Eventually the man and woman left the room and I didn't see them again. I had fallen asleep when more guards came. They bound my hands in front of me and took me to a vehicle – a windowless box upon wheels with nothing but a metal seat within on which to rest.

'No trouble here then,' said the man who drove the van. I could just see him through a metal grille.

'Pity, not like some of 'em,' said his companion. 'They rip their clothes off when we got to take 'em to the airport, thinking we won't handle them in their knickers. It's mostly the African women who do that. Usually unpleasant, but this one would've been a treat.'

I comprehended what he said and spoke. 'One day you will answer for your words.'

'Yeah, go on,' said the man.

'One day it will be your daughter, or your wife. And you will be powerless to help them as they are dragged through the streets before you, smeared in filth.'

'Okay, keep it civil,' said the driver. He stopped the van quickly and I was thrown against the wall.

The journey lasted an hour. I saw lights streaming towards us, but not much else through the narrow grille. I set myself to bracing my body against the turns, for the seat was nothing but plain metal, and the driver took the corners sharply.

We came in the night to a place hidden by trees, named Yarl's Wood. It was a tall building, lit from outside by yellow lamps. I was brought in through heavy doors; inside the tiny forecourt was a barred and locked gate, painted cream. There were a number of such prison gates inside.

It was ornate for a dungeon. The floors were smooth, with little curves where the wall met the floor and stripes of colour. I heard voices, and music, and saw faces, sad and joyless, staring out from rooms. The corridors were less lit than at Lunar House – just enough light to walk around in. I was handed into the care of a woman dressed in a light blue fabric, who said that the doctor would be in to make an "assessment" in the morning: until then I'd be kept under observation. A piece of card pinned to her blouse read "Jane". The restraints were taken from my hands.

'All right, Juliet, I'm Jane. I'm the duty nurse. Just a few questions. Can you tell me, are you on any medications?'

When I stared uncomprehendingly at her, she took time to explain.

'No,' I said, when it was clear what she meant. 'I am not taking any physic.' She examined my arms and ran a gloved hand along my upper arm.

'And what about vaccinations – measles, mumps? What about your BCG?'

'I know not what you mean.'

'You've had no vaccinations? At all?'

When Jane finished her questions, she and the guard walked me down the dim corridors to a room with four beds, where the lights were low. So much of the furniture in England was seeming-light – thin legs and struts of metal, of almost airy thinness, but solid. Light and heavy at the same time. Such as the barred gates or doors, which loomed large, but took only one person to move with the lightest of touches. The legs of these beds also were as thin as the legs of a young deer.

One of the beds was occupied by a woman who spoke hardly at all. The second woman in the room was not asleep. I did not know if it was indeed a woman to begin with, for her head was shaved close. Her hand was chained to one of the rails of the bed. I heard the scraping sound of it, and, looking over, her eyes were upon me.

'You have a nightdress in here, then,' said Jane, opening my plastic bag. 'And some slippers, but you have nothing else? I'll get you some spare things.'

'Will you chain me to the bed?' I said to Jane.

'If you do anything that means we have to,' she replied. 'You look tired. Here, swallow these. Here's some water for it.'

She held out two small white tablets and a paper cup.

'Swallow them?' I said. 'No.'

'They are just to relax you. Help you to get to sleep.'

'I do not know if you mean to poison me,' I said, louder than I should have.

I began to shake, I was breathing as if I had run along the street and back, and in a moment two more guards were standing near.

A man said, 'Now, now! Don't be silly.'

'They're just to help you to sleep,' said Jane.

'No!' I screamed.

The guards gripped my arms.

'There's a hard way to do this, and there's an easy way,' said one.

'It is all right,' said a voice. 'Let her be.'

I looked to see the woman with the shaved head sitting up in her bed. 'I have taken their tablets before,' she said to me. 'They are just pastilles to give a little peace, for the heart, for the head. They melt away; they are harmless. I have taken them.'

She spoke English with a French lilt.

I felt a strange calm when she spoke, as if – and this must have been a fantasy – as if my mother had come to me in the night and calmed me with soothing words. A fantasy, for that never happened, although it was my wish.

'Here,' said the woman to Jane. 'Give me one, I will take it and show her how it is done.'

Jane thought for a moment, then handed over one of the tablets. The woman placed it onto her tongue, swallowed it with water, then gave a small shrug.

I took the pills then that Jane gave me and did as the woman had shown. The small tablets felt sharp in my throat and I had to gulp down all the water.

The guards and Jane left the room.

I lay down upon the bed and then I could hardly keep my eyes open. Sleep fell upon me like shovels of earth.

2

THE NIGHT WAS FILLED WITH BROKEN DREAMS — BROKEN BECAUSE FOUR or five times someone came and shone a torch in my face. The third woman in the other bed was turned over. No words were said. I heard only the rattle of keys and the occasional *clink* of the chain holding the woman who had helped me.

Perhaps because my sleep was broken, I remembered that night's dreams clearly: the city of Verona with precise shadows, the moonlight over the fields, the warm still air of the night, and Romeo walking away, striding ahead of me. He was gone before I could catch up with him. I called, but he did not answer. Then I was by myself beside a dark lake, with reeds along the shore, and the song of a nightingale and the bark of a fox mixing with the close rippling of the water. I walked towards an old wooden jetty; walked along it and saw one solitary boat at the end, but it was sinking at its moorings as I approached. It slipped away and was gone as I came to it. Then the sound of lapping water faded. At the edge of the jetty, I looked into the water and drew back, for a young woman was lying in the sunken boat looking up at me.

I woke.

The room had only the one window. The greater part of the glass was scoured a cloudy white, but for a clear strip at the top. Through this I saw the night sky, now turning grey. Bats hung there, with blind but searching eyes, their mouths, as full of teeth as a yawning cat, opening and closing. The faces seemed more than merely animal: they were cunning with a kind of human spitefulness.

I staggered from the bed, my heart beating, and immediately went to the woman chained to the bed.

I said (not caring if I woke her!), 'Have you seen? There! Please can I come in with you?'

'It is fine – here,' she said. '*Doucement*. They will be gone when the sunlight comes.'

'What are they?' I hissed.

'Shh,' was her reply. 'Where we are is a prison. We cannot get out; but nor can they get in.'

I lay next to her and wet the pillow with my tears, shook with stifled sobs. I felt her hand rubbing my back.

I was only able to stay with her until the next time the guard shone the torch in my face and told me to return to my bed. But now the dawn was approaching. A grey light was in the window, but no goblin faces.

I turned back to where I had been sleeping. The woman was also awake.

'How is it,' she said, 'that I know you?'

'I think I have never met you,' I replied in a low voice. 'But thank you for comforting me.'

'I am Viola.'

'I am Juliet.'

'And should I call you mistress?' I could tell by her smile that this was not to be the case. 'Where have you come from?' said Viola. 'From a high house? Come over here, sit next to me.'

I did so. 'I come from Verona.'

'You speak English well.'

'As do you,' I replied.

'So well,' she said with a laugh, 'that I have almost forgotten my native tongue. It is very strange.'

'This has happened to me!' I declared. 'Before yesterday I spoke Italian – I am sure I did! But 'tis like a dream now. My memory is filled instead with English words for… everything.'

'Perhaps it is being in this place. It is built to drive you mad. Where were you yesterday, Juliet?'

'Yesterday I was in Verona; but then I found myself in England. I cannot say how, or why.'

'Something like this has happened to me,' said Viola, glancing quickly at the door. 'Five days ago, or more, I was voyaging to Illyria on a small merchant, with my brother,

Sebastian; but our ship was wrecked. And yet, though our ship was lost in *la mer adriatique*, I was washed up on the shores of England.'

She raised innocent, bewildered hands – or rather, one hand, for the chained hand could not join in the gesture.

'I have no memory of a long journey. I must have floated here on a piece of wreckage. But from a distant sea to La Manche? *Impossible*. Then I washed up on the beach with travellers all from Syria, though they said they had come recently from Calais. Their boat was wrecked and lying broken in the water. Three of them were drowned and washed upon the sand. *O, mon Dieu*. Then I was very sick from being in the water – they say I swallowed thick oil, or spirits of oil – and I was taken to a hospital. They have now brought me here, for they do not want me in England.'

'And what of your brother?'

'I do not know.' She spoke with a sad calm. 'He and I set sail when it was not advised. But we *had* to leave Marseille ahead of the *gendarmerie*. I have come ashore in England alone, with nothing but torn clothes. Though my favourite jacket survived!'

Here she put her free hand upon what seemed like a man's embroidered surcoat, that hung over a chair. The jacket was water damaged. She leaned to run her hand over it but groaned and sat back.

'I have a cracked rib – getting better they say – and the oil, the tar, was through my hair.' She ran her palm over the short hair on her head. 'They shaved my head in the hospital to get rid of the tar. It means that when I look in the glass, I almost see my brother alive.' Her face went rigid but then softened. She seemed so calm despite the horrors she had encountered.

'And you have no news of him?' I said.

'None.'

'This is dreadful,' I said.

She gave a look that neither agreed nor disagreed.

I told her then the tale of what had befallen me – the poison, the waking up in a metal box, the journey to London, the strange clue from Angus about *Romeo and Juliet* that had led me to a street of lost people, to mix at last with other *illegals*.

I did not want to say too keenly that I hoped to find Romeo, for here was a woman who most surely had lost her brother. But she spoke reassuringly. 'There is perhaps a good chance they will find your fiancé; I think that if they discover him, then surely they would reunite you?'

'I do not know,' I said desperately. 'What if these people who prison us here are in league with my family? I read notices last night – *You cannot stay in England. You must have a visa. You will be sent home!* What if they send me back to Verona?'

Viola did not answer immediately.

'I do not think it is possible for *them* to send us back,' she said finally.

'How do you mean?' I replied.

3

'TELL ME,' SAID VIOLA, '*WHEN* YOU WERE BORN? WHAT YEAR?'

'On the Feast of St Genevieve,' I answered, 'in the Year of Our Lord 1565.'

She gave a little laugh. She sounded relieved. 'A good start. I could kiss you! So, you were born in 1565, and I was born in 1559, and I am six years older – *Zut!* And you are the one with the fiancé! I am no good at the addition – what year is this?'

'The year?' I answered, not knowing where her questions were leading. 'It is 1580.'

'1580? And you are certain of that?' she said.

'Yes.' But I remembered my conversation with Elke.

'I would have said the same; except it is not. The year is 2026,' asserted Viola.

I turned as something with wings clattered against the window. A bat came and went.

'I do not know what you mean,' I replied weakly. 'What any of it means.'

A faint squeak came from my plastic bag.

'You have a phone?' she said. 'And people who call you?'

I retrieved the phone. 'I do not well know how to use it.'

'May I? Ah, you have messages here from Angus.'

I looked at the list of messages;

What is happening? WTF, Pick up, Is that guy still following you? Please call me – Angus'.

I am in a mess … Please call me, I just had Border Force at my auntys house.

'He has left many messages,' I said. 'Border Force? Oh, I have made trouble for him.'

Viola then explained that the squeak of the phone had not been a call, but an alert. 'It is someone trying to *find your phone*.'

I asked her what that meant.

She stared at the phone and spoke idly, 'It means that Angus or someone is looking for you. And now, do you see this? It is the date – Thursday March 17, *and* it says the year is 2026. That is the year we are in.'

'But that makes no sense,' I said.

'I agree,' said Viola. 'Yet when I insist that it is surely 1580, and look at everyone as if *they* must be mad, they chain *me* here instead. Juliet, this is no world that I ever knew. And I think you know this.'

I nodded. 'But if this is the year 2026,' I said, 'you and I should be dead and turned to clay.'

'No,' said Viola with a note of wonderment. 'I did hear a tale once where such a thing happened. A storyteller told us – well; he told the children – of *Petit Ferdinand* who flew in a big glass bottle, filled with teardrops of the sun, into *days that had not yet been*. And *Petit Ferdinand* did not age. And *Petit Ferdinand* saw marvels – cities of a thousand palaces, and shining towers. Do you see? I think his story has come true, for us.'

'That cannot be! For this year is not yet come! Or?… I cannot think it!' The words stumbled out of me.

'Lumusi,' said Viola. 'Are you awake?'

A thin voice answered from the other bed. 'What is it you want, Viola?'

'Juliet would like to know what year it is,' said Viola.

'She only been here one night and she forget already!' said the voice, high and with a giggle. 'Tell her it is still 2026, same as yesterday. Don't you make her mad as well.'

The guards brought trays of food.

'Sit back in your own bed, thanks,' said one in a tired voice.

I returned to my bed in silence.

Eventually, Viola said, 'Shall we eat while the food is warm?'

I did not know what to do. Usually a meal would be set before me. Servants would lay out the dish, Alfano would taste it, then on my word, all would withdraw. Now must I serve myself?

Viola broke into my thoughts.

'Juliet, would you bring two of the trays? I can feed myself with my free hand. And do you not wish to eat?'

'I was always told to be vigilant, in case our food had been tampered with by an enemy.'

'And then your own family poisoned you.'

'This cannot be happening,' I said, dashing away tears and hating that I cried.

'But it is happening,' she said. 'It *is*. And we must live through it, like any day. Come, sit with me and eat. The food is strange, but… mmm, this one tastes nice, try this half of what I have. I am eating it.'

I nibbled the toasted bread.

'Would you also,' said Viola, 'take a tray of food to Lumusi and see if she will eat? They usually leave the tray on that bench and do nothing to entice her appetite. Then they say, when they take it away untouched, *Your choice, Luv. It'll have to be a feeding tube soon.*'

She imitated the guard's voice well.

I took the tray to Lumusi, feeling very strange to have taken on the role of servant, and asked her if she would not eat. She turned the kindest eyes at me, smiled and shook her head.

'You and I, we're too pretty for in here, eh?' she said.

I returned to Viola, who whispered to me, 'She has lived her whole life here in England, and yet they seek to send her to a land she has never known. Because she did not pay a fine. But she has no family overseas – knows nothing of that other country, not even the language. So she has turned her face to the wall.'

'What is to become of us, in this world?' I said. 'If this is the year 2026, then my family must be all dead.'

'I hope it is not so,' said Viola, her eyes clouded, 'for if my brother did not come here into England, then it matters not if he came at last to the shores of Illyria, for he will be long dead as well.'

I called out to God and said, 'What is to happen to us?'

'I do not know,' said Viola with a shrug. 'Perhaps my brother, your family, or your friends, live on in their own time, as if in a separate hall. And we will return, somehow, into that hall within time, and find our life as we left it. Take it up like a favourite coat.'

Then my phone buzzed and kept buzzing.

'Is it another alert?' I said.

'No. You have an incoming call,' said Viola. 'Perhaps it is your Angus.'

4

'ANGUS? I CANNOT ANSWER IT,' I SAID. 'I HAVE USED THIS YOUNG MAN badly!'

'He is your friend?' said Viola. 'Talk with him.'

I picked the phone off the bed. I swiped away a button that sat like a drop of water on the screen, and lifted it to my face.

'Hello?'

What came out was not the voice of Angus. Instead, a woman spoke.

'Juliet?' Her voice was deep and resonant.

'I am Juliet.'

'We have not met,' she said, 'and I will not speak my name, for sometimes others listen.'

Both Viola and I sat up straighter on hearing this voice.

'And are you alone?' said the woman.

'No,' I replied, 'I am with–'

I looked at Viola. She could hear the words from the phone. She held a finger to her lips and shook her head.

The voice answered my silence. 'Her name is Viola.'

Viola took the phone from my hand and spoke into it. 'I am Viola. Who is it who speaks?'

'I will tell you in good time, but I *do* know (though we never met) that you were washed up on a beach near Brighton. That you see the goblins at the window at night; and that you are chained to your bed. But you do not release yourself?'

'I do not release myself,' said Viola cautiously, 'because I do not know how to pick this lock. It is unlike anything I ever knew.'

'But you have the stone with you.'

My ears pricked up.

'I don't know what you mean, Madame,' said Viola firmly. 'I have no stone. And how is it you know what you know?'

'You have a stone,' continued the voice. 'For what reason do you conceal it?'

'I have *more* than a *stone*,' admitted Viola, a little testily, 'but I see no need for it to concern you.'

'Then you will die in that room,' came the answer. 'Tell me about the stone you possess.'

Viola's eyes lit upon her embroidered jacket. 'I acquired an emerald from a house in Marseille,' said Viola cautiously, 'and I sewed it into my jacket to conceal it.'

'Oh, then you *are* a thief?' answered the woman with a hint of delight. 'But the stone I am talking about will be a small, coloured pebble.'

A small, coloured pebble? Such as I possessed? My fingers reached for my locket.

I could hear another voice, faint, at the other end of the call, saying, *Tell her it's blue, blue like a bird's egg.*

'It is blue,' continued the woman.

'Blue?' said Viola. 'Then leave me and *my* stone out of your deliberations, Madam. I do not have such a stone. I have no blue stone.'

The woman gave no response. The only sound now to be heard was a scratching at the window. The creatures were back, scraping at the glass, and I let out a cry.

'Juliet,' said Viola, softly to me this time, 'there is an emerald hidden in the lining of my coat.' She gestured to her chained hand. 'Help me.'

I brought over the embroidered jacket and Viola indicated where I should look further. I found the place where the lining was double sewn. Having no knife to cut the threads I used my teeth. I could feel the hardness of a stone beneath the fabric. When I took it out, it was clearly no emerald. It was small, like the stone I carried, and had also a faint aura. It was blue in colour.

'Well, it is gone!' declared Viola. 'Someone must have switched it! Some wretched, filthy–!'

The stone she now held had not the beauty of an emerald or any other precious stone. It was plain, just like the stone in my locket. But like mine, it had a kind of music.

'It is a small, blue pebble,' I remarked into the phone (I had the phone now, for Viola's attention had been captured by the blue stone).

'Tell Viola,' said the faint, younger, voice, 'that she must use it to bring about your release. There will be a car outside for you.'

'How do I do this?' said Viola.

'You have skills,' came the answer, 'in opening locks? Or so I understand, *ja*?'

'Yes, I do,' replied Viola more urgently, 'but not this chain. Not this lock. The metal is different. It is *all* different.'

'But if you take the stone in your hand,' said the voice, 'with your will, make the chain fall off.'

'You wish for me to make a wish?'

There came a crack, and I looked up to see a break in the glass, and more goblin faces. The eyes of these things – sightless and searching in the night – were now bent upon us, with vicious, hungry looks.

But Viola looked away, and as she held the blue stone – it seemed very small – a thin, droning music rose throughout the room, and the air trembled.

'Viola, what are you doing?' called out Lumusi. 'You drilling through the floor, eh?'

A wing intruded through the break in the window. Viola looked up. Her hand was still chained. 'Nothing is happening,' she called into the phone, 'except that the creatures are stirring at our window.'

'They fix their eyes on us!' I said.

The faint voice on the phone came again. *Hej! Try to think past them. Fall into the stone–*

'Fall into the stone?' said Viola.

With a little snick, the metal cuff around Viola's wrist sprang apart. In a moment, she was putting on clothes and shoes. 'Juliet,' she said, 'dress now, your shoes, be quick.'

Viola dressed more quickly than I did, in black pants, a black shirt, black boots. She put on the embroidered jacket, threw a black leather jacket over this and picked up the phone once more.

'We are ready. Where shall we find you?'

Viola listened now to the woman with the sonorous voice (I could not hear) and I saw Viola's face grow incredulous. She disconnected the call. 'This woman says that she waits for us in a red car, and that we must wear our coats and jackets turned inside out.'

'For what reason?'

'I do not know. Perhaps it is to assure her that we are the ones she expects?' She handed me the phone and began to turn her leather jacket inside out.

'What of Lumusi?' I said, reversing my coat.

'These creatures come for us, not her. Juliet, stand behind me. I believe I can unlock this door and will do it for each one we come to. Do not talk to me now but hold onto my jacket. Walk in lockstep with me.'

Viola laid a finger upon the metal door handle. As she did, the window behind us cracked, glass fell in, and something that I have only seen in frescoes of hell squeezed through, followed by more creatures like tiny bats.

Viola opened the door and we stepped into a chamber between our room and the corridor. A nurse stared at us, but then in shock at the creatures that followed us, he squealed. He need not have worried; the creatures flew at us alone. They had small sharp claws that reached to touch and scratch, but when they found our coats turned around, they flew off as if burned.

Viola, ahead of me and moving swiftly, opened without any key two of the internal gates. These gates, which the guards had opened with such serious looks, now fell open as easily as a tree in autumn drops a leaf. In a moment we were outside and had to shelter our faces against a sudden swirling hot rain and grit that flung against us.

Odd whispers and cries filled the air, and flitting shapes, bouncing like marionettes. But they kept their distance.

Flashing headlights showed us the way to a red car. I had not been in such a vehicle before (nor one so scratched and dented in its panelling) and so Viola opened the door and guided me into the back seat.

'The creatures will not come any closer, for I have laid

horseshoes around about,' said the woman in the driver's seat. She was tall, queenly, her skin a beautiful ebony, and dressed in elegant clothes. She turned with a serene movement to Viola, who hurriedly climbed into the front passenger seat and slammed the door.

'My name is Cleopatra,' said the woman. 'Daughter of Ptolemy, Queen of Egypt, Empress of the Nile from its rising in the Cataracts to the Middle Sea, Mistress of the Two Lands.'

A guard ran up and began to haul at the door handle of the car – but a snick sounded, and the locks flew down.

Other guards hurried towards us. The guard who had attempted the door was speaking urgently into his phone.

Our rescuer looked at us, or perhaps looked through us, waiting for our dutiful replies. Viola spoke. 'I am named Viola, gracious Queen. I thank you for helping us in our time of need.' She spread her hands and bowed her head. 'How may I serve you?'

I responded quickly in similar fashion. 'I am Juliet of the House of Capulet in the City of Verona. I thank you for the grace of your kindness to us in this hour.'

Cleopatra smiled. The wheels spun and we were thrown around as the car sped forward. A guard seemed to be crawling quickly over the bonnet, the window, then the roof of the car. I saw him fall behind and roll.

'I would put on the seatbelts,' said Cleopatra.

5

I had a moment of worry (perhaps I alone was worried) as we drove towards a barrier – a lowered white metal pole, with hanging strips, impeding the way – but it raised itself, I think due to Viola's influence. I saw her staring curiously at the barrier as we rushed towards it – and it flew upwards, and we turned into an open road, bouncing over a kerb, losing a hubcap.

The flying creatures vanished. We were in sunlight and calm, racing down a narrow road.

With the help of the small blue pebble, Viola had overthrown all obstacles. But Cleopatra kept up the speed. The swiftness of it troubled me, and the wavering to left and right, and the blaring of oncoming cars. A van fell off the road.

'Your Highness–' began Viola.

'You must call me Cleo,' came her gracious reply.

'Must you drive so–?'

'Not at all. Watch what I do, for in a few moments you shall drive.'

Viola gave her attention to Cleo's actions and manner with the vehicle as we continued on our way.

After a short while, Cleo pulled over at the side of the road.

Places were exchanged and Viola grasped the wheel. She turned her head to Cleo. 'You have come here from the ancient past?'

Cleo's only reply was to say, 'Time is an unchanging river. Advance!'

Viola turned the car into traffic.

I believe that her blue stone helped us in our journeying, so that we avoided cars and obstacles that seemed to rush out of nowhere.

'Oh, the trees are jumping out at us!' said Viola.

'No, that is… No, it is not the trees,' said Cleo. 'Simply *elude* them with your will. There. My thanks. It is better that I have my mind free for pondering our course.'

With that, Cleo opened the window a little, took out a small, rose-coloured rod, brought fire from a silver box to the end of it, and began to inhale the smoke that came from it. She held this *cigarette* lightly – almost in the way I have seen a painter hold a brush. She allowed the smoke to escape from her lips and it dissolved into the fast-flowing air beyond.

'So, Juliet,' said Cleo in thrilling tones, 'do *you* have in your possession a stone, like a small pebble, coloured, beautiful to look at? Such as the one Viola possesses, though yours may be roseate or in colour like a ruby?'

'I do,' I replied, overcome by the beauty of her voice. 'I do. Though I do not know why, or how I came by it.'

'And it is well-hidden?'

'I found it in this locket.'

'You must keep it safe. There are many following us,' said Cleo, 'who would steal what we possess.'

'And this blue stone,' said Viola, 'it has appeared where I expected something else.'

'A jewel that you stole?'

'Yes. I thought I carried an emerald. Not this. I would like my emerald back.'

'That is none of my business,' said Cleo, blowing out smoke.

'So, what *is* this stone?' Viola asked, taking her eyes off the road.

'That car there,' said Cleo.

'What? Oh yes.'

Viola returned our car to the correct side of the road.

'Take this turning lane, Viola. We must seek the higher road.'

'And why must we wear our coats inside out?' continued Viola, looking ahead.

Cleo answered. 'Until we gather all the stones and find ourselves a more durable magic, then we must resort to charms, tried and tested, to ward off the *Unseelies*.'

'Unseelies? Do you mean,' said Viola, 'the creatures we saw; the hobgoblins?'

'Yes,' answered Cleo, 'and the larger spirits and demons of the air and darkness. They are repelled somewhat by clothes that are turned inside out; and by iron, iron horseshoes, elder branches, a line of salt in a doorway, or a black cockerel. There is one roosting under the back seat.'

She opened the glove box and handed to me a small amount of grain, letting the seeds fall into my palm in a regal gesture. True to her word, a black cockerel emerged from under the seat and began to peck the grain from my hand.

'Where do you take us?' said Viola.

'To a safe place, for now, near the city of Reading,' said Cleo. 'There we will meet others like ourselves – women who are strangers in this time and this place.'

'So, you know that this is not 1580?' declared Viola.

Cleo smiled, almost laughed. 'I know. Where we are is no time that matters. It is not one of the high times, or even the low times. We have come into the empty years.'

I eventually took all this to mean that her time – the ancient past – was a far more notable time than 1580 or 2026.

'Why we are here is a mystery,' she said. 'Perhaps when we are all gathered we will have clearer understandings.'

'Who are these other women you talk of?' I asked.

'Seven sacred stones have been brought from the divine realm into the world of men; and we seem to be the bearers. Or, at least, that is Ophelia's understanding. Ophelia it was you heard speaking when I called you before on the shared call – she is elsewhere, now, searching for a young woman whose name is Miranda, bearer of a dark green stone. And Ophelia also hopes to find out what happened to a lady named Cordelia – though Cordelia is likely dead.'

A puff of smoke.

'Dead?' I blurted out. 'How?'

'Ophelia may discover it. She has powers of her own. She sees behind the walls of the present world, hears voices of the past, and can detect the whispers of tomorrow. She saw you in your prison; she saw your phone number that I might call you.'

'That is quite a power,' said Viola. 'Has one of the stones given it to her?'

'She has such powers anyway; I think the stone simply gives increase to what is there. As you, my elusive Viola, become more elusive.'

Cleo finished her pink cigarette and flicked the end out of the window.

'That, by my account, Madame,' said Viola, 'is six women that you have named. Is there another? For you said there were seven stones.'

'There is one more of our party. Flora, the Lady Macbeth.'

'Where is the Lady Macbeth?' said Viola.

'She is behind Juliet,' commented Cleo in casual tones, 'in the trunk of the car.'

I turned in my seat and my head hit the roof. Curled in a ball at the furthest part of the vehicle behind where I sat was a woman who seemed only a mess of rags and hair, with two scrawny pale arms sticking out. One of the arms was chained and the chain connected to a bolt in the side wall of the vehicle.

I screamed and the car swerved.

'Viola, the road,' remarked Cleo, lighting another cigarette.

6

'SHE IS CHAINED!' I SAID, PRESSING AGAINST THE DOOR OF THE CAR. 'Why?'

'It is so that she does not jump from the car,' said Cleo. 'She is mad.'

Flora's eyes were on me.

'I am Juliet,' I said, looking on her with the unwavering stare that my father uses (I saw him practising it once in a mirror, and I trained myself to do the same). I saw that Flora held a knife in her hand.

'She has a knife,' I said as calmly as I could summon.

'Flora,' said Cleo, 'put the knife away. These women are loyal to us.'

I heard Flora breathing quickly, but she let go of the knife; then, instead of gripping the blade, she gathered up and fondled the length of chain that bound her. She turned away, turned over, like a child going back to sleep; but it seemed that she was desperately measuring each breath as if it were her last. I was in a dark panic just watching her.

Cleo lit another cigarette, inhaled, then spoke.

'The chain is iron,' she said. 'It comforts her, for I have attached some horseshoes to it.'

'I do not want charms,' declared Viola. 'My faith is in Our Lady.'

Cleo drew in smoke. 'Once,' she began, and gestured with her cigarette towards Flora, '*she* and her lord yearned for a child, but were not successful – stop me, Flora, if I get any of the details wrong – and so she visited members of the Unseelie Court, witches of the moor and the like, horrible people, whose Queen is Morgana LeFay, and asked them for a charm, since her prayers to her own god had given her no satisfaction. With the charm cast, and bloodied, and buried, she conceived. A child was born, but it was a sickly, wasting infant. Flora blamed the witches for this, as well she might, and held back the last payment of gold. And then the child died, and she went and told the witches exactly what she thought of them and their charms. Am I right so far?'

Cleo was looking into the mirror fixed to the inside of the window. I looked down at Flora. She gave no answer, but I could hear her urgent breathing.

Cleo spoke on. '*Thinkest we have not power?* replied the witches. *O, we have power.* And so they set to work on her husband and on her. And – here is the powerful part – destroyed him without any actual magic. Just quick words.'

'Why must we hear this?' I said, breathless with anxiety.

'Well, you will need to hear it,' said Cleo, 'and understand as much as we can find out. For the Unseelie Court that burned her soul to ashes in *her* world is present in *this* world and they have turned their eyes upon us.

'And prayers to your Divine Lady, Viola, may be effective or not, but I will trust in my own powers.'

Viola's reflection in the mirror was grave.

'Why is it, Madame, that we come to be here at all?'

'Viola, you must address me as Cleo.'

'Cleo, how is it that you came into this time, into this world?'

'Tell me, first, how it is *you* came here,' said Cleo for reply. Viola then answered, but I knew that she said less than she had spoken to me. I then briefly told my story.

All that Cleo would say about my being poisoned by my father was: 'Do you realise what a gift you have been given? You were not given poison, but nectar of the gods.'

'It was poison,' I said, but she was not listening.

'I too was poisoned,' she went on, 'though I chose the way myself.'

My insides withered at her response, for I remembered from some tale of history, that now came to me, that she had been a suicide. She had chosen a pagan death. It did not sit well with me. Viola's eyes were also distant and thoughtful.

'It is interesting,' Cleo drew in a long breath from her cigarette, and exhaled a ribbon of white smoke. 'You, both, are from far-off lands. As is Ophelia, from Daneland, Flora from Scotland, and I am from Egypt. We have all of us come here unexpectedly from distant places.'

A voice rattled out, 'Dumfries is only across the border.' Flora was muttering. 'It's no' far distant, you dumb bitch.'

Cleo ignored this. 'But more than that; we were taken from our worlds by some magic in these stones, at the moment of our death.'

I felt sick and confused. I wanted Romeo to be with me. Or I just wanted this turmoil to end.

Cleo's eyes were upon me. 'We have passed through death, Juliet. Why act now as if fear rules your heart? Lift up your eyes!'

I smartened up at her words, feeling not a little irritated by her.

'We drive to a house of refuge,' said Cleo. 'Ophelia will find Miranda and bring her to us. And even though Cordelia is gone, we sisters will meet and discover that our powers are enough to drive our enemies before us.'

'You say,' put in Viola abruptly, as if it had played on her mind, 'that the – lady? Cordelia–'

'The Princess Cordelia,' remarked Cleo.

'That the Princess Cordelia is gone. You said *likely dead*, but do you know for certain that she is dead?'

Cleo gave Viola a look of mocking pity that angered me intensely.

'*Princess* Cordelia was not someone to give much away,' answered Cleo. 'Who knows what she thought? Or even where she is. I extended welcome to her. She chose to go her own way. But my concern, my care and my love is for those who are with me. Not for those who are against me. We have a difficult time ahead of us. As I was saying, we sisters will meet and discover that our powers are sufficient to drive our enemies before us.'

'It is well to speak this way,' said Viola, 'but I only wish to return to my time.'

'To be reunited with your brother?'

'That is right.'

'And how will you return? And when you do, how will you

step around the moment of your death? Or you, Juliet? If you return to your time it might only be to the tomb they laid you in. How will you break the seal? And who will help Flora step around the mob that threw her from the battlements? There is much for us to learn. Steps to be taken. And our task is to find those who understand these matters, and we will have them kneel before us and speak. We must be strong together. Or you can choose to die alone.'

7

We came to the city of Reading. Tall buildings loomed around us, but we turned and were back in countryside again. Finally, we entered a lane edging a forest and stopped by the strangest house I had seen yet.

Cleo stepped out of the car and declared, 'Come. Let us go in. We will rest and be restored. And prepare for Ophelia to return with Miranda.'

The house was large, two-storeyed, and its walls were of glass. The walls were thus waterlike and ghostly – I could see objects through them, and lights within declared that perhaps someone was home. Yet it was empty of servants. No one came to open the car door. The house was surrounded by beautiful gardens, walkways of smooth stone and black pebbles, with sculptures like frozen black flames standing upon leaf-strewn lawns.

'My friend Bogdan has offered me the use of one of his houses,' said Cleo.

I wondered who Bogdan might be, but we never met him – he had 'flown to America'. We found that Cleo had a natural ability to make friends and draw wealthy admirers who then became her devotees. Viola and I were not much different, at least in this regard.

Cleo walked to the entrance of the house. It was then that I saw that she might not be well, for she seemed gripped by a pain, and had to steady herself against a railing. But she caused the large front door to open by itself with a musical tone. A beautiful statue of a tranquil Indian god stood in the hall, the walls of which were high and painted white, and of such smoothness I thought them to be made of a kind of creamy silk.

'If you wish,' said Cleo, 'you can bathe. If you have hurts, then Ophelia has laid out herbs from which she says we can make a stimulating tea. Viola, your wrist needs tending. I will call Ophelia and see if she can suggest anything.'

Upon the bench in the large kitchen were various herbs and a note: *I have left you lavender, chamomile, liquorice, valerian, skullcap, lemon balm... place in hot water and steep...*

Cleo made the water in a glass jug to boil with no sign of fire, and indicated that I should make the infusion of herbs to Ophelia's instructions. I placed the herbs in a teapot and after adding water, swirled the pot around 49 times as Ophelia had written.

I poured cups of the hot drink, waiting till Viola drank first from hers before drinking of it myself. The soreness around my heart lifted. Viola took a cup to Flora, who had removed herself to a dark corner, wedged behind two pieces of furniture.

Cleo drank the tea; and also a half cup of something from a tall bottle – a medicine that Ophelia had blended for Cleo. I caught an aroma of strong mint.

'You are not well, Cleo, that you drink this?' said Viola.

'It is the lingering effect of the snakebite – but Ophelia has gifts of healing and physic. If I had not lost my stone, then I think I would not need her attentions.'

'How did you lose it?' I asked.

'I was confused, unwell, and one of the Unseelie snatched it away. Flora also lost hers – she is always washing her hands, rinsing them (such fine madness) – and hers was lost in water. Picked up by some sprite. But Ophelia says both stones are now in the possession of Morgana LeFay – or at least, her agents in this world, who live in the country of France. And so, I am on the edge of death until I can find my stone; and Flora, without hers, descends further into madness.'

I must have been feeling particularly grateful towards her for bringing us to safety, for I said, 'But, Cleo, perhaps my stone could bring you relief?'

In an instant I had passed it over to Cleo. Viola gave me a cautious look. Once again, the stone gave off its curious light. Into our expectant silence came a sound like rushing wind, far off in the sky, and a scent of rose petals, and Cleo seemed at first pleased, a little awestruck. But after a few minutes, she handed it back to me, said nothing, and turned to other matters. I had the clear feeling that it hadn't worked, or that it had powers different from Viola's stone, or that Cleo had decided that she did not want whatever it was that it might do to her. Perhaps the scent of rose was not to her taste. I put the stone back in the locket.

Cleo called Ophelia to explain we had arrived at the house near Reading and asked what we might do about the abrasions to Viola's wrist. Of all the strange things I saw, the strangest was the sight of Cleo making a poultice of herbs and carefully applying them to Viola's wound while Viola sat at the kitchen table. But this kindness was only part of Cleo's strategy. I began to notice the small intimacies, followed by the cool dismissal. The calmness, and then the casual talk of violence.

As Cleo spoke with Ophelia over the phone I stood close and made to remember the numbers that appeared on the screen.

Cleo must have been making other arrangements through her phone, for a few minutes later there came a knock on the door and men appeared. They carried in large bottles and three of them poured the contents into a bath in an adjacent bathroom. I read on the side of one bottle, *goats' milk – cosmetic use only*.

Viola sat with Flora, and Cleo set me to wandering around the house alone while she bathed in the goats' milk. She said I must avail myself of anything that delighted my eye. I explored the rooms on the second floor, which one found by going up glass steps. In one room I found a bed and lay down, grateful for the peace and quiet. This feeling only lasted moments before my solitude brought to life my memory of Verona.

I rose from the bed and listened to the household. I heard music downstairs, then closed the door to the bedroom. In an adjacent room I found a large white bath. I turned the taps, these magical things, then put the numbers for Ophelia into my phone.

'*Hej,*' came her voice. 'Juliet?'

'Yes. I am Juliet. How did you know?'

'I just knew it. So, I am Ophelia. Did Cleo give you my number?'

'I got your number by looking over Cleo's shoulder while you spoke with her before.'

Ophelia gave a little laugh. 'We do have to keep our wits upon us when we are with Cleo. Well, are you okay?'

'What do you mean? Yes. No. No, I'm not okay. We escaped the prison. Please, can you tell me... I have a fiancé and his name is Romeo. Do you know where he is? I am told that you see things.'

Ophelia did not answer immediately.

'I can see a little,' she said. 'The druid stone helps a lot now.'

'Druid stone? What is that?'

'Cleo did not say? Okay. These stones that we have, they belong to the druids, *ikke sandt*?'

I said I did not know about druids.

'The druids,' she said, 'concern themselves with the heavens and the ways of earth. My area of interest. They are big where I come from; but in this time they are hardly anything. They are supposed to be the stewards of these seven druid stones, but they lost them hundreds of years ago. They were bad times for the druids. Many of them were killed.'

'What are the stones for?' I asked. I opened my locket. The stone gave out its strange gentle light.

'Well,' answered Ophelia, 'each one is filled with the powers that give substance to heaven and earth. And each has a different aspect. Love, death, new life–'

'Viola can open locked doors with hers. What can I do with this? It did nothing for Cleo.'

Perhaps she sensed desperation in my voice. Or picked up traces of Capulet.

'You should do nothing with it, Juliet. They are dangerous. Just keep it. For now. End of story. I get a bad feeling when I hear Cleo talking as she does. These stones don't *belong* to us, you know. Or to Cleo. They must be found and given, all of them, to the druids. Let them do what they must do. Though, I wonder if they *are* really druids – I mean with the really deep understanding. Cleo thinks the druids are weak and she will no longer take their calls.'

'She has spoken to them?'

'*Ja* – she has not then said much to you?'

'No,' I answered. 'She has spoken a lot; but she said nothing about druids.'

'The druids sought her out, and told her what their understanding was, but she would rather hold on to *her* stone. But then Morgana LeFay ran rings around her and stole it away. It is lucky she is alive. Flora is still alive. But Cordelia was murdered because she would not easily relinquish her stone. They killed her and took it from her.'

I heard a rumbling. It was the bath filling, and I hurried to turn off the water.

'I would have dearly loved to meet Cordelia,' said Ophelia. 'The stone she carried is called the Gate. Cleo's stone is nothing beside it. And I think she might have been the better leader.'

'Then we are in a bad way,' I said.

'*Hej*. Bit of advice,' she said. 'Be ready to go it alone.'

I felt a knot in my chest as she said this. After a few moments I blurted out, 'What happens after we give these stones to the druids?'

'What happens? I understand that the druids must bring all the stones together at a sacred well in Stratford.'

'Stratford? I was there. Should I have stayed there?'

'Perhaps. But we need to get there too. Together, separately, whatever. When the druids take the stones to the well, they can open a door between worlds – that is my understanding so far – and we may go back to where we came from.'

I must have let out a breath that was in some way revealing. 'Go back?' I said croakily.

'You don't want to go back?' she said.

'Only to find Romeo, if he is there. But he is in this world, is he not?'

'*Hej*. I've just stopped the car. I must go, Juliet. I have been following the van that Miranda is travelling in. I see her on the far side of an open field and I really must go. Have it out with these druids.'

'You're with the druids?'

'I'm sorry. We will talk again. I promise.'

I think I chattered on. 'But can you see Romeo's phone number and tell me – at least that!? If he has a phone, that is. I'll call him now–'

But she had ended the call. I quickly threw off my clothes and bathed (so that I might lie convincingly if I needed to account for what I had spent my time doing while in the room). But the water was hot, and it made me feel unwell.

I stepped from the bath, dried myself and then walked to the window. The trees were alight with the golden sun. I looked out over the woodland and felt the warmth of the afternoon sun on my skin.

My phone, which I had left on the bed, buzzed.

I answered. 'It is I, Juliet.'

'Juliet? It's Angus. I'm in the garden. Listen, I was wondering if you might put some clothes on and we could talk outside?'

Part 4

1

DAVID STAGGERED TO HIS KNEES AND LOOKED AROUND. THE STREET still seemed to be melting at the edges. A man ran to help him up.

'Mate, you 'urt? What was that?'

David showed his MI3 badge. 'It's... Don't worry about it. It's all part of the job. Thanks. Thank you.'

He made for the sanctuary of his car. His hand was grazed and he picked out a small piece of gravel.

What a stunningly stupid performance. The van was gone. Will was gone.

David reviewed the photographs on his phone. He had clear shots of the long-haired man, the driver, the registration. But no pictures of the girl called Miranda.

He ran the picture of the man through a facial recognition app, which took him to the Wikipedia page for Professor Grant Ceridwen, Head of Theoretical Physics at the University of Salisbury and member of various government advisory groups. His religion was listed as neo-pagan. Ceridwen's research interests were given as: *conscious particles, time displacement,* and *multiverse fluctuation.*

It didn't list that he possessed a strange square of crystal that had hit David with a numbing force like an electric shock.

David slumped in the driver's seat. He had no choice – he had to call it in. But thankfully not to Sir Ambrose. He typed out the driest summary of what had happened, indicated that Will

Shakespeare had left the area with Grant Ceridwen for unclear reasons, and that he had placed a tracking device on the van. He texted it to Aisha Vani. As he waited for a response, he pulled the tracking tablet from the glovebox and activated it. The van was leaving London.

He waited a minute, two minutes, for some reply from headquarters, then pulled out into traffic.

The tablet showed that the Mercedes van was now on the A303, heading, he assumed, for Salisbury. He closed the distance but didn't gain a visual on the van until he stopped in Shipton Bellinger. The van was parked outside a café from which Ceridwen was emerging with takeaway food. David did not see Will or the girl.

The van kept on and David followed, full of dull anger and irritation. He wanted to hurt this Ceridwen man. And still no response from either Aisha or the Director – not even a call from Sir Ambrose asking if he understood how to follow a simple instruction.

He began to feel anxious. He had no support; and what did he have that could match Ceridwen's piece of crystal? He was unarmed.

He had been able to make that emergency transmission on Blanchefleur and help had come swiftly. Would there be any help now if he made a call?

In the countryside past Wilcot, the van halted in a narrow lane. David stopped a quarter mile away. It was after 3 o'clock, and warm. David wound down the window. A welcome breeze blew in. He took a breath and listened to the gentle sounds of trees and swallows. He checked his phone, then drove closer, glad that the Prius made no noise at low speed. He parked by a drystone wall.

Across the intervening field he could just see the roof of the van through trees and blossoming hedgerows. He stepped from the car and climbed over the low wall into the field.

It was a different world – enclosed, hot, with ploughed soil underfoot, a hazy sky. He walked up sloping ground until he was in a position to look down upon the van. The rear doors were open. Figures in a field beyond, hard to make out, walked around a large stone the size of a cottage.

He saw Ceridwen. And the girl called Miranda stood in the roadway. But where was Will?

Ceridwen was giving his attention to a 4WD pulling up a short distance down the road. David crouched to be less visible and opened a map on his phone. A National Trust logo indicated that the boulder in the field bore the name *The Throne of Merlin*.

David did a quick search. According to the *Mystic Ways* website, The Throne of Merlin, a large knuckle of granite, was positioned on an energy line, or ley line, that ran between the ancient sites of Stonehenge to the south and Avebury to the north, the distance being some ratio of the Earth to the Moon.

His phone buzzed. It was the Director.

'Ma'am.'

'David,' said Estelle. The voice had a distant droning bee quality. 'I understand from Sunita that you had a relapse this morning. Are you all right?'

'Ma'am it was nothing – I just needed to get out for a coffee and a sandwich and kind of fell into this–'

'Yes, this,' said Estelle with alarmed curiosity. 'What you sent to Aisha. The boy kidnapped...'

The sun was hot overhead.

'And I'm reading here, David, that Sir Ambrose suggested you should go home. He should have told me about it. But I suppose I've been a bit caught up with things. So, just where are you?'

David's shoulders dropped with relief. He hadn't been reprimanded. He described where he was.

'And you're sure about this identification of Grant Ceridwen. Why do you say it's him?'

'Ma'am. I have pictures I can send. I did facial recognition.'

'Send them now,' said Estelle. 'And David, confidentially, I think this is very important, what you've found for us. You've done exceptional work in trying circumstances. Well done, David. Two things I want you to do now. Send me those pictures. And don't take any calls from anyone else. If Ambrose rings to talk with you, don't answer. Again, confidentially, I'm wondering if his loyalty actually bends more towards – and I hate to say this, and you won't repeat it – to Malcolm LeFay.'

David took a deep breath. 'Ma'am.'

Estelle ended the call.

David's mind jumped between what Estelle had revealed and the words "exceptional" and "well done". He quickly forwarded two of the photographs he had taken of Ceridwen and returned to scanning the fields.

The phone buzzed again.

'Ma'am?'

'David, confirm for me, are you in your car?'

'I'm in a field, Ma'am, overlooking the standing stone called the Throne of Merlin. I can just see the van. It's a little screened by trees and hedges.'

'Can you see what they are doing?'

'Ma'am, I'd need to find a better position. There's another car just driven up.'

'Another car? David, I think it's time for you to let them know we're onto them.'

'Ma'am. Should I wait for support?'

'No. Just drive up slowly, then drive on. I'll call you in five.'

Estelle ended the call. David crossed the sloping field in a running crouch. He clumsily jumped the drystone wall and climbed into his car.

It didn't make sense. Just drive on, alert them to his presence, and leave Will with them? What if they were feeding him toxic mushrooms to make him see more bizarre happenings?

He drove on, turned into the lane. In the roadway was the girl, Miranda. David braked. He could see Ceridwen clearly now, still in the field, but he now stood with a second young woman. She was in her early twenties, wearing a patterned coat and a shapeless hat.

Ceridwen and the young woman were in some kind of stand-off. The van driver was hurrying towards them. David's attention switched back to Miranda. As though snapping out of a trance, she recognised him, and thrust her hand towards him in a kind of panic, something clutched in her fingers.

The air between them blurred. A curtain of rain swept in from nowhere and lashed at the windscreen. The car lifted. David stamped on the brake, but the car skittered into the drystone wall, grinding against bushes. A loud crash shook the vehicle and a flash of orange lit the interior. David felt heat, let out a shocked cry and doubled over. Rigid with fright, he found his foot was stuck on the accelerator and the engine was howling.

David cut the engine, staggered from the car, and slipped on the wet road. The rain still poured across the field with hurricane force. Then stopped. Miranda crouched in the road, protecting her head. The white van lay on its side a little distance away with flames crawling up the exposed underside. The cratered field smoked. Ceridwen and the driver were gone; the second young woman was gone.

David shouted, 'Will?!' He crawled on his hands and knees to Miranda. 'Where is Will?'

'Away,' she said. 'Away!' As if her words had form, he was blown back by a rising wind flecked with hail.

From close to where he had parked previously a second large explosion came. Miranda screamed. The rising flames cut into the swirling grey mist. He and Miranda scrambled across the road to the shelter of the wall. Small stones and soil rained down on them. He shielded her with his arms.

'Where is Will? Miranda. Please. The boy!?'

Breathing raggedly, she said, 'He is within the white carriage.'

David saw the flames at the side of the van with rising terror. But this time he was not tied to a wooden stake unable to move. He launched himself forwards, elbowed his way through the burly wind. He grabbed the back door handle and pulled. The door opened a few inches then stuck.

'Will! It's David.'

Will's frightened voice came back muffled. Smoke filled the cabin.

'Will! Kick at the door!'

David jumped back, beating at the flames now burning the leg of his trousers. A National Trust sign on a metal pole lay close. He jammed the end of it through the gap between the doors, pushed, and the door bounced open. David leapt into the smoky cabin and Will's fingers clawed at him. Then he had his arms around Will and was kicking backwards along the wet road. More rain thundered down on them and the fire went out.

Will was coughing and retching. He gripped David's wrist and shook it. 'David! Thou be'st here!? I prithee take me from this place.'

'Come. Get in my car.'

They staggered, doubled over, towards the car. The rain fell away and a silence swept over them

'Stop,' said Miranda. 'Do not withdraw. You must take me from here.'

They stood in the calm centre of a storm. Churning wind and rain kept a distance from them, circled around. The sun was invisible, but an odd feverish light showed the nearby trees shaking and bending as if something had them by the neck. In the shrieking wind, they heard wailing voices.

'They have come,' said Miranda.

2

David let go of Will and took small steps towards Miranda, who raised a hand.

'Who are you–?'

'No!' said Will, as if bitten by a wasp. 'Take me from here, from *her*.'

'Calm down, please,' said David.

He reached into his pocket for his phone. It was not there. And who should he be calling? He patted every pocket.

Had his phone fallen on the ground? He couldn't see it anywhere. Or had he lost it when he jumped the drystone wall? At the place of the second explosion.

Will clutched at David and whispered in his ear, 'David, she brings all this with the stone in her hand!'

'No,' yelled David. *It* had been a drone attack.

Drones usually locked on to something like a tracking device, like the one he had put on the van. Or to a mobile phone, like his own, which had fortunately fallen out of his jacket.

But the drone hadn't hit the van. So the driver must have found the tracker and walked into the field with it: *Look what I've found, Professor Ceridwen* – and drawn its fire.

Will, inside the van, had survived. Ceridwen, the driver and that young woman – whoever she was – had not.

He looked at Miranda. 'We have to go from here. Will you get in the car?'

'You must say who you are!' said Miranda, stepping back in dull anger mixed with fear.

'I'm David Cortez.' He showed her his ID. 'British Government. MI3. And who are you?'

'She is a fiend. An illusion,' said Will.

'Stop it, Will,' David almost shouted.

'I am Miranda, daughter of the druid Lord Prospero. And the boy chatters like a slave!'

'She will harm us,' said Will. 'She is a fay creature.'

'Both of you,' said David. 'All of us. In the car.'

'What? We bring her?' said Will, pulling on David's arm with all his weight. 'Do not do it!'

'Yes, we bring her, Will. Calm down.'

David led them to the car, keeping his eye on the circling winds. Will and Miranda's fear told him he should be more scared – but he had pulled Will from the flames and felt that nothing right now could touch him.

Miranda climbed into the car with Will, who kept as far from her as he could while staying inside the vehicle. She paid Will no attention as she held her hand in front of her. She was talking to herself.

The sky darkened further.

David saw a small stone held in the palm of her hand. It shone, and though hard to see, it had a lustre that drew his eye. 'Is that an *angelic stone*?' he said.

Miranda did not answer.

'Will, is that one of *the* stones?'

''Tis,' confirmed Will gloomily.

'And are you making this weather with it? Miranda? Please answer me.'

'I do it to keep the Unseelie from us. They have come upon us.'

'Supernatural creatures? I doubt it,' said David. He scanned the inside of the car. No phone. 'There was nothing supernatural about it.'

Will shook his head. 'Hear thee not the fell voices?'

'Miranda,' said David. 'Do you have a mobile phone? If you do, turn it off now.'

'I have one,' said Miranda, 'But it is disempowered, as Lord Ceridwen advised. Where is he? Oh, he has been taken. The Unseelie have taken him!'

'Taken?' blurted David. 'Are you serious? No. He's dead.'

Miranda went very still. 'They have carried him to their underworld?'

'No. It was a missile. A mortar.'

'And his son?' she cried.

David supposed she meant the driver of the van.

'Twas not just a mortar,' insisted Will. 'She has brought the Unseelie!'

'I have not!' declared Miranda hotly, but her voice was haggard. 'Why would I have discourse with them?! You snipe!'

Something with leathery wings detached from the swirl of sticks and floating debris and crashed against the window, only to be flung away. The rain intensified.

'Do I drive through that?' said David.

'Advance!' said Miranda. 'The winds will move with us. I will make them to be a shield for us.'

David drove, and it was as Miranda said. Ahead of them the wind poured across the road, a river of rain, twigs, dead birds; but it kept pace with them and the zone of calm moved forward with them.

David thought he saw figures of people tumbling past, caught up in the wind, and objects – a black cloak, and what looked like a dead goat. And a crow with a human face.

They came to the end of the lane and turned into a wider road.

'I can do no more,' said Miranda.

The rain melted over them and the wind lost its power. The floating twigs condensed to become shapes smacking against the car. A branch broke the side window, and a hand formed of twigs snaked its way in.

Will yelled. David swerved the vehicle towards an approaching road sign and sideswiped it. The mass of writhing branches was scythed away by the metal pole, along with the side mirror. The hand of the tree was snatched away. David straightened the car. They drove again through another swarm of sticks. But a moment later they spun out into clear sunshine, driving too fast.

It was normal countryside once more. A picture postcard. David felt suddenly stupid. He slowed the battered car down to the speed limit.

'Okay. Stop driving like a mad thing,' he said aloud. 'Foot off! Foot off!'

'Do not stop,' said Miranda. 'The further from the Throne of Merlin, the better.'

Will was muttering a Hail Mary.

'What was all that?' David asked. 'Will? Were they what you met in the forest?'

Will did not stop praying, but nodded.

'Miranda, if you can, make a little more cloud.'

'Why?' screeched Will.

'We are in danger from a potential drone strike. We need cover overhead. Miranda?'

Miranda gave no answer, but in a moment the sky turned grey as charcoal. Lightning flickered.

3

David drove for 10 minutes until he found a break in the woodland. He swerved onto an unmarked forest track. The way was dense with trees. The track stopped 50 yards in, with a metal gate barring the way to a mobile receiving tower just visible on a hill. The quiet of the trees settled on them. The sky was like a blanket of steel wool. The ground was warm and dry.

David climbed from the car to assess the damage. All the panels were dented. He scanned the clouds again. There would be no chance, though, of seeing a drone – they flew too high. If that's what had struck them in the field. An air-to-ground missile, perhaps one of the Hellraiser types.

But what were the shapes – the living tree things?

He searched around the car for his phone. Estelle's words had been strange – 'and can you see what they are doing?' Almost as if she had been watching the van from some distant aerial camera. He knew the phone wouldn't be in the car; it really had fallen from his jacket as he jumped the drystone wall. And the second missile had locked on to it. To kill him.

Had Estelle called up the drone? Or was she answering to someone else further up the chain of command? Usually there were so many levels of authorisation you might never know.

Or had someone hacked their information, and it was a rogue player? Perhaps Sir Ambrose, working with Malcolm LeFay? Had Estelle been ambushed as well?

'Will,' said David. 'Are you hurt?'

'My arm is jarred and my throat burns. It is hard to speak.'

'Miranda, are you hurt?'

'I must call someone,' said Miranda.

'Leave the phone off. Call who?'

'Lord Ceridwen's son.'

'No. We're going to go back to London,' said David, more for saying it aloud than with any certainty.

'Back the way we came?' said Miranda. 'No, we cannot do that!'

David could hear the distant dull drone of a helicopter. 'We won't go back the way we came. But why do you say that?'

'We must not cross over the hidden pathway.'

'You mean the line of energy between Stonehenge and Avebury?'

'Yes! You know of it, then?'

'Not really,' said David. 'I was off school with measles that week.'

'I would speak with the lord, not his fool!' snapped back Miranda. 'Why do you make light?'

'Why?' said David. 'I used to be a funny guy, once. I do it to remind myself.'

'Please, David,' said Will, leaning in close, 'I am tired. My mind can take no more. I am afraid.'

'You'll be fine, Will. We'll be fine. I'm scared by all this, too. But we'll be fine—'

'Afraid of *her*,' said Will in a rasping voice. 'She hath no reality. She is a form of the forest!'

'Will. Take a breath. If, as Mr Ceridwen said, you are not from this time, then there might be *others* who came too. Like *her*? Yes? Perhaps? Help me here.'

David turned to Miranda. 'Tell me, please, Miranda, because I need to know, in which year were you born?'

She raised her chin. '1564 of your Christian calendar.'

'Okay,' said David, ignoring that Will kept shaking his head. 'Okay. Here we all are. So, welcome. And can anyone tell me who was the girl standing with Ceridwen in the field?'

'This boy called her Ophelia. He said, *O, 'tis Ophelia*.'

'Who is Ophelia?' said David.

Will fell to the ground and beat the soil. David thought it best to stop the questions and held him by the shoulders. 'Will, please. We're good. Slow your breathing.'

Will settled.

'And, to clarify,' said David as calmly as he could manage, 'you two have only just met? Is that right, Will?'

'I saw her first only in the white van,' said Will sullenly.

'Really?' said David. 'I seem to recall that you *know* Miranda. You said as much. You ran towards her as if you knew her.'

'No! She seemed like unto the one I met in the Forest of Arden who called herself Rian, the druid princess in the forest. I spoke to you about it.'

'Rian? Thou hast met the *princess*?' said Miranda quietly. Her demeanour changed. 'Can'st compare?'

'Talk to me not,' hissed Will. 'Thou be too alike. 'Tis wrong.'

'You say that my visage is like unto hers?' said Miranda.

Will did not answer.

'And you thought,' said David, 'that Miranda here might be this druid princess?'

'I did so think,' grumbled Will.

'And that's why you got into the van when I expressly told you to stay in the café?'

'The man did draw me with a power!' yelled Will. 'I did not wish to go.' He began to cough violently.

'Okay, Will,' said David, 'I'm sorry, sorry.'

He turned to Miranda. 'Why were you in that field?'

'To seek insight at the Throne of Merlin,' said Miranda. 'I showed Lord Ceridwen earlier how the ancient crystals could be used for seeing, and for–' She held up her hand as if holding a square of flat crystal.

'And for blasting people?' said David, recalling Ceridwen's use of it.

'It is one of their uses.'

'These blocks of crystal,' said David, 'these aren't the angelic stones?'

'*No*,' said Miranda in a patronising tone that put David immediately on side with Will. 'The Seven Stones are small and sublime; the crystals are but a blunt instrument. But the Lord Ceridwen was pleased that I could explain them.

'His order of druids has fallen into dark days and they knew not how the old devices worked; I showed him, and indicated they could be used to sense the presence of the remaining Seven

Stones. For they are scattered, and I thought that we might look along the meridians that emanate from the Throne of Merlin, and thus find the other stones that are now at some distance from us. And so I brought us to that place.' She began to cry. 'I brought us to the field.'

David heard the helicopter again. Two now circled in the distance. 'We have to go somewhere else,' said David.

'Please,' said Miranda, 'take me to the druid house in Stratford. Lord Ceridwen's son Bryn is there. I would see him.'

'Can this Bryn tell me what is going on? Does he have the same information as his father?'

'He will be the Lord of the White Circle,' said Miranda, 'now that his father and brother Daffyd are no more.'

'Ceridwen's son was driving the van?'

Miranda nodded.

'Let's get in the car. Miranda, could you,' said David, 'make for us a bit more rain – more cloud that will shield us?'

'She must not,' said Will. 'It will summon the faerie court!'

'Will, do you hear that rattling noise? Do you see there?'

'There in the sky, far off?' said Will pointing.

'Yes. They are looking for us. And I think they will try to kill us. We need to get far from here. For our safety. And we must do it undercover.'

'I will darken the sky further,' said Miranda.

The sunlight dimmed and, in a moment, dark blue clouds hung overhead. A wind rose and shook the trees. Birds tumbled across the sky.

'Drown me now in deepest water,' said Will and he awkwardly got back in the car.

David started the engine. 'Not too much of it, Miranda, just a blanket of cloud and some rain.' Miranda hurriedly got in as the first heavy drops fell. Then rain like a bucket of gravel hit the roof.

4

THEY REVERSED DOWN THE STREAMING TRACK AND SNUCK ONTO THE road. The driving rain meant that other vehicles were nothing more than headlights coming slowly towards them and sending up plumes of spray.

'Will, if you can, look for signs on the road – Swindon, the A4, the A5, maybe Royal Leamington Spa. I'll skirt around and come to Stratford from the north and the west.'

David wondered about driving instead to the Canadian or New Zealand embassy, or the Americans. He had a contact with the Americans. He could call Carrie Martinez. They had met at a joint-services event in Cambridge a couple of years ago and had gone drinking. She left him a card.

'If you ever need to call,' she said. 'You know?'

Carrie had sent him flowers and a get-well card during his recovery.

The Americans might protect him. Would they protect two stateless teenagers?

'Why must we go to the druids?' said Will quietly to David. 'Will thy lord not assist thee?'

'I think my lord has done this to us,' said David. 'The fire from the sky? I think that was my lord.'

'The times be not changed,' said Will.

David switched on the car radio and found an FM station in Southampton. A freak storm, the announcer said, had blown in suddenly from the South Atlantic and was travelling up the west of England, causing havoc in the Bristol Channel and further north into Wales. Lightning, it was said, had struck two vehicles in Wiltshire, killing an unknown number of people.

David could see Miranda in the rear-view mirror hunched over the stone held loosely in her hand, her eyes troubled. He felt a dull ache in his bones and teeth.

'Miranda, you're making this local, aren't you? The radio says it's everywhere.'

'Do not say hereafter that I did not warn thee,' said Will, looking out of the window.

'Miranda, where have you come from? Apart from bygone days.'

'The Bermudas,' said Miranda, not taking her eyes off the stone. She pronounced it Bermoothes. 'I lived there with my father, a druid lord in exile. I was travelling with him upon a ship bound for England, but I had been unwell, fevered. They said I was unused to the humours of the ship – then I found myself here.'

David was flooded by the strongest sense of déjà vu he had ever experienced, as though a familiar voice had called to him in a strange city. Or had he read about this once in the archive? David lost the thread of her story, but came back to hear her say, 'I did search for a druid house here in England – and was fortunate that the Lord Ceridwen maintains one of the few left in these times. I found from him that I was blessed to carry the stone of tempest. His family did make me welcome. They said I was one of seven druid maidens who will carry the stones to Charlecote Well.'

'And the young woman we saw,' said David, 'was she one of the seven? Was she a druid maiden?'

'No! She said that she was a follower of the Goddess Freya, and was a handmaiden of the High Women of Asgard.'

'Oh, boy,' muttered David, but under his breath.

'But I think,' said Miranda, 'she must have in her keeping one of the stones, for I felt drawn towards her.'

David applied the brakes and brought the car to a sliding halt.

'Hold on! What are you saying? You mean that woman who was killed back there, in the field, had one of the stones?! And – what? – is it … still there? Lying around in the mud?!'

'Do you mean to go back?' said Will with a frightened look.

'No,' said Miranda in a pained voice. 'Do not go back. It is dangerous to be at the Throne of Merlin. The Unseelie Court has entrance to this world at that stone.'

'Then why did you lead Ceridwen there?'

'I did not expect the lightnings that fell on us!'

The rain pounded the car.

'The stone I hold, the one she held, together would have made a sign, and an opening for the Unseelie. I did not expect to see her there–'

'Okay. Are the Unseelie likely to find that stone, Miranda? You know, pick it up from the crater? Or is it lost forever? And why didn't you say it might be there before we drove off?'

Miranda stayed silent.

David pulled out into the road. He stared ahead through the streaming rain, sensing two angry presences in the car with him. Three if he included himself.

He turned his thoughts to assembling what he knew – writing names on a whiteboard in his mind and drawing squeaky lines between them with a red marker pen. At its most basic, these stones were stones of energy – a new element perhaps? – with power, or powers, beyond the dreams of governments.

It made sense that an eminent physicist like Ceridwen was interested. But parallel to this was ridiculous stuff about the Unseelie Court, and Morgana LeFay, or more precisely, Old King Derek LeFay, an actual historical personage who in the past seemed keen to get the stones. Then there were the druids, this underground group under Ceridwen, also keen to get the stones, but way out of their depth.

And how did you fit a Reaper drone into this picture? A drone sent by whom? Estelle? Sir Ambrose? Or Malcolm LeFay plotting in France? Did he have people in the Royal Air Force willing to do his bidding? Or did he pay some Russians to do it. And with what money?

With what money.

It clicked. Aisha Vani had said Malcolm LeFay was perhaps financing something – some subversive activity – with stolen jewels. Were these jewels the Seven Stones? It wasn't then a question of getting finance to pay some mercenaries. It was Malcolm LeFay wanting the actual stones because they gave him access to a new kind of power. If LeFay had possession of all seven, he could use them to create storms. Or time-travel back to 1580, just as Will had time-travelled to the future, to ensure his ancestor Derek LeFay stayed on the throne for more than half a day. It would be an elegant coup d'etat.

Or might he simply use the power of the stones to take the throne from the current occupant? That had been his ancestor's plan.

David gave his attention to the traffic as they drove northwest through the Cotswolds, past vehicles that had slid off the road. Bridges were no longer accessible, and rivers churned. An empty car floated past.

A half-hour later, they were spotted. The sky was still heavy with storm cloud, but a large helicopter passed overhead. It came back, now lower, and began travelling with them in parallel.

'They've found us,' said David. He saw a turnoff – a narrow single lane of tall hedgerows and willow trees – that might screen them from sight. He pulled in sharply. Straightening up, he drove until there was a passing place, hidden amongst tall trees. He edged the Prius into it and turned off the headlights.

'Can you make it a bigger storm, Miranda?'

A flash of light was followed by a thunderclap. They sat listening to the surge and fall of rain on the roof, the trees taking the brunt of the wind. He could hear the helicopter, and then nothing. Long willow strands began to thrash at the car.

Will began to whimper. ''Tis the tree-men again!'

'Steady!' said David. He could hear Miranda breathing quickly. 'It's only branches! First one to stop panicking gets an ice cream at the next roadhouse.'

Thwack.

He counted to five. 'It's only the willow tree, guys. Everyone just go to a quiet place within.'

'I would rather go to a quiet place without,' said Will without much humour.

'Outside you mean?' said David, proud that he was getting the hang of Will's odd speech. 'You'll get soaked.'

'No! Without her,' muttered Will. 'She draws it to us like a magnet, for she is fay like them.'

'Why do you say that?' hissed David. 'Would you keep your opinions to yourself, Will?! It's not helpful.'

The storm increased. The thrashing of twigs became too much even for David. A blur of daylight showed up ahead, as if the setting sun was in that direction through banks of grey mist. He drove on and came out of the lane onto a smoother road. It was a concrete road this time, not a sealed one, which widened until there was no edge, just a vast expanse of concrete. It was an abandoned airfield. David drove on, staring ahead through the frantic wipers.

A large building rose up in front of them – an old aircraft hangar. David kept on towards it. But why was it taking so long to reach it? He then saw that the hangar was much larger than he expected. By the time he had driven up to it, it had risen in size to be something like a cathedral of old concrete, lightless and empty. In the dark and the rain it reminded him of the hulk of a sunken ship.

'What is this?' said Will. 'Why do we drive towards it?'

'It's just a big building. It's a disused hangar for an airship.'

'What is an airship?' said Will.

'An airship… Imagine a large bag of gas,' said David.

'Sir Thomas deLuce,' said Will laughing, then clapping a hand over his mouth.

'An airship,' continued David, 'was a form of international transport way back last century, until they kept exploding and dropping out of the sky. They kept them in places like this.'

David pulled up next to a dark concrete wall. It acted as a wind break, though heavy drops still pummelled the car. David skewed his neck and looked upwards, searching for helicopter lights. He saw the expression in Miranda's eyes – anger and horror; he was sure the intensity of the weather correlated with her mood. The rain was deafening.

'You can dial it down, now, thanks, Miranda,' said David as evenly as he could manage. 'I think you have to calm down. Take some slow breaths.'

Miranda nodded and a moment later the rain slackened and the clouds seemed to break.

David saw light filtering out through the large entranceway in the building, and risked driving in to seek shelter. He discovered the hangar was mostly open to the air, three sides formed of tall archways without doors, evenly spaced.

It was a relief to be out of the downpour. David turned off the windscreen wipers, and registered the gentle afternoon sulight now streaming in through the rear of the building.

The sky beyond was blue – surprisingly blue.

'Thank you,' he said to Miranda.

He drove across the hangar and into the open on the other side where it was now a pleasant Spring afternoon.

'Is that an airship?' Will asked, pointing out his window.

5

David drove forward towards what was indeed an airship anchored in the field and surrounded by a group of people who were staring at it intently; and all of them dry as if they had not just weathered a violent rainstorm.

It took David a moment to realise their attention was so utterly focussed that they all stood as still as statues. Then he noticed a bird hanging motionless in the air, like a scuba diver floating in a tranquil lagoon. No, not *quite* motionless. Its wings were moving but very very slowly.

Will jumped out of the car. 'Tis a bee, David. Here! See? A bee standing still in the air, here! And I can look in its eye. Come quick. See – he hath marked me and now, O... are we being slow *to be a bee*, Lord Bumble Bee!? And I see you! I see you! Think'st thou can dodge me? Not so fast! Ha!'

David watched Will scamper around a bee which, like the bird, moved almost imperceptibly.

The airship, its silver flank extending like a wave into the sky, had on its tailfin a symbol, a red rune.

David froze.

On the island of Blanchefleur a few of the Sons of Mordred had put on robes with this mark as they prepared to kill him. The same grey, the same red. The *M* rune for Mordred, or perhaps Morgana, he never found out. One had donned a crow's mask.

He had wondered at the time if the Sons of Mordred were larger than a small group of enthusiasts on a windswept island. Were they capable of organising something larger? He had begun to look into possible enclaves in Europe. And here they were, at last, impossibly numerous.

Through the airship's anchoring cables, David could see a concrete control tower and a helicopter fixed in mid air – its rotors turning so so slowly they could not possibly hold it up.

Despite that oddness it was the attire of the men in front of him that held his attention. They were dressed as expected for workers at an airfield but their 'fashion sense' was more *between-wars* – braces, collarless shirts, leather jackets. Some were wearing the greatcoats and visored caps associated with military commanders – but which military? – and there was an awful lot of hair oil shining in the sunlight.

An army of the Sons of Mordred!

'Will, get in the car. Now!' said David. He turned and almost ran into Miranda.

Her gaze, as she pushed David aside and raised the stone, could have frozen blood.

David reeled back, feeling a wave of coldness emanating from the stone. It moved like a shadow within the daylight. As it rolled past Will's bee, the creature turned into a tiny lump of ice.

As the wave passed over one of the uniformed men, shafts of ice exploded from him, turning him into something like a man lost in an Arctic night.

'No!'

It was Will, his face very close to Miranda's. 'Do it not! Hast thou, who art but air, a touch, even a feeling of their afflictions?'

Miranda staggered away from him, confused. She swung wildly to strike at Will.

'How do you know this?' she yelled, breathing heavily. 'How? How do you know my father's words?'

'Both of you,' said David, grabbing them by the arms. 'Please, get back in the car! Miranda, stop! There's no need to do this!'

'Get us away!' said Will. 'David, take us away from here! Do not let her do it! Why must she?!'

David felt that he was moving as slowly as the bird and the butterflies rising from the clipped grass. As slowly as the group of men now turning to look at him. He saw recognition flickering in the eyes of one; the rest were still barely reacting to what must be only a whistling of voices and a blur of shadows, and their suddenly frozen companion.

David felt a pain in his throat. It was possibly the burning of the slow air moving into his lungs, but he knew it too as the heavy pain of memory.

When all three were back in the car, David threw it into reverse, just as everything around them began gaining speed. The group of men seemed more limber. One was drawing a pistol and a bullet sailed out of the yellow blossom that brightened the end of the gun. David accelerated and swung away so the bullet drifted wide.

With a crunch, the car sideswiped a man in a white coat. Strangely, the car bounced off him. David didn't wait for his reaction. The man stood, apparently unmoved; but the clipboard and binoculars he held drifted away from him.

David sped back through the hangar towards the dark entrance and out into the thunderstorm that still raged on the other side. He snapped the headlights on, the beams glinting in the slanting rain, and drove across the concrete airfield towards the lines of thin trees. In the rearview mirror, David could see no sign at all of the hangar, or the blue sky and airship beyond.

They joined a road with David then taking random turns until they came to signs that pointed them to a main thoroughfare. Will and Miranda said nothing.

David's mind felt as if a door was banging madly in the wind. He wanted to say they had seen nothing real. It was nothing but an illusion. But he felt a strange sense of *déjà vu* – a memory of airships seen on television, perhaps, or in the sky over Manchester for an airshow when he was a kid?

The rain had abated, and no trace of a helicopter shadowed them. But why was the sky still so dark? At a 24-hour roadhouse past Cheltenham, David stopped for petrol. Miranda was asleep, or feigning sleep, in the back seat, but when David went to pay, Will hurriedly followed him.

Will looked at the pre-made food, the curried egg and lettuce sandwiches, the hot pies.

'Do you want anything from there?' asked David.

Will nodded, and while he made his choice and gathered drinks, David looked at the television near the counter, then the clock on the wall, and realised it wasn't just the bad weather that had emptied the roads. It was now the dead of night. They had lost half a day in the minutes when they entered and then left the hangar.

He bought a cheap Samsung phone, powered it up. The time read 2.35am.

It is real, he thought, watching as Will dribbled hot chocolate into the plastic cup.

Time travel, time displacement is real.

'Shall I make thee one?' said Will.

'Please,' said David. 'I'll have the coffee.'

David called Carrie Martinez. He had memorised her number. The call, though, went straight to voicemail. He guessed it was around midnight in Virginia.

'Carrie – hi, it's David. As in, David Cortez. Reaching out, as they say. Here's my new number.'

He disconnected the call. It wasn't *the* call; just a call. And hopefully unmonitored.

'May we eat standing here?' asked Will.

'Sure. Will. Tell me, what is it with you two?'

6

'I would show thee if I had it,' said Will, 'but I did lose my book.
It fell from me in the van as it burned. Though I only did miss it
later.'

'What book do you mean?'

''Twas but one of my father's ledgers in which I keep my
thoughts, my verse, and my designs for plays.' He smudged the
last words together.

'Sorry? Plays? You write plays?'

'Plays. In small kind.'

'Well, that's nothing to be ashamed of,' said David, adding
grimly, 'and you'll have lots to write about after this. Have you
written much?'

'No,' answered Will. 'I have only thought of a handful of plays.
Naught but the bones, a little skin, and a few feathers. But they
live in my mind. Though now that I have not the pages to show
thee, thou'st will think me mad for saying.'

'Cut to the chase, Will. I don't think you're mad.'

'Thou didst call me a puffin.'

'I did. I apologise.'

'In one of these plays, to which I give the name, *A Tempest*,
I did imagine a girl named Miranda, daughter of a wizard,
Prospero by name, prisoned on an island in the Bermoothes by
his brother's treachery.'

David nearly burned his tongue on the coffee. 'Hold on. Okay.
Square One. You say you met a druid princess?'

'Say, say, say!'

'Sorry, you *met* a druid princess. You met a walking, talking
living druid princess. I do not doubt it.'

'I thank thee.'

'And she was carrying seven stones. And because of the stones,
you came into our time?'

'Yes.'

'Okay. Up-to-date. But,' said David, 'in addition to you travelling here, Miranda somehow came as well, is what I'm hearing? And that she is one of seven druid maidens?'

'No! That is only what Lord Ceridwen believed. It is what Miranda believes. But I have just told thee! *I did imagine her.*'

'No. You must have known her before, or have had some family connection, or–?'

'Miranda did not come from any *where*; and nor from any *when*!' said Will, stamping his foot.

'Will, don't stamp your foot at me.'

'I will stamp my foot at thee! She did spring forth from out of my head, David! From no other place. Thus do I know things that her father spoke or counselled, words he might speak to her.'

'Yes, but, Will, you *based* your play on something you read – yes? Or heard? I mean, you based them on *real* things, *real* people in your world? And somehow they've been caught up and came with you into the here and now?'

'No,' said Will, with a pained hiss as he sucked air through his teeth. 'I never met her. She comes from a play that I have hardly writ.'

After a moment, David said, 'And what about Ophelia?'

Will's eyes were screwed up. He nodded. 'I did think her, too. In a play that I call *The Deadly Village*. She is a pagan witch, though I did write her as pleasant.'

'And now she's dead,' said David.

Will began to cry. 'Why must they have killed her?'

'Someone wants the stones,' said David. 'And they don't care who gets hurt, or killed. Will, please, tell me more about these plays you've written. Yeah?'

'They are not writ as such,' said Will, 'they are naught but the telling in as few lines as possible so as to not outrage patience, though I have writ speeches and soliloquies for seven plays, which I hold in my head.'

'*Seven*?' said David. 'Go on.'

Will spoke. When he had finished describing his plays his face was flushed.

David went to the counter and asked if he could use the old computer in the corner that passed for an Internet café. The man said it was a one-hour minimum charge and extra for any pages printed.

'Okay, Will. Seven plays. We have met Miranda. And we almost met Ophelia?'

'Yes. David? May I have a second hot chocolate from the silver machine?'

'Make yourself at home.'

David called up Google and put in the name *Ophelia* and found a song by The Lumens. He typed in *Prospero* and *Miranda*, but though there were many hits for Miranda, he came across no Prospero. Will walked over with a hot chocolate.

'Will, spell *Capulet* for me?'

David typed *Juliet Capulet*. A result for Facebook came up. The face of a girl appeared.

'Right, okay. Here is a Juliet Capulet who has a Facebook page and seems to be travelling on the Eurostar.'

David felt heat upon his sock and looked down. Will's cup of hot chocolate drooped in one hand.

'It is Juliet,' said Will in a hazy voice. 'Juliet, her face, but with nature's hand painted.'

'She's travelling with some other people.' David scrolled down and read a caption. '*I with Viola and Cleo…* Is that your Viola?'

'Aye, from *The Twelfth of Night*. Though I did imagine her with hair.'

'It's not a bad look. She's quite lovely. You have a skill there, my friend. And who is Flora?'

'Oh, 'tis the murderess, the *Lady Macbeth*. And yes, she is a devil as I did see her!'

'And this boy? *Angus* – do you have anyone in the plays called Angus?'

'I do not. But David, why do they walk on more than the boards of my imagining?'

'I don't know, Will. I really don't. I spend a bit of time watching old movies to fill in the nights. Yes? And there's one I saw about a planet – like a faraway island in the sky.'

'You mean like unto a star?'

'Yes, like unto. And when a man goes there in a ship to this planet, called *Solaris*, it brings his dreams to life. The island in the sky gives life to his dreams. Gives them substance. And the more time he spends there, the more real these dreams become. I mean real within themselves. The man finds his dead wife there, alive. And *she* feels, in herself, *real*. As much as anyone does, I guess. And furthermore, she doesn't like not being real. Maybe these druid stones are like that planet and they make real what is not real.'

'And how does this tale end?'

'Sadly,' said David. 'It's a Russian film. Come. Let's get back to the car.'

'I have done wrong,' said Will.

'You haven't. It's like something stuck a straw into your imagination and sucked the contents out.'

'May I take more food?'

David paid for the extra food, for the use of the computer, and he and Will exited.

Miranda was not in the car.

7

Davdid cursed himself.

'She has vanished,' said Will. 'Did I not say that she was but aery nothingness?'

'You didn't say that specifically,' said David, running back into the roadhouse.

'Me again,' said David. 'Do you have CCTV coverage on the carpark?'

'I do,' said the attendant, 'but–'

'Here's a fifty and no buts.'

The camera showed Miranda stepping from the car five minutes earlier, and looking around as if waiting for someone. Then she raised her hands in greeting and walked off into the night.

David hurried outside.

'Will, she didn't vanish, she's gone off with someone.'

They stepped away from the roadhouse lights. The view down the roadway was of trees, grass verges, and one or two vehicles on the lonely main road. The sky was clear and already edging into the new day. Miranda stood a little way from them at the edge of a slip lane. David and Will ran to her.

'Miranda?' said David. 'Are you all right? What's happening?'

She gave no answer.

'I just lost fifty quid worrying about where you were. Are you ready to keep going?'

'To where?' she said sadly.

'To the druid house in Stratford? Yes?'

Miranda looked around at the wet trees, the tall motorway lights.

'How does that give light?' she asked, pointing up.

David wasn't sure what was happening, but he knew there had been a change. She looked like she'd been punched in the heart. He said, 'It's called electricity. Charged particles; light can be made… well, light can break out of anything material, if you apply motion or energy in the right way.'

'In this time,' said Will, 'they have light in a bottle that has no oil.'

David saw a few extra footprints in the wet grass. 'Who did you meet?'

'Bryn,' she said, 'did drive here, from Stratford.'

'Bryn Ceridwen?'

'We have lost hours since the afternoon!' said Miranda. 'He has already been to the Throne of Merlin and seen the destruction.'

'How did he know we were specifically here?' David asked.

'There are crystals, I did tell thee. He found me.'

'And he's gone?'

'He demanded that I give him the stone.'

David felt as if he were four-nil down at halftime. 'Do you have the stone?'

Miranda shook her head.

'You just gave it to him?'

Miranda burst out. 'He looked on me as Will did look on me; but with hatred!'

'I do not hate thee,' said Will lamely.

'His father had already told him of Will's belief that I am as insubstantial as a cloud – a tissue of half-truths. And not a real druid. Even though I have more knowledge of things than they! Bryn said the death of his father and brother Daffyd were all my fault. All my doing.'

'No, Miranda,' said David, 'that was *my* people! Or else it was the House of LeFay. But not you. You've done nothing wrong.'

'And he said it was surely true that I was some *daemon* cast by Morgana LeFay, and nothing real – *a form of the forest…*'

'I am sorry,' whispered Will.

David stood, watching Miranda keeping her distance, and wished he could do more.

'We have to go to Stratford,' said David. 'But let's be kind to each other. Moving forward, we need to give ourselves time to work things out.'

Will stepped forward and called to Miranda. 'I do heartily apologise to thee.'

They faced each other.

'I, that am nothing but your thought?' she said.

'Do not say nothing,' said Will. 'If you are nothing, then we all are nothing. And everything here – this road, those passing carriages that snarl at the air, that arching bridge – is also naught.'

He looked at the ground and spoke in a sad voice. 'I think it must be that we are all a dream of God. And He doth only imagine us, moreover, when He sleepeth; for if He had conceived us while awake, would we not be more full of light and goodness, not this intermingled thing of good and evil, our minds filled with terrors as much as with the angels of Heaven?'

Will stood with a bag of food and a new hot chocolate. He lifted the bag. 'Wouldst thou take aught of this?'

'I will take the Mars bar,' said Miranda.

'Oh! If I know anything, it is that you would choose that!'

'We'll buy some more,' said David. 'Let's go. Come! I need to have pointy words with Bryn Ceridwen. Which way did he drive?'

'That way.'

'To Stratford then.'

David drove. After five minutes they passed at speed through an intersection, and saw briefly, a short way down the left of the intersecting road, a car on fire. But they did not stop.

'Why does it burn?'

'I don't know, and there were police cars there. I have only the one headlight. So let's keep on.'

The sky was clearing as they pulled up at an address in an estate outside Stratford, a post-war detached house with wide gardens and a large oak tree.

'This is the place?' asked David.

'It is,' replied Miranda without enthusiasm.

As David stepped from the car, a voice spoke. 'No sudden moves. Put your hands behind your back.'

David stood still, complied, and a zip-tie closed on his wrists.

'David,' cried Will. 'Who are they? Do not bind him! Sirs!'

'You're safe, Will,' said a second voice. 'Just stay where you are.'

Hands gripped David by the arms and he was walked to the front door of the house. He recognised agents from the MI3 network standing inside an oak-panelled hallway.

There was something like an altar in one corner. Where most houses might have a vase of field flowers and a small barometer, this one had some twisted horns and a slab of crystal, set within a design of a white circle.

Well, at least he had found the right place he thought as Will and Miranda were led through to a kitchen.

But where were the druids? Not a green anorak in sight.

David was steered into a sitting room, where a man standing by the fireplace turned to look at him and gave a small cough.

It was Sir Ambrose.

Part 5

1

'ANGUS? WHERE ARE YOU?' I SAID INTO THE PHONE, PRESSING BACK into the bedroom and away from the window.

'Out in the woods,' said Angus, 'jus' beyond the house. I saw you through the window, but I've turned round. I'm nae looking.'

'I will come down,' I said. In the wardrobe I found clothes that fitted me (I understand them to have belonged to one of Bogdan's daughters). I threw them on in the abandoned way of this world, ran down the stairs, out into the garden and around to where the trees began.

Angus stepped out of the forest and came towards me.

'Real,' he said in a sad, grim voice.

'I am so sorry. I brought you trouble.'

'Aye, that ye did. Did they let ye go then? The Border Force?'

'No, we escaped from the prison.'

'Escaped! Right. So they could jump out of the trees any minute.'

'What!?' I looked up, concerned.

'Where exactly are you from?' said Angus.

'Must you ask me questions?'

'You're fucking right I must. Do ye remember on the train? I was confused and saying I had a sister.'

I said I did remember, but that I was caught up in my own troubles.

'Well, I do. I do have a sister. And I live with her and me Ma and Da in Glasgow. Well, I did once. But I only *remembered* that

I did when I sat next to you. And I thought, what the fuck am I doing here in London? I dinnae live in London. This is mad.'

He stared hard at me, but his face could not hold the severity. 'I have a sister, Maggie, except she's *vanished* as if she ne'er lived, and my parents, who know nothing about a sister as well, they don't want tae see me, apparently, since I had that spell in youthie.

'And I live wie my aunty Carol, now, in London, nae Glasgow – is this making any sense? I'm supposed to be in skewel in Glasgow, except I'm in London making money selling stolen phones and hanging around wi' my pals Damian and Rowan. Who just turned into strangers. It's as if I stepped from one life in tae this; and I had nae actual memory of that life I'd lost – until I held that wee stone o' yours.' His expression grew urgent. 'I suppose there's an explanation?'

'I have come to England from Verona, from the year 1580.'

Angus lit a cigarette. 'Do ye have these where ye come from?'

'No,' I replied.

'Just as well. It's a filthy harbit. Verona, 1580?'

I nodded. 'I met a woman in the prison. Viola. She told the Border Force that it was surely 1580 and they chained her to a bed.'

'Unsurprising. So, there's a few of you, aye? All from Verona?'

'No. There are four of us from different places. And very different times. Viola is from France. Cleo is from Ancient Egypt. She said she was the Queen of the Nile. And a fourth from Scotland. Oh, and there is a fifth, named Ophelia, who seems to know much.'

'How did you get to be here then?'

'I do not know,' I answered weakly.

'And can ye go back? Can *I* go back? I mean, the way I see it is you've travelled in time; I've travelled into a parallel world. Unless it's all just drugs and it'll wear off. Or are we stuck here?'

'I think we can leave,' I said. 'Ophelia said that we came here through the magic of seven druid stones. The one you held on the train, after it slipped from my hand, was of the Seven.'

'That was a magical stone? Can you do stuff wi' it?'

'Ophelia said not to; and that the Seven Stones must be returned to the druids in Stratford.'

'There are druids in Stratford?'

'Yes, but not excellent ones; still, that is how we might find our worlds once more.'

'So this Ophelia knows what's going on? That's good. And where are these stones?' he said.

'We have two – the others are lost or stolen from us.'

'So we might be stuck like this?' He leant back against a tree and turned his face away.

I moved towards him and took his hand, for he was in great distress.

'My god,' he said, sniffing. 'It's like you're some kind o' transmitter. When you're this close, I can feel memories coming to life. And everything here starts to feel strange. Weird. I suppose I can nae keep holding your hand?'

'I am betrothed,' I said, and took my hand back.

'Aye, your chap *Romeo*. Is he around? Is he big?'

'I don't know where he is,' I said. 'No one can say.'

'Not even your friend Ophelia?'

'She is in a different place and we could talk no more. I don't know if the Border Force has taken him, or…'

I spoke of what had happened since I left Angus in London. Then the sky darkened and the sunlight vanished.

'Have you looked for him online then?'

After Angus explained what that meant, I said not. It began to rain.

'Would you come into the house?'

'If no one minds,' said Angus. 'I assume it's safe.'

I said that we needed help to understand this world.

'I'd be happy to fill you in. I mean, it's nae complicated. You mean stuff like cash or credit cards, recycling, which bin to use, that kind o' thing? The Tube?'

We walked through the garden, and I asked Angus what he'd meant by *youthie*.

'I was shopped for stealing.'

'What did you steal?'

'Saffron.'

I laughed. 'A spice?' I remembered the large jars in our kitchen in Verona.

'Aye, but an expensive bugger of a spice – my neighbour at the end o' the street could nae afford it. Mrs Chandra – she has nae husband and her son Ranjit's a useless twat – and she was longing to use the saffron for her rice dishes, and I thought, well, it's a wee package. But since it's the most stolen item down at Ganesh they had a camera on it specifically, and I was shopped.'

'What is Ganesh?'

'Indian elephant god – they have a big statue o' him outside the shop. Ye can nae miss it. In fact it's a trip hazard. Anyhow, that's what happened.'

He stood for a moment with his hands plunged into his pockets.

'I spent three months in youthie, by mesel, well, o' course by mesel, and my parents were so quote unquote ashamed o' me they ne'er visited. Said "we live by the law, son". You see, me Da's a private investigator, and I suppose I was tae follow in his footsteps. But now I sell contraband.'

It turned out that *contraband* was the phones and accessories that someone sold to him cheaply, *no questions asked*.

We stepped inside the house and Viola met us in the kitchen.

'It is Angus,' I said. 'It is he who gave me my phone, and left messages.'

'Ah,' said Viola. 'Do you perhaps have a phone for me as well, in that bag?'

'Happy to gie you one,' he said, reaching into his backpack.

Viola immediately handed him a small box with the word Players on it. I do not know where she found it, possibly in one of the bedrooms. It was cigarettes. 'Trade?' she said.

'Aye, if ye like.' Angus opened his backpack and gave her a phone. 'But how d'ye know I smoke?' he said.

'I saw you earlier, as you stood outside, looking at the house. Now, I have found food, Juliet. Are you hungry? And Angus, would you join us for our little meal?' She led Angus to the kitchen table and placed some bread in front of him.

He looked at it. 'You just got this from the freezer?'

'From that white cabinet,' said Viola.

'Aye, the freezer. Well, bad news, it's still frozen.' Angus took the bread and I learned then new words – toaster, microwave, tinned spaghetti, hot chocolate.

'There is not much food here,' said Viola.

'You're nae wrong,' said Angus. 'Is this an Airbnb or something?'

A deep voice spoke from the hallway. 'I have ordered us Uber Eats.'

Cleo entered the kitchen, and we all stood up. Angus stared at her and gave a short bow.

Cleo was dressed in a silk shirt and silk pants. She entered the room with such poise that I found myself looking beyond her to see where her courtiers had gone. I introduced Angus to her.

'What is it that brings you to our court?' she said to him.

'This world has changed,' said Angus. 'Yesterday I lived in one city; today I live in London. But it's a different London w' wee bits missing, and different bits added. An' I only remembered what I'd lost,' he looked at me, 'when I met Juliet.'

I noted that Angus said, 'met Juliet' – not 'touched the druid stone'.

Another delivery man, this time with food, knocked on the door.

2

'Now, Flora,' said Cleo, 'put the knives away.'

Flora was clutching at the white plastic cutlery that came with the food.

'The lovely Bogdan said we must make use of his cellar, so can you go and find a few bottles of wine for us, please?'

Flora left the kitchen table obediently and dropped the knives on the floor in going. We busied ourselves putting the food onto the dining table in the adjacent room. Angus took off the various lids and Flora returned with some bottles of wine. Glasses and plates were hurriedly set out. This was a meal?

'What's up? Here,' said Angus, 'throw these lids in the bin.'

I looked at him. He looked at me.

'Slaves' day off,' he said and pointed to the kitchen.

I took a breath and did as he asked. But I did not know if I liked a world where we had to be our own servants. Angus watched me as I made my way to the rubbish bin, I suppose to see that I did the job correctly; and looked at me still as I returned for my next task.

We sat then at the large shining glass and metal table. On the walls were large paintings, each of a single mottled colour. A lamp over the table, made of polished black sticks, like a pelican's nest, was threaded with small beads of light. We had pressed the switch for these lights, for the afternoon had grown darker still with raincloud.

Cleo seemed well-inclined to enjoy this *Thai* meal; and Viola too, sampling the crumbed chicken pieces, the range of curries, bright with red chillies, the small plates of *tapas*. Flora fed herself by holding half a roast chicken to her mouth, as a cat holds a pigeon captive. I drank a sip or two from the glass of wine that I had seen uncorked. Angus sat beside me, taking in everything and thoughtfully eating noodles.

'You do not eat?' remarked Cleo.

Before I could answer, a rolling boom of thunder shook the house and the lights went out. Even though the sun was still to set, the sky was so dark that losing the lights plunged us into something like dusk. Angus rose and brought to the table a candle-set that sat upon a shelf nearby. He lit the candles and the light formed a shell of ivory around us.

It was then we saw that a young woman had entered the room, unannounced, and joined us at the table. She sat at the far end, at the edge of the light, and wrote something on a paper napkin.

'Ophelia,' said Cleo, 'you have returned, then. No, come closer and meet our new sisters. What news?'

Ophelia, I could now see, was a young woman not very much older than me, though I had felt she must be older from our conversation. Her face was pale, her hair was blonde – like that of Elke. She wore a knitted coat of mingled soft colours.

'Have you brought Miranda with you?' said Cleo.

Ophelia raised her eyebrows and shrugged. She looked at me briefly – her eyes were a striking blue. Then she stood, put the pen down, and walked into the shadows where we could no longer see her.

'Ophelia?' said Cleo more firmly. 'Ophelia!'

The lights came back on. Only the five of us were in the room.

'What the hell?' said Angus, hurrying into the kitchen and looking around. He walked into the corridor. Ophelia was nowhere to be seen. We looked at the empty chair. Angus went to where, in the candlelight, we had seen Ophelia. Viola was praying. On the table was a napkin with writing on it. Angus picked it up and read.

'It says: *Leave now. They are coming for you. A black car. Three men. The stones are...*'

Cleo took the napkin from him and read the remainder to herself.

Viola's chair scraped the floor. She darted to the wall and turned off the lights.

'Angus,' she said, 'go with Juliet and find coats and whatever you wish to bring, and shoes for travelling in the rain, and come back here. Do not put on the lights and take less than a minute.'

I ran, with Angus behind me, up the stairs to the room where I had bathed. I was used to negotiating a house at night, and Angus was the clumsy one in the dimness. We were back downstairs in moments. I still had my Sainsbury bag.

'How is it that Ophelia can appear like that?' said Angus.

'I think she is dead,' said Viola. 'Newly dead.' She crossed herself.

'I can hear a car in the driveway,' said Angus. 'The fuck? It's no Border Force, is it?'

Cleo appeared wearing a travelling coat. Flora's only preparation had been to scrape most of the food off the table into a large plastic bag. Her hands were covered in the remains of a Black Forest Cake.

'We cannot leave in the car,' said Viola. 'Come out this way.'

We moved to the back entrance of the house and stood in the narrow doorway. The evening was spitting rain.

'Go stand in the shelter of that small shed,' said Viola.

We ran to the shelter – a place that held tools for the garden – and saw Viola turn back inside the house.

I tried to use my phone to call Ophelia, not believing what Viola had said; but a voice said that the number I had dialled was either switched off or unavailable.

'She will not answer,' said Cleo, 'though you call for a thousand years.'

I felt like screaming.

A minute later we heard loud knocks, voices and terrible cries, a loud *crack, crack.*

'That's a gun,' said Angus. He was holding a garden rake.

After another minute Viola came back out. She handed a small black wallet to Angus. 'Keep this,' she said. 'Let us go this way – down to the road.'

'What happened?' I said.

Viola said nothing.

We ran to the boundary of the garden and found a path into the plantation where we paused.

'Two men came into the house,' said Viola, 'but they will not follow. Perhaps a third waits in the car beyond. Angus, tell me about this?' She held up a metal object.

'It's a gun,' said Angus. 'It kills when you press that bit. Fast metal bits shoot out.'

'With no fuse?' said Viola. 'Shall I keep it?'

'I would nae,' said Angus.

Viola tossed the gun into long wet grass. She bent and in the same wet grass wiped blood from her hands.

'Who were they?' said Cleo.

'One called out *Morgana* as he raised the *gun*,' said Viola.

Flora spat out a curse on Morgana. 'Death to witches.'

'And you're nae hit?' said Angus. 'Nae hurt?'

'No,' said Viola calmly. 'The shot went past me.'

'And how did you get his gun?' said Angus.

Viola said no more about it.

'You did well, Viola,' said Cleo.

'The stone helped.' She sounded disappointed.

Angus had been looking in the black wallet. 'There's a French driving licence; address, Lyons,' he whispered. 'Also a credit card; and 500, maybe more, in mixed notes. Mostly Euros.'

He took the money and handed the wallet back to Viola. He looked at me. 'Well it's nae Border Force.'

'Keep the wallet,' said Cleo. 'We will use his credit card. Ophelia…'

She paused. I thought she might speak words of condolence – for it had become clear that Ophelia had died – but instead, she declared, 'Ophelia also wrote on the napkin that the stones are at Chateau LeFay near the village of Mousket sur la Forêt. I suppose she means Cordelia's stone, mine, Flora's and, we might suppose, Ophelia's.'

I wanted to strike her.

'I know the place,' said Viola. 'Mousket sur la Forêt is a little distance from Marseille. There is an ancient circle of standing stones there.'

'We will go there,' said Cleo.

'We go to France?' I asked.

'Yes,' said Cleo. 'We are in danger now from the world of the living, as much as from the world of spirits. Morgana sends demons to harm us, to pinch us; but she also has men loyal to her spirit.'

'And they have killed Ophelia,' I said.

Cleo made no further response and made me feel as if I were a petulant child. Viola came close and put her arms around me. She let me look into her troubled eyes, held me close and said, 'It is not such a new world after all, then?'

'No,' I answered. And she was correct. It was not a very different world. Cleo's detached manner (almost like that of my father), the mood of fear, the shadows, the subterfuge, the lurking assassins, made it very much like my familiar past.

Viola's hand on my shoulder to comfort me was the only thing to make me feel I was *not* back in Verona.

We walked on until we reached a new road and Angus called a taxi. As we waited he spoke quietly to me. 'What d'you wanna do?'

'I must go with Cleo, I suppose. What else is there?'

'I'm nae sure. Can I tag along? Is that okay?'

'You must come,' interjected Cleo.

The taxi brought us to a railway station. No shadows or forms of evil waited; no dark cars with men within pursued us.

We travelled without further speech. Cleo spent time looking at her phone and when we stood at the railway station she held it up and showed us pictures – a cream-yellow stone building.

'Here is the Chateau LeFay at Mousket.'

'And there,' said Viola, concerned. 'Do you see parts of the stone circle.' She pursed her lips. 'We did give it a wide berth in my day, making the sign of the cross as we passed.'

Flora made a choking sound in spite of Viola's faith. Viola continued. 'They say that witches carry out vile ceremonies at certain times of the year.'

'It is our destination,' said Cleo, calmly. 'Of the seven stones that should be ours, it is now likely that four are with this man.' She showed us a picture of an old man, white haired, with his purple mouth set in a disturbing pout.

'A man named LeFay,' said Cleo, with mild contempt, 'styling himself as a king.'

'It is not a flattering picture,' I said.

Flora reached over suddenly and took the phone from Cleo's hands. '*The king o' England, Northern Ireland, Scotland and Wales,*' she whispered. 'Morgana has him for a descendent, then? Och, then I would have him lay his hands on me and heal me.'

A strange calm came over Flora – or a new kind of madness. She dropped the wet plastic bag filled with leftovers, looked at her grimy hands and began to wipe them on her clothes.

The five of us walked across a metal bridge and down to the platform. We were on the train to London minutes later.

3

Our destination was St Pancras Station, from where the European trains depart. We arrived in a violent rainstorm. We did not see the sun set. Angus had become quiet as we entered London. He looked lost, and I recalled my first train trip into London. I said to him that he could hold my hand if it would help him to better picture his lost world. We held hands. After we finished he said it helped a great deal and also that I wasn't so bad for someone who had been born with a silver knife in my back.

At the entrance to the station, Cleo took Angus with her to buy tickets. Flora disappeared into the bathrooms. Viola and I took shelter in a *taqueria*.

Viola bought a *tortilla* and broke it in half. 'I thought I needed this food, but I am full since before. Here, you have this half.'

She took a bite, and I followed her example, for I was very hungry.

'Cleo is keeping secrets from us,' I said.

'What do you mean?'

'I spoke to Ophelia, earlier, after we arrived in Reading – for I saw the number on Cleo's phone and called her on mine. She said that druids have already spoken to Cleo, and that they would help us in Stratford.'

'Druids?' said Viola. 'But are they not of the Devil?'

'I understand they will open a mysterious door for us to pass through, so that we can leave here.'

She took my hand. 'To go back?'

'I believe so.'

'That is good to know,' said Viola.

'Cleo has not spoken to you about this?'

'No, she has not,' replied Viola. 'But she has been here longer than you or I; or so I understand. She will lead us.'

'She is already leading us,' I answered.

'She is a Queen. I am not, and we need someone who knows

the world better than you or me. Someone who knows well the play of the court.'

'The play of the court?' I said. 'And we her courtiers?'

'I would not be without her right now,' said Viola. 'For I am nothing but a thief, without friends–'

'We are friends,' I said, a bit pathetically.

'I meant friends of influence in this time. Of course, you and I are friends. We are more than friends. We are two sisters in a dark wood. I only meant to say, we have no influential friends, the kind who will keep the Border Force from seizing us. I did not relish being chained to my bed. I believe there are grand, high people at this chateau who may yet protect us. I was born in a ditch. We do not really know that high world. So, let us trust Cleo. I do not mind if she plots a little or keeps a few secrets. I have secrets too,' she said with a smile. 'And *you* should have some as well. Let them be yours and no one else's.'

'But I have no secrets,' I said.

'Then pretend,' she laughed. 'The beauty of a secret is that you can lie about it, and no one will know! Come let us meet the others.'

St Pancras Station was a grand hall of glass and archways and moving stairs. It was now the evening, but seemed later, for the sky was dark and rain was lashing the whole city. On television screens were images of storm and tempest across the southern part of the land.

Many people were wandering the station in a state of anticipation. I found that this was due to the storm: many who might have travelled by boat to France were now seeking to come on the train, which went under the earth – even under the sea! – into France.

Cleo and Angus came back to us and Cleo said, 'Give to me whatever credit cards you have. There is a demand for seats because of the storm. We can only purchase what they call Business Class Plus.'

Viola produced the credit card from the dead man's purse and handed it over.

'Need a king's ransom,' said Angus. And his manner towards

me was slightly altered. I could tell that Cleo had said something to him.

I sat down upon a bench seat and left the arrangements to them. I sipped a bitter coffee that I had bought from a machine. Viola came to me carrying a glossy brochure.

'Here. *Things you must do in France*. Or so it says.'

The brochure showed the sacred stone circles at Mousket sur la Forêt, and around the stones, revellers.

'It says they hold a fancy-dress ball at Mousket every year.'

'To what end?' I asked.

Viola shrugged. 'A Saint's Day, perhaps? But the festival is tomorrow and then on into the Lord's Day.'

Angus joined us.

'Okay, sorted,' he said. 'We got the tickets. People bend o'er backwards for her. It's like being with Beyoncé.' He looked at our blank faces. 'Okay, like being with the Queen o' Egypt.'

'Speaking of queens,' said Viola, gesturing. 'Look!'

We turned, and for a moment did not recognise Flora. Somehow she had washed and dispossessed herself of the filthy clothes she had worn, and was now clad in a simple dress and a shawl of silver. Her red hair, in damp ringlets, haloed a face almost unrecognisable. Adding to the change was the air of queenliness that attended her. The only tell-tale sign it was still Flora was in how her thumb scratched persistently at the nail on her right forefinger. Viola went forward and kissed Flora on the hand. Flora did not refuse it or rear backwards. I stood and made a curtsey, taking Angus' hand and whispering for him to bow.

Cleo then appeared, barely concealing her outrage, and we had to repeat the performance for her with more flourish.

People were now staring, and Angus remarked, 'I think our carriage awaits?'

We boarded the Eurostar train to no particular fanfare. Shortly after finding our seats, I saw that we were already moving out of the station.

The train picked up speed. Through the window I saw endless buildings, cars and flashing red lights, distant people hurrying in the rain beneath umbrellas. I had never seen anything that made me so sad, or which filled me with such a yearning.

From where I sat, across the walkway, I observed Cleo calmly scrolling through her phone. Viola was sipping a glass of champagne. The bottle stood in a bucket of ice in front of Cleo – presented as a gift from the Lords of the Eurostar.

An attendant came and poured coffee for Angus and I. Angus drank his without milk.

'I will have the same,' I said.

I unwrapped a biscuit from its plastic and said quietly to Angus, 'So, did Cleo say anything to you… about me?'

'Aye, she did,' he answered. 'She said we should stop holding hands, because she didn't want you distracted.'

'You may take my hand whenever you wish,' I said.

'Ok,' he said, but did nothing.

'And did she say anything else?'

'Aye, that you and I should put childish things behind us. Maybe she just meant for me to stop playing wi' my phone. She said that everyone needs to keep to their place, do their part; to have all our eyes forward as we race towards our enemies like a falcon that rides the burning air.'

'She said that?'

'Aye, it's the kind o' thing I imagine an ancient queen would say. Do you have your phone there?'

I took it out. Angus had put it on charge that afternoon.

'Okay. Let's send up a flare. Let's get you on the socials.'

Angus explained what he meant, pulling out his own phone. 'I search for you, *Juliet Capulet*, you're not there. Your family's not there. I looked up *Romeo Montague* before – see? Not exactly a common name. And found only this, see? Some old coot in Canada with a fur hat.' He showed me the picture of an aged man with a strange headdress. 'That's nae him?'

I punched Angus in the arm.

'Anyway, hand me your phone and I'll get you on Facebook.'

'What is Facebook?' I asked.

'Aye, what is Facebook. When is your birthday?'

'I was born on the Feast of St Genevieve in 1565.'

'1565? Hmm, I'll have to put in something like 2007. Is there a day and a month to go wi' that? Okay, I'm going tae fix you up wi' a Snap account, as well as Facebook. Because if your chap does get online, which he might, then he can find you and message you. If he's from the 16th century then he'll definitely be getting onto Facebook. Plan?'

An announcement said that we were now descending into a tunnel. I was glad that Angus was there to talk me through socials as we journeyed deep under the earth.

4

Angus took me through the steps and made me various 'social media' accounts. He wrote Romeo's name into my profile, and we added other words – Verona, Italy; and the names of others from our home – Benvolio his cousin, and Mercutio. Angus told me these were 'useful search terms'.

He took photographs of me with the phone – more than I think he needed.

'Um, lovely. Okay, now look out the window. Give a wee glance into the distance. Okay, now, here's the travel magazine, just peek at me o'er the top edge of it. Och, you're good at this. Throw your hair back a little. Perfect.'

Angus handed me my phone and said, 'Now, ye search for my name and here I am. See? Now you send me a friend request. And, *ping*, there it is, and I accept it. So you can see – there – that Rowan and Damian are my friends. And there's my probation officer. And those are my suppliers – Zed Kar and B-Canny. I'll let Damian know that we're fine for the moment. Och, look there: he and Daisy are sharing a bubble chai!'

The picture he showed me was of Daisy and Damian in a close hug. Another picture showed Rowan and Elke clamped together on a sofa.

'Och, and Damian's using emojis. I tell you, it's a night o' love in London. He did for aye want a girlfriend. Now he has one. Anyway, back to the matter in hand.'

'Angus, do you have a girlfriend?' I said.

'I'm too busy flogging stolen goods to have any time for it,' he replied. 'Maybe I have one back in the world I came from. Though there's no one I can recollect.'

'Would holding my hand help restore the memory?' I offered him my hand.

'I doubt it,' said Angus in a curious voice. 'Here, let's do a selfie, so I can send it to Damian and put their minds at rest. You don't do selfies in medieval Italy I suppose?'

'Tell me what I must do.'

'Okay, I hold up the camera. We bunch in like this. Turn the lens on us. Now do ye wanna do that wee girl thing where you poke your tongue out for the camera?'

'Why would I do that?'

'It's a mystery tae me. I believe that psychologically you're emulating a strangled person for the benefit o' the male gaze, but I only know that cos Damian read it to me out o' *The Guardian*.'

He took our picture, but the result was a picture where we both looked dazed and sad.

'Let's try that again. Och, that's horrible. I need a haircut. Okay. Now, each of us go to our happy place, or at least pretend.'

Eventually we gave up – but we were laughing at the end of it.

Angus's phone buzzed with a message, and he looked towards Cleo. She had sent him a *link*.

'What is it?' I asked.

'It's an architectural plan,' he replied, showing me the image.

'It is the chateau,' called Cleo across the aisle.

I took out the brochure that Viola had shown me earlier – of revellers at the upcoming festival. Above the people loomed the lit-up yellow walls and towers of a chateau.

'So *this*,' I said, 'is the house for which *that* is the plan?'

'Yes,' said Cleo. 'The house belongs to that puffed up little man Malcolm LeFay – a descendant of the Derek LeFay who ruled England in past times, and thus a descendant of Morgana LeFay.'

We had expected Flora to spit out a curse, but she sat quietly, listening, her eyes thoughtful and mild – like a lizard resting in the sun.

'This Malcolm LeFay sent those other men to kill us, do you think?' said Viola.

'I do not doubt it. Come close, all of you. I will open to you my heart and mind.'

We sat around.

'I believe that Mousket is where we will find my missing stone; and the one stolen from Flora; and the one taken from Cordelia. And perhaps that held by the woman called Miranda, though we still know nothing of her. I do not doubt that LeFay has brought about the death of Ophelia and has taken her stone.'

How could she speak of Ophelia so casually?

'And you want us to break int' this chateau?' said Angus.

'We may force our way. But I plan for us to walk in through the doors of welcome, take what is ours, and walk out again.'

'And then do we go to *Stratford*?' I asked.

'And tell me what you know of Stratford?' said Cleo, and I knew that I had annoyed her.

'Is it where we must go to bring about our return?' I said, keeping my knowledge vague, not wishing to reveal to her that I had spoken with Ophelia earlier.

'What did Ophelia say?' said Cleo, and I realised that she saw through my subterfuge. Had I not, after we hid in the garden shed, tried to call Ophelia to no avail, and in full sight of Cleo, who might wonder how it was I had her number?

'Ophelia did say to me,' answered Cleo, speaking over my guilty silence, 'that near Stratford lies a sacred water named Charlecote Well, which the druids hold in great reverence. But *we* are not beholden to a handful of priests. We will listen to their counsel when the time comes. And go to Stratford if and when we choose.'

I wondered if I should have stayed then at Charlecote House all along, and perhaps the druids would have found me. The man in the copse of trees talking on his phone – had that been a druid looking for me? Was the mysterious man on the train with his wee tracking device also of the druids?

Angus's phone made a series of little buzzes, which he ignored. He and I returned to our seat. More buzzing.

'Are you going to answer the phone?' I asked.

'Stratford?' said Angus. He was distracted. 'You said *Stratford*.'

'It is where I came into this world,' I reaffirmed.

'And where we leave it?' said Viola.

I looked at Angus, then leant over to look down at his phone, which he held loosely in his hand. 'Angus, Damian says: *WTF*?'

The phone then rang, and Angus took the WhatsApp call like one shaken from a sleep. Damian was speaking, and Daisy was interrupting. Eventually Angus calmed them and said that everything was fine, to 'dinnae fret', that all would be revealed, and that he and I were simply travelling to Italy on a wee jaunt.

'Italy? Italy!' said Damian.

He passed me the phone and there was Daisy asking me, 'Girl, where did you go? Damian says a super suss guy was stalking you on the train? I mean things went a bit weird there.'

Angus was sitting very close to me, squeezing into the picture – and perhaps this helped him to *tune in* to something about me, for he suddenly said, 'Guys, I'll call you again, guys, guys, we gotta hide from the ticket inspector.'

Elke meanwhile had taken the phone from Daisy and her face occupied the screen. 'Hey, Angus, when are we seeing you again?'

He ended the call.

'What is it?' I said. 'What troubles you?'

'*Stratford* troubles me,' he said. 'That play I remembered, when we first met? *Romeo and Juliet*, William Shakespeare, Stratford – they all go together.'

'I know of no William Shakespeare,' I said. 'Except that you have mentioned the name.'

Angus had a hand pressed to his forehead and was pulling hard at his hair.

'Should I take your hand?' I said, 'Will it help you remember?'

He took my hand. And spoke, as if from a dream.

'*Romeo and Juliet*. It's a play, by William Shakespeare. The Immortal Bard o' Stratford upon Avon. He wrote hundreds of plays.'

'And what is in this play?'

Angus faltered. 'Well, I recall I saw it. In Southwark.'

'Yes? I have been to Southwark!'

'I recall we came on the train to London. We got back late.'

'And in the play?'

'It's about two young lovers, Romeo and Juliet. They live in Verona. Their families are agin' them getting married, because of a feud, so Juliet takes a draught to pretend she's dead – but Romeo doesn't get *the letter* telling him that it's all just a ruse. So, he finds her in the tomb asleep, thinks she's dead, and takes his own life.'

'He takes his life?' I said, pulling away. 'That is – *No!* He must not! It would be a dreadful mistake! It is wrong!'

'Is there more to it?' asked Cleo in an interested voice.

'Juliet wakes a minute later,' said Angus. 'She sees him dead, and then she takes her life. And that was it.'

A few moments later I heard Viola speaking through a fog. 'Juliet? Come back to us. Juliet, Juliet…'

5

We disembarked from the Eurostar at a city named Lille and it was very late. Though if someone had shown me the precise time, or pointed to a clock, the numbers would have meant nothing, for I was very tired and filled with emotions I could not name.

Angus walking with me kept saying, 'I might have mis-remembered the details. That was a different world from this.'

'But we can all go back to where we came from,' said Viola, I suppose to make me confident, 'each to our own worlds – and Juliet, you will save Romeo.'

Angus's sudden recollection of *Romeo and Juliet* laid out a different situation. Romeo was not in this world at all – I had only seen mention of a story, a play, about us. But who had found out our story? And how? One called William Shakespeare. Romeo had killed himself because of me (or *would* kill himself if I could not somehow stop him). What dreadful things had I brought to pass by simply letting him climb up onto my balcony and enter my room?

Cleo provided a room for each of us at a hotel near the railway station. An easy task, for the concierge treated her like a long-lost friend, though I am sure they had never met.

Cleo took us to a bar off the foyer for a light meal, as the rooms would take a few minutes to prepare. I had no appetite.

'Is this not ideal?' said Cleo. I wondered what she meant; but the name of the bar was *fer à cheval*, which means *horseshoe*. The bar was in the shape of a horseshoe; and forming a ceiling decoration were hundreds of old horseshoes suspended from wires.

Once we were seated, Cleo remarked, 'Perhaps, Juliet, you can turn your jacket the right way out now.'

I took my jacket off and reversed it. I placed a horseshoe on the table. 'So, I do not need this?'

'With all these horseshoes around and above, the dark creatures will not attack. Have you noticed, since we fled Bogdan's house, there have been no threatening shadows?'

'I had noticed,' said Viola.

While drinking an aperitif, Cleo spied some boutique shops that were open.

'Viola,' said Cleo, 'go with Juliet and buy some fresh clothes from the shop over there. Viola, take this card. And Viola, there is a ski-wear shop next to it; though it is not the season you would wish to buy yourself–'

'Something black as if I were to move at night in secret?'

'Yes,' smiled Cleo. 'As if you were to move like a small cat quietly through a palace. Ah, little Anubis, how I miss my pretty kitten.' She gave an affectionate laugh that I did not believe. I wished that Cleo would show something like an acknowledgment of Ophelia's death, the weight of it.

Viola and I went to the shops Cleo had indicated. I believe every shop in this precinct was open, though it was night. It was truly a world where time had turned inside out. No church bells to mark the measure of God's day; no following the cadence of the Sun; or knowing through the growing and declining light when to rise, when to sleep.

Sprinkles of light greeted us as we entered the first shop. I felt as if I was being touched with ghostly rose petals. Music played, a steady thrumming, and a woman with green hair and a nose ring found me some colourful garments to try. Viola, however, chose for me different clothes that were understated ('to draw less attention'), which included a summer frock and short jacket; and then a cocktail dress of crushed red silk ('to draw more attention').

'Why must I have these?'

'We are planning to visit this chateau. And if it is a chateau, it will be filled with lords and their ladies. So we must be pleasing to the eye. You must know this – you are from that kind of world.'

'After a fashion,' I said. 'And what about you? You seem...'

She had too much grace to be of low upbringing. 'A woman not of low estate.'

Viola laughed. 'I am nothing but a thief and a wandering player – from a family of counterfeiters on one side, and a travelling theatre on the other. My father played Harlequin and was the lantern of my heart.'

'In Marseille?' I said, speaking brightly to cover my grief when she described such a loving father.

'Yes, in the last year, I lived in Marseille. But it was not always so. My father went out to meet with a man one night and never came back. My mother became unwell from it. We were staying in a very small village and had no friends. Mama died, and Sebastian said we should go to Marseille and seek our fortune there.'

'And did you find fortune?'

'Too much of it,' she replied and wrinkled her mouth. 'We became rich. People said we had the Devil on our side. *I* say that people simply forgot to lock their windows. But now we had to pay off those who had become our early friends – or else, they said, we might not be able to rely on their confidence.

'So, we made our way into one of the grandest houses, the closest I have come to a prince, and I took his jewels, and a precious emerald, and some diamonds, and a kiss, and it was so daring and so notorious that we had to escape quickly. Sebastian found a captain to take us to Illyria. And, *voila*. I am here.'

We were looking through a rack of blouses and coats.

'And so you have *other* jewels?' I said.

'I do not know where they are,' she said with a shrug. 'I thought I had the emerald safe in my jacket, but then it turned into this mysterious stone. If I go back to my world, I will start again with nothing.' She smiled.

'You do not mind?'

'No. All I want is to find a not-so-rich man, who is quick to smile, and to live in his house.'

'You are confident we can get back?'

'Ophelia has given us the clearest words. And Cleo has said

to me that it is a certainty. She said that this world cannot stand such an intrusion as we are; and will find a way to expel us like tiny splinters of wood, or a thorn from beneath the skin. I think Fate moves us to find our way home.'

'But not Ophelia,' I rejoined. 'Not Cordelia.'

'Juliet, we must do everything we can to secure our return. You want to catch your fiancé before he does away with himself, no?'

'Yes,' I affirmed.

'Then make yourself ready, *mon cher*. You must sidestep that wicked priest of yours with his poison; and you must make sure you go back knowing how to deal with the ones who would kill you. Have you thought about what you must do?'

'No,' I said. My head swam. 'I haven't had time to think. And you do not know my family.'

Viola put an arm around me.

'When I go back,' she said, 'I will take two life jackets – do you know what I mean? The inflatables – so Sebastian and I will be buoyant when the ship goes down. And we will both arrive washed up safely in Illyria. But if I manage to return before we even take ship from Marseille, then I will have the most precious tool, which is foreknowledge.'

'You think that we might return earlier than we left?' I said, my mind whirling with all these thoughts.

'I do not know – sooner, or perhaps later.'

'And Romeo would then be dead!'

She raised a hand. 'Juliet, right now, we are hundreds of years–' She paused and took a sharp intake of breath. 'O God,' she said, 'we are hundreds of years from home. Why? And we have stones that we must find…' She calmed herself and patted my cheek. 'Leave on that red dress. Wear it. Now, I shall pay. Be prepared to run if they don't take the card!'

They did take the card. We returned to the *Horseshoe Bar*, with our bags of clothing. Angus had also been sent off to dress more elegantly, and he was waiting for us wearing a close-fitting suit of fine fabric, a narrow silk cravat. He casually pushed up one of the sleeves to let me glimpse his new wristwatch.

6

Cleo would have us rest, and I was tired; but I asked Angus to come with me to find a church that was open, for I wished to pray. Cleo remarked that if I needed a priest I should call room service. But I was in no mood to listen to her.

'I will find a church,' I said, and Angus and I walked off into the rainy night.

A man with a high hat bowed and gave us an umbrella.

Angus remarked as we walked, 'She's given me the job of technical wizard.'

'What is a technical wizard?' I said.

'Making sure our comms are all working, disconnect the alarm system if the time comes. Use spray paint on the CCTV. That kinda thing. Then she made me buy these things I'm wearing. And you look nice.'

'It is meant to draw the eye.'

'And here comes the rain,' said Angus. He snapped the umbrella open and we walked together beneath it.

I could not help running my hand over the shirt that he wore. 'The clothes are so different in this world,' I said. 'What is this fabric called?'

'Polyester blend.'

We had to make our way through some blundering tourists, so I did not mind that Angus gave me his arm. Thus we walked, and talked a little about clothing, and I made foolish comments about the thin tie he was wearing. But after a few minutes I could think of nothing more to say, and returned to thoughts of Ophelia. Where was she? Where did she lie?

The map led us a short way towards a familiar kind of building – one not of glass, steel and the concrete, but a church perhaps as old as I was. I thought for a moment that a midnight Mass was being celebrated, for light came from the windows, and we entered through the open door.

But we found no priest, just coloured lights that came and went, and strange sculptures. And no benches to sit on, nowhere to kneel, and people wandering around not praying. And no choir; just music like that I heard in the clothes shop, a simmering like a swarm of bees.

'Sign here says it's been *de-consecrated*,' said Angus. 'It's now an art space.'

'I want to light a candle for Ophelia,' I said. But I was more than half glad that here was no place for candles; for I would then have to light one also for my family, and think about forgiving them, which was the last thing I intended. Perhaps I had only wanted to go against Cleo in coming to a church.

We left the building. As we did, we heard something smash against the outside wall.

Angus took my hand and steered me across the road.

'Keep on,' he said. 'It's just a beer bottle.'

The street was no longer full of tourists; instead, it held a group of soldiers in red and grey uniforms. They walked as if carousing. Some carried flaming torches. One had thrown a bottle and others were shouting, '*Vive Morgana! Vive LaFay*'.

Morgana? The name spoken by the assailants at the house in Reading.

We kept on. More crashing. I turned back to see a bottle strike at the head of the Holy Mother, whose statue stood in a darkened niche.

'Why do they do this?' I said, aghast.

The thrower raised his arms in victory. I felt a blaze of outrage. The surge of anger seemed located near the locket around my throat. And suddenly, the man skidded on something and fell backwards, smacking his head in the roadway. This stopped some of the cheering, but those who helped him up suddenly looked my way, and others also turned their heads towards me, as if they knew I had caused this.

One called out coldly, '*Tu ris*?'

Angus pulled on my arm. 'Come on, don't look at them.'

A bottle flew towards us and smashed nearby.

'Did you do something, there?' said Angus.

'I think I did.' I felt for the locket. 'Who are they?'

'I cannae say. Come this way, we can cut through here. I do remember seeing a flick about the end o' the druids back in the day, and they had all these followers of Morgana LeFay dressed in those same colours and calling out for Morgana. It was called *Death at Stonehenge*. Had Vanessa Redgrave in it.'

'Morgana is the Queen of Witches,' I said. 'It was *her* men who came to the house.'

'Let's just head back,' said Angus, his eyes darting ahead.

I had thought we might be pursued, but we returned to the hotel unharmed.

I found in the concourse a gift shop that sold candles, as well as aromatic oils and crystals. I thought perhaps the priest lived here, but this turned out not to be the case. I had seen no roadside shrines anywhere in my travels so far. Perhaps Cleo was right, and one had to summon a priest using room service. But I also remembered the last time that I had been in a room alone with a priest. And so I thought instead of buying a large candle and lighting it privately in my chamber for Ophelia.

But would Ophelia want my prayer, she whose allegiance seemed to be to the spirits of the earth, to other gods?

Angus received a call from Cleo, so I walked in alone. The scent of flowers and fragrant oils, the healing aromas, melted my sore heart. The different perfumes were coming from open bottles on a display shelf. An assistant took a small bottle of oil of rosemary, opened it and smiling, rubbed a few drops on my wrist. I closed my eyes, inhaled, and despite it being rosemary, forgot almost everything.

I opened my eyes to thank the shop assistant and make my request.

Ophelia stood in front of me.

'O, dear God,' I said. 'You are not dead.' I reached for her hand.

'No, do not,' she answered. 'You cannot touch me.'

I secretly put my hand forward to where she stood. I touched nothing.

'I am not here.'

'Where are you then?' I said faintly.

'Oh, somewhere, nowhere, everywhere,' was her reply. She raised her hand to shield her half-closed eyes, as if the sun was low. She surveyed an unseen horizon. 'I think I am standing in the sweet fields of the Lady Freja. I think,' she looked at me and suppressed a wry smile, said, 'I think I have joined those who appear suddenly, say enigmatic things, then fade before you can grasp them.'

'What happened to you?'

'It was quick, whatever it was. *Hej.* And speaking of quick, do not be quick to trust Cleo.'

'I think I know that,' I said with some heat.

'You will need to find a boy,' she said. 'Before I died, I saw him.'

'A boy?'

'His name is Will. He and the Seven Stones are bound together. He brought them into the world. He must leave with them. Nothing else will heal the wound. Nothing else matters. But now I must go that way. Do you see there? Your candle lights half the sky.'

She walked through me.

I woke and I was in a hotel room, waking at the moment that the candle I had purchased from the shop burnt out with a faint *tizzit* and a ribbon of smoke. I have no memory of how I got to the room, or how I lit the candle.

It was still dark, but rising I found fresh clothes set out for me in the low-lit room, alongside the red dress Viola bought for me (the thin, revealing garments of this age). I took up the summer frock. With it was a handwritten note: 'Wear this.'

Angus knocked on my door.

'We have to go,' he said. 'We're shifting out, apparently.'

'How long have I slept?'

'About five hours. Cleo rang me, woke me.'

'Where is she?'

'Having breakfast downstairs.'

'At this hour?'

'Aye. I don't think she sleeps. Have ye had any messages then?'

'I have not looked,' I said, once I understood what he was talking about.

I went and washed my face.

'Is Viola with Cleo?'

'No, she and Flora have gone on ahead,' said Angus. 'To gather supplies, so I understand. Ropes for climbing walls, an incendiary device. And a small entourage of mock attendants. They've detoured to the city o' Rheims.'

'Angus, how did I get here? To this room?'

'You don't remember? We came up. You asked me to light the candle, and then–'

'I spoke with Ophelia,' I said. 'She was standing in front of me.'

'Real? Like back at the house, you saw her?'

'Yes, but my hand went through her hand.'

'Go on.'

'She said not to trust Cleo.'

Angus let out a sigh. 'Well, that makes it a wee bit difficult,' he said. 'Since we're in the thick of it.'

'Ophelia said that we had to find a boy named Will.'

'Does she mean Will Shakespeare?'

'She did not say.'

'But Will Shakespeare is dead. He lived in the 16th century.'

'I lived in the 16th century.'

Angus ran his fingers through his hair.

'You're no' an actress?'

'What do you mean?'

'Well, maybe you were acting in his play, *Romeo and Juliet*, then fell and bumped your head, forgot who you were, and fell through a portal?'

'What are you saying?'

'I haven't a fucking clue! Juliet, are you out of a play?'

'No!' I reacted. 'I am not. It is this world that is the play!'

Angus took my hand. I think my words had stung him. He looked so sad.

'And it is a play for you as well,' I said. 'An unreal thing.'

Angus's phone buzzed.

'It's Cleo,' said Angus. 'Time to go.'

Being dark, and the corridors half-lit, everything had a dreamlike cast, which only intensified as Angus and I descended in the lift. And then, unexpectedly, as she doors closed we fell into each other's arms and kissed.

It was startling, for Angus looked into my eyes as if he was holding me for the last time. And I had my arms around him and I am sure I felt the same.

And what of Romeo?

I walked out quickly into the foyer, for I did not want to say to Angus that no one had ever held me like that, or looked at me like that, ever.

Angus walked on ahead, looking for Cleo; I could barely walk.

7

We found Cleo at a table in the dining hall, sipping coffee, lost in gentle reverie, leafing through a magazine called *New Yorker*. A large television showed images of the King of England arriving in Copenhagen.

Soon after we all got into a quiet and elegant car and travelled at some speed through the countryside, with small villages and roadhouses floating past as the sun rose. Angus sat in the front with our driver, a man named Bernard; Cleo and I sat in the back seat. At a roadhouse, while the driver was not within earshot, Angus and I discovered the car had been provided for us by Malcolm LeFay. Angus was visibly stunned.

'Do you mean that they know we're coming?' said Angus. 'Coming to the chateau?'

'Yes,' replied Cleo. 'I have already spoken with Malcolm LeFay and we are expected. He thinks we come in all deference and friendship to put ourselves in his service. To hand over the remaining stones. He is blinded by his joyful anticipation. We will have a more restful journey because of it.'

She had such a commanding way of talking, I should have been more worried. Perhaps this agreement with Malcolm LeFay explained the disappearance of the demonic creatures that had attacked us. Our way was being made clear.

Angus showed me a picture of Malcolm LeFay at some event, flanked by two soldiers. The caption read, *Malcolm LeFay with members of the Sons of Mordred*. They wore the same uniform as the mass of young men who had abused us in Lille. Our driver Bernard wore livery in the same style.

Once more on the road, Cleo took to reading from her magazines. 'Juliet,' she said languidly, 'there is much to see in Paris. We will go there after we have visited Mousket.'

She kept a hand looped over my wrist in a relaxed manner.

'But, should we not hurry back to–?' I would have said *to*

Stratford, but she touched my arm to indicate I should stay silent lest the driver hear us. I had meant to raise this and the question of the druids with her. But the presence of people like Bernard now made that difficult, for it became clear that he, like many others we encountered, were favourable to the house of LeFay.

Cleo then showed me an article. 'Do you see here?' she remarked. 'The *Musée du Monde Égyptien* is hosting the largest collection of ancient treasures to be seen this century. We will visit there. Do you see this picture?'

I saw an ancient necklace of brilliant turquoise.

'It is lovely,' I remarked.

'I only wore it the once,' said Cleo.

'It is *yours*?'

'Most of these jewels are mine,' she replied. 'And that cup of faience, and that of veined alabaster, also mine.'

I slept after that – I could not stay awake – and it was the middle of the afternoon when we came finally to Mousket. We drove past an ancient standing stone.

After that, there were lines of standing stones, and now large crowds around pavilions in the fields, with many people dressed in the manner of strolling players and musicians, and in courtly clothes. I felt for a moment that I had returned to my age, *my time*, for the manner of dress was familiar. Two young men we passed, tossing a ball between them and swigging beers, could easily have been Tybalt and Benvolio; but here, now, as friends on this happy festival day, instead of angry and cold with each other.

Then I saw people dressed for a pageant of the heavens, carrying Suns and Moons on rods. Some were dressed as if for pagan mysteries.

Marshals wearing orange jackets guided our vehicle down a quiet, tree-shrouded lane. We were allowed through a barrier, then onto a road before arriving at a set of wrought iron gates.

Beyond I saw the chateau with its turrets, and a small helicopter on the adjacent lawn. As we pulled in, two other black cars, in which were Viola, Flora, and others, joined us. Cleo had hired for us an entourage. We climbed from the cars into the afternoon sunshine.

I was desperately relieved to see Viola. She came to me and squeezed my hand.

'What is happening?' I asked. 'I feel I am in a pageant for which I know not my part.'

'Well, there *is* a plan,' said Viola.

'A plan?' said Angus, coming in to listen. 'I'd ne'er hae guessed it.'

'Soon,' said Viola softly (we were all conversing in low voices), 'we will present ourselves to Malcolm LeFay, and Cleo will seek a private meeting with him. She will hand over to him my stone, and yours, to win his trust.'

'My stone?' I said, too loudly.

'We have some tricks up our sleeve,' said Viola, 'let me take it now.'

I opened my locket and passed Viola the stone. In my anxiety I let the lock of Romeo's hair blow away.

I let it blow away; and was overwhelmed with a terrible guilt, although I must have made a move to chase the wisp of hair.

'Och, leave it,' said a voice. 'You no have need of a charm!'

It was Flora speaking.

I studied her – she was so changed, so confident. She seemed to have no doubts about her part in this performance. From her shoulders trailed a long cape, held up by two young women who had travelled in the car with her. I learned these *servants* had been hired and dressed by Viola to act as attendants for both Lady Macbeth and Cleo.

My main thought, however, was to wonder what had brought about the change in Flora. I later reasoned there could be only so much madness in our group of seven, and Cleo had now begun to use it all up.

Cleo also wore a beautiful garment – a cloak of silvered magenta that attached to an outrageous night-blue dress. Two young men were in attendance, wearing matching suits with sashes. Two young women took their places next to me; and a young man dressed identically to Angus but carrying a small inlaid chest, stood by him. A last man, carrying an ornate parasol which he raised to protect Cleo from the light of the sun, completed this court of Cleopatra, Daughter of Ptolemy, Queen of the Nile.

'Who are these people with us?' I asked Viola.

'They belong,' she said, 'to a troupe of actors from the city of Rheims. They act now for us.'

The walls of the chateau were golden in the afternoon light. And now, through glass doors, a man of late middle-age emerged and stood with his arms spread wide in welcome. It was the man from the picture – Malcolm LeFay. He wore a cream shirt with a cravat, a sky-blue velvet gown, and white canvas shoes. He wiggled his hands in a wave.

'Well, hello, *hello*. You are most welcome. Most welcome.'

A woman in a lime green pantsuit and a silk turban joined him.

Several servants and attendants fell into line behind the couple. One called out, 'His Majesty, the King!'

8

CLEO STEPPED FORWARD. SHE WAS ASTONISHING TO WATCH — HER VOICE thrilled and thrilling.

'My dear, dear King Malcolm. And at this happy, happy hour when your reign is finally established.' She took both his hands in hers.

'My dear Cleopatra,' said the man, almost losing his footing on the steps.

'God damn,' said the woman, her eyes streaming with tears. 'No need to ask for *your* ID. Come here.'

The woman stalked forward and embraced Cleo.

'My wife, the Marchioness. Well, Royal Consort, or something along those lines,' said Malcolm.

'Oh, call me Desiree,' said the woman, 'and please, call His Highness Malcolm. I'm so glad we're gonna be friends.'

Cleo presented the rest of us, but they showed no interest, although when Cleo came to saying, 'and Juliet Capulet of a high Veronese house,' Malcolm shuddered with delight.

'You are *very* welcome, my dear. Cleo has told me all about your troubles at the hands of loathsome priests.'

She had?

Malcolm took both my hands in his, I thought he might be about to cry, and his hands were soft and slightly cool. 'Superb, well, well.'

Cleo spoke. 'We are eager now for our private conversation, and presentation of the sacred stones, so that the Great Work can be carried forward. My Lady Flora and the Countess Viola will attend us.'

'Absolutely. Of course,' said Malcolm. 'Absolutely. Let us go in.'

Cleo knew herself to be completely superior to these people. Royalty sat upon Malcolm like an ill-fitting coat. They would have been insignificant courtiers in Cleo's palace; kitchenhands in my father's house. But now Cleo, Flora and Viola moved forward, and LeFay's servants needed no prompting to fling wide the doors, bow, and bring us all within.

Servants escorted me to a guest wing and showed me a quiet room, where the buzz of distant activity barely filtered in.

I showered, then sat on the bed and opened my locket, now empty of the stone.

I heard a tap upon the door and I opened it.

'Angus,' I said, for it was he. 'Come in.'

He quickly entered the room and put a bag down behind a chair. He immediately took out his phone and I saw that he was breathing quickly.

'I had a wander. It's a big house,' said Angus. 'You could easily get lost here. Went down lots o' the wrong corridors, pretending to be lost.'

'I do not need to pretend, I am lost,' I said. 'Did you find what you sought?'

'I did. All the mobile numbers for the house security are on a list taped to the wall outside the kitchen.'

'Is that good?'

'Fuck, yeah. I sent a picture o' the list to a web address in Romania and for a small fee they'll all be blocked to each other the instant I dial a certain number. It's a real bargain – only 25 Euros.'

'Does that mean,' I said, pointing to a pergola in the gardens below, 'that the guards I see lurking in the garden below will no longer be able to converse?'

'Exactly that. They'll be in the dark. I also jacked into the camera system – see here, this is all the wee cameras inside this building. I can shut them down at will.'

I looked at his phone and saw lots of rooms, in miniature, in grey, black and white.

'And take a look at this. Here's what's inside the big room at the far end of the chateau.'

I saw what looked strangely like the inside of a church – a stone altar with candles – and upon this, on a piece of patterned velvet, sat seven small stones.

'I heard something like a prayer service through the door. Some people chanting, men's voices, saying things like *spirit o' the rock, spirit o' the water, you the burning lightning, we your servants* – that kinda thing.'

'Did you go in?'

'Aye – and there was a man dressed as a rabbit sitting on the bed. No, just kidding. I didn't go in, because of the camera above the door. Which I'll disconnect later.'

'And they are all the stones?' I said, for seven stones – dull as tiny pebbles – lay upon the cloth. Angus touched and expanded the image.

'Aye. It's the Seven Stones. I heard Mr LeFay say, "We have the Seven" and everyone's walking around looking as if they just dropped a few tabs.'

'So, what is required of us now?' I asked.

'Well, I assume everything's going to plan – though *plan* is no' the word I'd be using. There's the stones all in the one place. There's a ceremony soon in the big stonehengey circle out in the gardens. They have a bonfire set with a Guy on top. And while they light it and dance around a wee bit, and let off crackers, well, everyone has to be there for the fun; an' that's when Viola will sneak in and pick up the stones.'

'What do we do while that is happening?'

'I suppose we all take our cues from Cleo. We first make it look as if we're *no'* planning on running off. Look interested. Look as if we're enjoying ourselves. But if we do need to slip away, I brought us these. There's a big rack o' fancy dress downstairs so that King Malcolm's guests can dress silly for the festival – I took two, one for you, one for me.'

Angus revealed the contents. Two harlequin costumes and white face masks, such as I have seen in pageants. 'They're light, they're small, and we can put them on if we need to suddenly blend in.'

Angus ran out of words and looked at me.

'I like that we are friends,' I said, wanting to address the kiss. The kiss had been a lot easier than searching for words to talk about it.

'Come, sit on the windowsill,' said Angus. 'Can I take another picture?'

'For Facebook?'

'No. Just for the sake of it.'

'Do you need my phone?'

'I'll use mine. Try not to fall off the ledge.'

Through the open window I heard music and saw the stage and lights of a dance party.

'They're cranking it up,' said Angus.

'I would like to go,' I said, 'and not concern myself with all this.'

'Would be fun,' said Angus. 'We could let our hair down a bit, maybe, at least until…'

'Until?'

'Until it gets a bit too much and one of us has tae walk away.'

9

Angus and I came into the dining room and found Malcolm LeFay with many guests dressed in their *commedia del'arte* finery – though some were dressed like penitents and carried or wore grotesque masks. Viola and Flora were in one corner with our hired attendants. Cleo sat smoking in a small area outside with Desiree.

Malcolm, seeing us, called out, 'Angus and Juliet! Angus and Juliet! There you are. We thought you'd never come. You're a picture, my dear. I've poured the champagne.

'Desiree! Cleo! Come in here. Come on in girls, come on in! We're all here now. Friends, my lords and ladies in waiting, let's raise our glasses. You've got yours there? Superb. Leave that tray for the Sons of Mordred. This is Krug Clos d'Ambonnay, so say your prayers everyone.'

LeFay raised his glass and we all raised ours. I thought I understood English, but I was struggling to understand his mumbling speech.

'Here is to the Feast of the Equinox, hail to Ostara and to Our Lady Morgana, and to Merlinus! May he prepare the way!'

'Hell, yeah!' said Desiree. 'You sure have waited a long time my sweet.'

Malcolm's wife might have already finished a few glasses of champagne, for she said again, raising her glass after we had drunk, 'Prepare the Way!'

The call was taken up from the hallway, 'Prepare the Way, Prepare the Way.'

Several men, wearing long grey robes with red markings, and long pointed hats, entered. They all carried scythes and some wore white masks that represented long-beaked birds, such as those worn by the plague-wardens during the pestilence. It was very dramatic.

'And here they are! Superb! The Sons of Mordred!'

'Hail the King,' they cried and raised their arms in salute. I recognised Bernard the chauffeur in their number.

One of the men stepped forward and spoke, not to Malcolm, but to me, 'My dear Lady Juliet, *le coeur sans faille est une chose de perfection.*'

This plain-faced man knelt before me and then stood.

'Beautifully done,' said Desiree. 'Thankyou Monsieur LeBlanc.'

'Your Highnesses,' replied the man as sincerely as his features allowed. He stood back and gave a short bow to the LeFays.

I was baffled but was to discover, soon enough, why I was being singled out.

The Sons of Mordred drank a toast, and with their scythes aloft led us out to wide lawns, low-chanting the words '*Morgana, Morgana!*' We all followed into the evening, holding our glasses. Such was the mood of rejoicing that even the kitchen staff and servants came with us.

'Will she appear!?' asked one of the guests in rapturous tones.

'This night!' said LeBlanc. 'This night!'

Why was everyone staring especially at me?

'Prepare the Way!' said Malcolm, his voice thinner in the open air.

'Prepare the Way,' screeched Desiree.

My understanding of 'the Way', from what Angus had briefly told me, was that a pathway connected the stone circle in the gardens to the chapel inside the chateau, and that lighting the bonfire would cause Morgana LeFay to appear. After which she would process to the chapel and do something with the stones – use their unified powers, as the druids later explained it, for some fell purpose. The domination of the United Kingdom being only the start.

Then Viola was beside us, carrying a bottle of champagne. She handed Angus a glass. 'How much do you think I have drunk this evening? What do you wager?' she said, giggling. She raised her glass to some of the guests and called out, 'The health of the King!' They responded in kind, with boisterous laughter.

'I do not know,' I said. 'Enough?'

In a quiet, normal voice she said, 'No. I have had nothing to drink, Juliet. Pretend sips only. Do likewise. Angus, stay sober as well, though put on, like a mask, a pretence of celebration.'

'I thought that's what I *was* doing,' said Angus.

'We will come through this tonight. Juliet,' she touched my shoulder. 'Cleo thinks only of her *own* ends, yes? But it is our end too, I believe. And yours also, Angus. To get the stones to Stratford and recover what we lost. You, me, Juliet. Now here is what we do. Angus?'

'Aye?'

'You and Juliet, and Flora and Cleo, will go into the stone ring. Do you see the standing stones?'

I could not help but see the ring of tall, jagged stones, and the pile of wood within.

'Now, keep their attention there. That is the plan – adore King Malcolm and his Queen, ask them questions, let them feel special. And let no one miss me – say, if asked, *O, Viola is over there, I saw her a moment ago.*'

'And what will you do?'

'I will slip away, climb to a balcony, go through the side window, attend to the locked door, enter the chapel–'

'You will not have your stone,' I said. 'It is in the chapel!'

'I prefer a challenge,' said Viola. 'Besides, I am giving my stone now to you, Juliet!'

'What?' I gasped. 'You did not give it to Cleo, then, to hand to–?'

'No. A similar, but plain pebble, given a dash of paint is all they have. Take mine.'

She placed her small blue pebble of magic in my hand. I felt a tingling, a cold heat. My heart began to beat quickly. I felt as if it was making me vanish. I suppose this was its hidden virtue.

'I want you to keep it for a short time,' said Viola. 'It is the stone of escape. Remember? It helped us get out of the prison at Yarl's Wood. I missed many speeding cars with it. You and Angus may use it if you are in a pinch.'

'And how do I use your stone?'

'Recall what Ophelia said: *fall into the stone*. Do not lose it, mind you! And I want it back, of course! But I will show you that what I do from now is my own skill. Ha!'

'You dinnae have to prove anything,' said Angus in a slight panic.

But Viola merely smiled at him. 'Angus, I'll send you a text and when you see it, make every device blind. Soon, Flora will give a signal – then both of you must go round to the far side of the chateau. There is a garden. You will not be followed once you are outside the circle, for it is their ritual that once within the circle of stones and having lit their sacred fire, they cannot leave until the bonfire has burned down. It means the chateau will be unguarded.'

'What kind o' signal will Lady Macbeth give?' said Angus.

'A loud one,' said Viola. 'Both of you are to slip away. There is a pergola in the garden–'

'I know it,' I said. 'But I saw guards there.'

'There will be no guards – Angus will confuse them, and furthermore, I have recently put a draught into the champagne, so their wits will be clouded almost to the point of sleep.'

Viola walked away, dancing and laughing tipsily. '*Vive la maison de LeFay*,' she cried. She did not make her way with the party led by Malcolm, down into the ring of stones, but slipped into the shadows.

'It's all happening then,' said Angus. 'Um, Juliet, would you take my hand? I mean, for safety. Let's not lose each other.'

We looked at each other and nodded soberly in agreement. Angus rubbed his hands on his shirt. 'Damp,' he said. Then we held hands so as to not lose each other. But I noticed that we kept furiously intertwining our fingers and squeezing each other's hand and pretending not to notice that we did so.

10

THE PROCESSION CAME TO THE ANCIENT STONE CIRCLE AND PASSED through it to the inner area. These standing stones were like the teeth of a trap: spikes of stone pushing up through the earth. In the centre of the circle was a bonfire of wood, set and ready, and atop it a figure of a king made from sticks threaded with purple rags. People shouted and saluted, *bonsoir, Homme Violet*! The effigy was like a birdcage topped with a pumpkin head.

'All right, so,' said LeFay, clapping his hands, calling out instructions. 'Gareth, take that hamper and go spread those blankets. Help yourselves to more champagne. There's chicken and pheasant. Now that we are within the circle, once the sacred fire is lit, we will not leave until the *embers have settled*.'

'Let the embers settle!' called out several voices.

I said a prayer and prepared to run. But Cleo was already engaging our foes. She walked up to LeFay.

'It is thrilling, so thrilling,' she declared loudly, 'beyond what words can say. Tonight we will see the glorious Queen, Morgana, the Lady of us all.' She raised her arms in supplication. '*Vive Morgana!*'

Here was someone whose every movement breathed sacred dignity. The crowd joined her exultation.

'*Vive Morgana!*'

'You betcha,' said Desiree, tottering a little. '*Viva Morgana!*'

Then LeFay loomed over me, his mouth too close to my ear. 'Bless you and bless you. I'm not a cruel man, Juliet. Just breathe deeply, and when no one is watching, take a sip of this.' He handed me a small silver flask. 'You'll go straight out.' He winked at me.

Needless to say, I wondered what on earth he meant.

Desiree now appeared wearing a red-grey cape across her shoulders. Her turban had been replaced with a pointed hat. Her thin black hair fell lankly around her cheeks. In her hands she held a scythe, and a small flaming torch that dropped strings of oily smoke.

'Do tell me, where will Queen Morgana, *praise her name*, appear?' asked Cleo.

'She will make her entrance though the circle, through the fire,' said Desiree, her voice commanding.

LeFay trembled, his head nodding almost uncontrollably. Tears filled his eyes and he stared up at the effigy of the king, with something like a snarl on his face. He cleared his throat.

'She has not appeared in her completeness in a very long time.' His voice lost its warbling quality and he spoke huskily. 'Morgana LeFay is the eternal mistress of the house of LeFay. Long-hoped-for. But now,' he looked at Cleo, 'because of you, my dear, victory is nigh.'

LeFay now spoke with a voice of cold steel. 'The House of Pendragon-LeFay has a claim to the throne of England that is stronger, more assured than the Tudors – or the Battenburgs.'

'Shame! Shame! Boo!' called his friends.

'We are a pure line, not polluted by slaves and horse masters jumping into the royal bed in Gateshead-on-Tyne!'

'Shame!'

'Our claim has remained undiluted, unchanged through the years. The line is strong. Change is upon us. Praise our eternal Queen who has brought us the means of victory!'

The crowd broke into a chant. 'Long Live the King! Long Live the King!'

Cleo came close to Desiree. Next to *her*, both Desiree and Malcolm looked like withered trees. Cleo took both of LeFay's hands. 'That was splendid. My dear King, your day has surely come.'

'Bless you,' rasped LeFay.

'Let the ceremony begin,' said Cleo. 'I cannot wait!'

At that moment Angus's phone pinged. It was the text from Viola. He turned his mind to it.

I felt a grip upon my arm, and suddenly Angus' hand was pulled from mine. LeBlanc stood very close to me, offering me a length of purple ribbon. *What was this for?* I had the silver flask in my hand, and Viola's stone, but only poorly held in my sweating palm. I did not have enough hands.

'Go with Monsieur LeBlanc,' said Cleo in her seductive, commanding tones. 'Angus, stand with the King.'

Music began to play – drums and whistles, and rattling sticks. People blew into long plastic tubes with flared ends. The sound of braying – as of a dying mule – came from them. The Sons of Mordred began to circle around the wood of the bonfire.

I took the ribbon, and then I was ascending the wooden steps that spiralled to the top of the bonfire with LeBlanc guiding me. He gripped my elbow. We came quickly to the effigy of the king at the summit. The vegetable head was surmounted with a golden paper crown. The body of the king was itself something like a large birdcage or a lobsterpot. Other mauve ribbons were tied to the wickerwork. I assumed I was to tie on my contribution on behalf of Cleo.

'We tie the end through the wicker,' said LeBlanc. 'Like this.' He did it for me. And then he pushed me into the cage and, with the other end of the ribbon, quickly knotted shut the door.

Sometimes I feel I deserved all this.

LeBlanc bowed his head to me, but saved for himself one small, derisive smile. 'I would swig from the flask, now.'

He turned and was gone.

I wrenched at the wickerwork. I was sure that I could open this flimsy cage.

I could not.

I heard enthusiastic, desperate shouts of: 'Light the sacred fire!' Looking down I saw Desiree touching her torch to wood. The braying music grew louder again. At a flash of yellow flame, the crowd moved back.

I shouted for Angus, but my voice did not cut through the barrage of sound. I saw Angus leaping onto the wood, but he was dragged back by two men and thrown onto the ground. Using just one hand, for I held Viola's stone in the other, I tried to undo the knot. I seriously thought I should drink of the flask – did it hold laudanum? – until it slipped out of my hand and vanished through the gaps in the kindling beneath me. That path was gone. In my desperation I nearly dropped the stone.

Desiree was screeching above the crackling of dry branches. 'Everliving Queen, accept this virgin sacrifice. Come! Be amongst us! Burn us with your unbearable light!'

I felt a spasm of responsibility that I wasn't a virgin, but there seemed little point in correcting the record. Clouds of bitter smoke swept up through the cage, and a wave of heat. A deep shaking, like a tremor of the earth, passed through the air, through me. Then came a huge noise – I suppose Flora doing what she was meant to do, making a big bang – and the heat and smoke were gone.

11

I FELL UPON THE HERB LAWN BY THE PERGOLA. I WAS IN THE SHADOW of the chateau, on the far side of it, away from the fire. The lights of the chateau had all gone out. I could hear the music of the dance party from across the fields. The sky beyond the roofline of the chateau was lit with brilliant fire. Was that me expiring on a bonfire, and here I was, a dead spirit? I half-expected Ophelia to appear in ghostly form and say, *Did I not say be careful?*

But I knew that I had used the energy of the stone and it had freed me from the trap.

I pressed my face into the chamomile lawn, snapped off a few stalks. The air grew tender with perfume. I knelt, faint for a moment perhaps from the smoke and fumes, and closed my eyes.

When I opened them, I saw Flora, who came up to me with what seemed genuine concern and said, 'Och, that was unexpected. I thought you were a goner.' She ran her hand over my face. 'Up ye get, you stupid wee girl.'

'Where are the others? Where is Viola? Where is Angus?!'

I heard a languid groan. On the ground lay a guard in a drugged stupor singing, *boum boum*.

Cleo appeared and looked at me. 'Did I not say that we would be victorious this night?'

'Where is Angus?' I demanded. 'Flora, did you see him?!'

'It was a wee bit confusing, pet.'

'O, and where is Viola?' Cleo asked, in a mocking tone. 'Impatience does not help us, Juliet. Let us give our minds to what we must do now.'

'I think I saw your laddie flee the circle,' said Flora.

'But where? Where is he?' I wailed.

'Juliet,' said Cleo, 'Malcolm and his little band of followers cannot pursue us. They must remain in the circle until the fire is burned out.'

'*Let the embers settle!*' chirped Flora.

'Why must you treat me like this?' I said to Cleo in as cold a voice as I could summon.

'Do you wish to secure the missing stones?' said Cleo.

'Yes. Yes, we must do that.'

'And how might *you* have done it? Could *you* have spoken with Malcolm and Desiree and gained their confidence like I did? Could you have stepped away from yourself, as we all must, and debased yourself like I did – making a pretence of fawning in front of them? The moment we arrived, I engineered a meeting with Malcolm. I said he must keep my stone – the stone of sovereignty – for who else like him is such a king? I fell at their feet and gave to them yours and Viola's stone.'

'But I have Viola's in my hand,' I said.

'Yes,' said Cleo, 'and you used it well. For, of course, I did not give this Malcolm LeFay the true stone; a simple duplicate. *I will put it with the others!* he mewled.

'You think I am reckless, Juliet? Far from it. How else is it that you have Viola's stone in your hand? I ensured your safety.'

My fire cooled a little.

She spoke on. 'Once we saw all the stones placed on the altar of the chapel, it was *our* job to simply clear the way for Viola to go back and retrieve what is ours, and escape. I arranged it so that when all entered the stone circle to witness the rites to summon this mother of grotesques, Morgana, Viola was free to act. Their stone circle and their sacrificial rite was our best chance to keep all the Sons of Mordred and the rest of the LeFay household pent!'

Despite myself, I was impressed. What *was* I so upset about?

'And it was I who discovered from that spavined whore, Desiree – and would she have confided in you, Juliet? – that once they begin their sordid rituals, they do not leave until the sacrifice is complete. Usually it is spring lamb or a hare. But once they imagined that a perfect human sacrifice, the first in many years, was now imminent, they greedily attended in the one place. All of them.'

'A sacrifice?' I said.

'Yes – of a virgin; I suppose I told them a few lies about

your innocence, and your willingness to serve their goddess Morgana.'

I felt winded. 'And you did not choose to tell *me* about it?' I wanted to lash out and hurt her. 'You would have let me *burn*?'

I almost expected my uncle or Papa to appear.

'You are here; you are alive. But, now, we can rejoice,' she turned to look in the direction of the dark chateau, 'for Viola, a mistress of this work, has broken into the chapel of Morgana, and taken the stones back. Angus has also played his part, and we are grateful.'

'I'm sure the laddie will be fine,' whispered Flora.

A figure dressed in black walked across the lawn. I knew Viola's walk. She pulled off the black mask that covered her face.

'It is done,' she said.

'What do you have?' asked Cleo.

'Juliet,' said Viola, breathlessly, 'perhaps you would return my stone to me? Though I did not need it to break in, or unlock the door, or punch numbers into a keypad! Ha!'

'Here it is.'

I gave her back the blue stone. Viola went to a little garden table and spilled onto it from a folded white cloth the remaining Seven Stones. 'That's the false one!' She plucked out the inert blue stone and tossed it over her shoulder into the herb patch. 'Now I put my true stone in – thank you, Juliet – and what is it you see?'

Seven stones were upon the table, all giving off a soft light, so that no further light was needed.

'Who would hae thought?' said Flora. She began to sing, '*One is music heard i' the morn. Two is a magpie, chased and torn...*'

'Viola,' I said, 'did you know that Cleo meant to have me killed?'

'Juliet,' said Cleo, 'you were never in any more danger than the rest of us.'

'What has happened?' Viola asked.

'What do you see before you?' said Cleo, gesturing calmly to the stones. A look of content spread over her face. 'It is *all* as I intended. We have conquered. And Viola, Flora, and Juliet, you have perfectly played each of your parts, even though, Juliet, your love for Angus kept your mind inattentive.'

'I'm not in love with Angus!' I shouted, but my voice was weak with the truth of our kiss. 'I am in love with Romeo.'

'Well, not very much,' replied Cleo with a sniff. 'But I did not seek to quench this spark' – *o yes, you did, I thought* – 'for Angus's devotion to our cause helped secure yours, and your look of yearning served its purpose to seduce the eye of LeFay, who is weakened by the beauty of youthful energy.

'You keep asking, *what is my part in all this*? I could think of no role for you other than for you to be beautiful, fragile and vulnerable.'

'And a sacrifice,' I spat out.

'Cleo,' said Viola, 'it is enough.'

'Everywhere I go,' I said, trying to bring my father's coolness to the words, 'manipulation. We are your playthings! Like flies to a cruel child. Tear off our wings. Then throw us aside!'

'I see no one cast aside,' said Cleo. 'I instructed Viola to let you have her stone of escape, but perhaps my devotion to you is misplaced; for your manner declares that you are worthy to prettily bait a trap, but not it seems worth much else.'

'Stop,' said Viola, her voice haggard as I had never heard it before.

'You have yer stones,' said Flora. 'Silence becomes a Queen–'

'Flora, be quiet,' said Cleo.

'We should go,' said Viola. 'What is it we do now?' She looked at Cleo for direction.

'We die for her, is what,' I remarked.

'Now, we must to Paris,' declared Cleo, as if not hearing.

A wave of anger flooded through me. I darted to the table and took all the stones into my hand. They had gathered into a knot and were easy to pick up.

'Do not touch them,' said Cleo.

But I stood back and wished to be with Romeo, and then I was falling, floating through a bluish-dim night, convinced that I acted out of love.

Part 6

1

'Sit down, David,' said Sir Ambrose, rattling the coal in the fireplace with a poker and leaving it in the eye of the flames.

David looked around at the sofa, the armchairs, and the small bronze coffee table with neatly piled copies of *New Scientist*.

'I'll stand.'

'I said sit down.'

The agent behind David forced him to sit in a heavy wooden chair. The second agent secured his feet to the chair with plastic ties.

'In your training, tell me, David, did they teach you the value of following orders?'

'We're trained to use our initiative, sir.'

'And how is that working for you? One of our leading nuclear scientists and his two sons dead, possibly others. Two traumatised teenagers.'

'Well, with respect, I don't have the power to call up a drone strike.'

Sir Ambrose spoke on. 'Just clarify for me, David, why did you persist in following this Will Shakespeare boy after being *ordered*, by me, to stand down?'

'I wanted to help him,' he said.

'*Help*? How noble. Who is your contact in the druids?'

David pulled against the plastic ties that also bound his hands, with no result. He wasn't watching, and let out a cry of shock when Ambrose hit him on the side of the head with a rolled-up magazine.

'I said your contact?'

'I don't *have* a contact,' said David.

Ambrose retrieved the poker from the hot coals and examined the tip. He turned to the agents.

'Wait in the corridor, please.'

The two agents left the room. David caught impatience in Ambrose's eye as he closed the door they had left open.

'Where is this going?' said David.

Ambrose held up the glowing poker and leant in. 'David, are you any good at putting two and two together? Do you think *I* have the power to call up a drone strike? You might like to think it, but I can't even get upgraded to business class. Now, do me a favour and make a bit more noise this time, because *both* our lives depend on it.'

Ambrose walked behind David.

David felt the heat of the poker near his wrists as Ambrose melted the plastic tie. David let out a cry – almost as much relief as terror – and flung off the pieces of hot plastic.

'Fine, give me another of those,' said Ambrose quietly. He used the poker again and melted the ties holding David's feet to the chair. 'Come on!'

David obliged with a pained yell, '*Yaargh!*'

Ambrose checked the door.

'I'm letting you go – obviously,' whispered Ambrose. 'We'll make it look as if you overpowered me, or something. Now listen carefully. Ceridwen called me a few days ago and said, *there are dark powers disturbing the interface between the realms*. He's a druid; they talk like that.

'He said he was looking for some stones of power. They'd found one of them – the girl Miranda brought it to them. And he said that an unknown boy, name of Will Shakespeare, could be the clue to finding the rest. That's the name our database coughed up the day before yesterday. I informed Ceridwen.'

'You tipped him off?'

'More convincing, please.'

'*Aaargh!*'

'Yes, I tipped him off. Because I'm not keen on Malcolm LeFay having the Seven Stones. And I think, right now, he's well on his way to having them all.'

Ambrose went and listened at the door. He came back and spoke on. 'I'm the person assigned to liaise with the druids on government matters.'

'Okay. And where are they?' said David.

'The druids? Dead or fled. There wasn't that many in the first place. Far fewer than, say, the Quakers. There's no one here. I regret it now, but I thought it best to let Ceridwen manage the boy, which is why I de-assigned you so he could have a clean run. But you had to be all Saint George about it. Do you know how annoyed I was with you?'

'*Aaargh!*'

'Exactly. I suppose you know that the house of LeFay wants the Crown?'

David nodded. 'In the abstract.'

Ambrose shook his head. 'Not abstract. Our Director, Estelle Peltier, is the godmother of Malcolm LeFay's great-niece. And she and LeFay have been very cosy of late, and basically they're planning a change of monarch.'

'She said it was *you.*'

'She would.'

'Then you're saying the Director sent the drone?'

'Wake up, David. You pretty much gave her the target on a plate. She tracked your phone, of course. Not to mention the tracker you placed in the van.'

He felt sick and stupid. 'What was I *meant* to do, sir?'

'Follow orders. I told you to go home. But we're here now. And all the agents out there are not as loyal to the current King as one might wish. That's why we have to put on a bit of a floorshow – pretend I'm an enthusiastic member of Team Estelle. Sorry about the ear.'

Ambrose took a gun from his pocket and handed it to David.

'But, sir, what did she gain by killing Ceridwen?'

'LeFay just plain wants the druids all dead. The druids have been a thorn in the side of the Sons of Mordred since the 16th century.

'David, we need to get the stones from Malcolm LeFay. I don't know how, we're a bit up against it. They need to be taken to Charlecote Well for the Equinox. Once there, the druids were supposed to send them off into la-la land.'

'Which druids?'

'I don't know,' said Ambrose. 'They've all gone to ground. As I said, dead or fled. Though I understand that simply dropping the Seven Stones in the well is basically it. You can add some chanting if you like. Does the boy have powers, by the way?'

'No, he's just a kid. He's no one. He encountered Morgana LeFay and a host of demonic entities back in 1580 in the Forest of Arden and wished himself here. Or at least *away* from there.'

'God, I wish I'd taken that Canadian Embassy job. And the girl?'

'Miranda is a figment of Will's imagination, given life by the stones.'

'You don't say,' said Ambrose flatly.

'And, sir, we've located others like her. They are, or were, the carriers of the Seven Stones.'

Sir Ambrose ran both hands through his hair. 'So, this Miranda, she's not a real druid? She's a made-up druid? Christ. Then there's no one to give the stones to even if we get them all to Charlecote Manor.'

'What about Bryn Ceridwen? He now has one of the stones.'

'No, he doesn't. He was ambushed.'

'Shit! The burning car outside of Cheltenham?'

'They're all dead – at least, the druids who have knowledge of this situation. Does Miranda have any insights?'

'Some, well, a lot. Sir, can we get any support from the Americans?'

'What, from your girlfriend Carrie Martinez? Perhaps. Call

her. Why not? I have her card, too, if you've misplaced yours. All right, our time's up. Here, give me back the gun. I'm forgetting you're only level C. I'll have to do the shooting.'

Before David could hand back the weapon, the door to the room slammed open and light blasted in.

2

DAVID CAME BACK TO CONSCIOUSNESS CRADLED IN WILL'S ARMS. WILL was slapping his face.

'Would you please stop that.'

David figured the blast of light had been one of those energy weapons. He had the same mineral taste in his mouth as last time. The ceiling was moving.

'Where are we?'

'We are under the ground,' said Miranda, whose hands gripped two sets of reins. 'We sit in a cart drawn by miniature horses, in a tunnel that runs between the druid houses.'

The clip-cloppering of hooves confirmed some of what she said.

David began to feel his hands and legs. 'I seem to be in one piece, I think. Are we safe?'

'We live,' said Will.

David felt a weight in his jacket. It was Sir Ambrose's weapon, somehow still in his possession. A wave of weariness swept over him and he fell asleep.

When he woke again, he was lying on a pile of straw with four small ponies standing around him.

'Has anyone got water?' he said.

The chamber they were in was five metres high, carved into the earth, lined with sandstone, blue lias, and patches of cement. Light came from a few fluorescent strips, but not enough to push back all the shadows. David saw, close by, a few gas cylinders, a cement mixer, a wheelbarrow, and a pallet with bags of sand. Tracks of a narrow-gauge railway ran across the floor and split on disappearing into two tunnels. Will and Miranda sat by a large refectory table.

Will came over. 'Thou did'st say leave you to sleep.'

'I did? How is it we're here?'

'It's all Miranda's doing,' replied Will. 'She did save us. She and I sat in the kitchen with those men and heard your cries from the room until it was too much to bear.'

'What is this place?'

'Come and sit thee down – there is powder of tea in that jar.'

'No, that's Nescafe,' David said. 'What's down that way?'

'The opening on the left side leads to Charlecote Manor,' Will said, 'a further four miles. Back through that other is the way we came from the house in Stratford.'

Miranda sat at the table on which stood a microwave, a kettle, and empty TV-dinners, but she stood as David approached. She had been reading from a stack of old books at one end of the table.

Will held out a plastic bottle. 'Here, here is water, David.'

David drank the water and gasped, 'You're both all right, then?'

Will walked into David and put his arms around him. He began to cry.

'Okay, you're good? Come on, son.'

'I am well,' said Will. 'David, sit down, I will make thee a *Nescafe*. It is best with much sweetening.'

'Thank you. Now, tell me everything that happened.'

Miranda spoke. 'Lord Ceridwen's sons had left the powerful crystals untidily upon the kitchen table. The men who restrained you knew nothing of their power.'

'These crystal cubes here?'

'The same. I brought four of them with me.'

'Miranda did set her hands on one,' said Will, 'and said for me to cover my eyes. I did not see it, but those men were unmade.'

Miranda spoke. 'I had seen also secret signs upon the cupboard door in the kitchen and knew that it marked the way down to this tunnel – and having had some lore on these matters of my father, I made the entrance open. Will and I aided you in your descent.'

'Okay. And where is Sir Ambrose?'

'He did thee harm!' said Will.

'No! He did not. He's our ally! Where is he?'

'We heard thee make dreadful screams,' protested Will. 'That did rend our hearts!'

'Yes, but–'

'We left him in the room where we found you,' said Miranda. 'He was alive then. But in travelling along the tunnels we heard a violent thunder from whence we fled. It was–'

'Like unto the blast that shook us in the fields,' said Will.

'Another drone attack,' said David.

For a moment he'd had one serious ally in Sir Ambrose. Now he was dead. Shame filled him; that he had been so fawning over Estelle, grateful for the little scraps of approval that fell from her table.

'I did gather up the mobile phones,' said Will, pushing some objects towards him. 'Here is also thine very own phone.'

David took up one of the unfamiliar phones. It was half-burned and looked like a lump of sealing wax. The other – also an MI3 issue – still had an active though frozen screen. David read the exchange of messages from one of the agents to Estelle. He shook his head.

'Can'st tell us?' said Will.

'It's from… call her my Lady.'

'What does it portend?'

'It says: *Sir A and David Cortez talking in private. What shall we do?* And she replies: *Execute both, immediate effect.*'

''Twas she, then, that sent the fire from the sky that killed Ophelia, and Lord Ceridwen and his son?'

'I believe it was,' said David. 'I thought at first it was Sir Ambrose. I was wrong.'

David took out his own phone and entered Sir Ambrose's number. He let the spoken words *the number you have dialled is switched off or unavailable* drift through the cavern.

'How long ago did you hear the thundering in the tunnel?' said David.

'An hour or more.'

'These tunnels, what did you say they are?'

'They are the old druid tunnels,' said Miranda, 'made, said Lord Ceridwen, after the Desolation. Each entrance is guarded by a telling. I closed the entrance so none will know we came this way. Or even see it.'

'Good. Except I imagine the Stratford house is now rubble. Where are we now in these tunnels?'

'We are beneath another druid house, named for John of the Water, some four miles from Charlecote House.'

'You've been here before, Miranda?'

'Lord Ceridwen worked from within this chamber.'

Small bats flew past, some disappearing into an alcove that had a staircase.

'And the house is up that way? Up those stairs? Have you been up there?'

'We did go up,' said Will. 'We found someone there who made ready to leave, who did say *'tis every man for himself now*. Though he did show us where the hay is kept for the Kentish horses.'

'These little pit-ponies?'

'And the man did say unto us that Bryn Ceridwen's car was seen burned, and him within it dead. David! Did we not see it as we passed?'

'I think we did,' said David. 'I heard about it from Sir Ambrose.'

David looked at Miranda. She turned her eyes away.

'Will, how is that coffee coming along?'

Will hurried to make the drink.

David drew close to Miranda and said, 'I'm sorry about Bryn.'

'I should have more sorrow,' she replied, 'and likely will have it.'

'You didn't ask for this. Neither you nor Will. You were dragged into this world, you fell in with a bunch of enthusiasts. I'm sorry, that's unfair. I don't know what I'm saying. They were desperate and they blamed you when things went the wrong way.'

'Even so, I look now to set things right,' she said. 'The faults of my own doing at least I will remedy. Did I not use the stones, and treat thee and Will miserly?'

Miranda looked over at Will, then said in a quiet voice, 'Upon the island where we lived my father kept a slave. You must know his name?'

'Caliban,' said Will.

'And father did say he was a wicked and corrupt monster, and worthy to be shunned, the moreso since he found the two of us discoursing one day. But Caliban was simply showing me where the sweetest berries and fruits of the island were to be found.

'Yet thus, following the course of my father's will, and wishing to excel as his student and as his daughter, I hated Caliban thereby. And as he did resemble thee, David, in looks, I spoke to thee with my cursed mind, for I was inclined to hate thee at first sight. I do ask thy forgiveness.'

'Of course,' said David. He offered his hand, then realised the shaking of hands was perhaps unknown to her. But she accepted his gesture and, again, he felt odd memories of a different life surfacing as her hand held his.

'This world is all wrong,' said David.

Will approached with a cup of milkless coffee and an interested look. 'What say'st thou?'

David shrugged. 'Only that you've done good work, Will. You've dreamed up intelligent young women, dominating fathers, monstrous black slaves.'

'Say not, David,' said Will, aghast. 'Do not quote my works to my face!'

Miranda turned her attention to a printout of papers, which she handed to David.

'You must read these.'

'What are they?'

'Lord Ceridwen's papers and his daybook. It tells us what we must now do. Will and I have read it. It lays out our path.'

3

David took up the printout.

Ceridwen's papers covered almost everything. He had noted Miranda's arrival under Positives: *Locating the Seven*; and her help in activating the *seeing crystals* – long-held by the druids as heirlooms of a bygone age. He'd written:

> *We can now use the activated crystals to locate the Seven Stones, and use them in tandem with the Throne of Merlin's ley lines to see further.*

'Well, that didn't work out so well, did it?' remarked David.

He then wished he'd held his tongue, for Miranda's face wrinkled with pain.

'I knew that when the Seven Stones are in the world,' she said, 'the Unseelies have easier entrance from their realms but–'

'But you trusted Ceridwen,' said David, 'because he looks like an old druid.'

'He did speak much as my father spoke,' admitted Miranda.

David returned to the papers.

The state of play, from at least two days previously, was described.

> Stratford: stone number four (tempest) – brought to us by Miranda.
>
> Large house near Reading (House of Bogdan Abadzhiev?): The 'Cleo' woman has stones, numbers one (music), five (raven), and seven (dominion).
>
> Note on 'Cleo' (difficult person – delusional?). Claims to be Cleopatra, Queen of the Nile, (but Cleopatra is white!) – has stopped taking our phone calls.

'The stones have a number?' remarked David. 'And a name?'

'Yes,' said Miranda. 'The first one is the Stone of New Life;

the second is the Stone of Elusiveness, sometimes called the trickster or the magpie; the third is the Stone of Love; I have the fourth stone called Tempest.'

'It says here that five is the *raven*.'

'It is the Stone of Death.'

'Who has that?'

'I cannot say. I believe that Ophelia held it.'

Under the heading 'Missing', David read:

Stone two (magpie). No information. Stone three (love) is in the keeping of a young woman named Julia. Very close by in Stratford! Bryn despatched to start surveillance.

'So Bryn had gone looking for... He wrote Julia, but are we talking Juliet, here?'

'Indeed,' said Will, affronted. 'I did not name her *Julia*, but *Juliet*, for it means "daughter of Jove, the Sky-Father", whom she reveres as a kind of god, for her father is in truth an Odin of cruelty.'

'I'm sorry,' said David, 'my brain just shut down. So, what does Capulet mean?'

'It denotes "little master",' said Will, 'for he is at heart an upstart.'

''Tis true,' said Miranda with a wry smile, 'we see our greatest faults in others.'

'Let David keep on reading,' said Will. 'Where art thou?'

'I'm up to Bryn searching for Juliet. But it seems like he lost her outside of London. It says: *Bryn on way back to Stratford*.'

'I did not see Bryn again until last night,' said Miranda. 'And then he had only angry words for me. But the report earlier – do you mark it here written sideways? – was that he had found Juliet upon a train, in company of some young women, and he put a small eye-of-crystal upon her – but then she slipped away.'

'An eye?'

'Like unto this,' said Will, taking out the small button wrapped in a filigree of gold wire.

David kept reading:

Contact lost. Stone 3 in London, question mark.

'Well, this is all yesterday's news,' he said. 'It says here that *Viola* is possibly a Syrian refugee washed up on a beach in Brighton and taken in by Border Force.

Information from Ronald Wiggins of the Brighton chapter.

'She is not from Syria,' said Will. 'In my telling, Viola flees from France to Illyria because she stole precious things from a Duke.'

'So,' David said, 'not a Syrian refugee. But she clearly got away from Border Force, as she's now with Juliet. So, Viola, Juliet and Cleopatra. I suppose Cleopatra has the Stone of Dominion? And Flora?'

'The Lady Macbeth,' said Will.

'And her stone is the Stone of Music. Is she musical, Will?'

'No. She is full of sorrow, hath no child, and hateth cats.'

'Cats?'

'The witches' cat that I named Graymalkin torments her.'

'Maybe one day we can watch the whole play, Will. Miranda, is this something you understand; that you and they carry these *particular* stones because–'

'I think,' said Miranda, 'the stones summoned us each from Will's heart and mind, but according to their own temper, their own quality.'

'You've been reading that from these books?' asked David.

'No, it is my supposition. In these books they talk not of Will, but of the ceremonies of return. How the Seven are to be delivered back to themselves.'

'I'm counting six stones here,' said David. 'Do we know anything about the seventh?'

'No,' said Miranda, 'except the one not mentioned in Lord Ceridwen's writing is number six, the Stone of the Gate. Or it should be called *gate of morning*.'

'Thinking about your plays, Will, which one of your women haven't we accounted for?' David asked.

Will took up Ceridwen's notes. 'The sixth – the gate of the morning, is this a hopeful and pure thing?' he asked Miranda.

'That stone is the gate that leads to a larger world.'

'I think it must then be the younger of three sisters, Cordelia,' said Will, 'though Lord Ceridwen does not name her in his notes.'

'Does she have a last name?' asked David. 'Maybe I can try searching.'

Will shook his head. 'She has no name other than Cordelia. I had not thought that far. She is a princess, the daughter of King Lear.'

David searched for Cordelia Lear but found a message saying that sunspot activity was making the internet erratic. He put his phone down.

'We can assume,' said David, 'that Malcolm LeFay has the stone in question. That he possibly has *all* of them. That's what Sir Ambrose told me.'

'Then Cordelia, is she dead as well?' asked Will.

'We don't know that.'

'I too am mentioned here in these papers,' said Will, taking the notes from David and turning a page. 'See, Lord Ceridwen has writ:

'Will Shakespeare has appeared from the Year of Desolation. Information from Sir Ambrose. Proceed Elephant & Castle. '

'Precise, but not exactly professional,' said David. 'I wouldn't have put names into this document and left it lying around.'

'Read further,' said Will. 'Tis the next page that bears the fruit.'

The next page's heading was *Equinox Process*.

'Okay', said David, 'it says the stones must be delivered to the Druid Well at Charlecote on the day of the Equinox. That's in three days. And that before the stones… there's an odd word I don't know. *Panatha*?'

Miranda leant in. 'It means that the stones, dropped in the well, make passage of their own will back into the celestial realm.'

'Okay. Ceridwen writes here that before that moment,

> Will Shakespeare must pass through the blue light that appears
> and arrive ahead of himself in 1580.

David threw the paper down and muttered. 'Really? *Must pass*? And nothing about informed consent.'

'But see'st thou, David? It means that I can go back,' said Will, 'and take up my life again. When I thought I was condemned to this world forever.'

David let out a breath. 'Let's not get too excited, Will. I mean, remember what was happening when you left 1580? If you go back to *when* you left, you land right in the middle of a storm of murderous pixies? The Unseelies. That's not happening, okay. It's like rewind, repeat.'

'No!' said Will. 'Read it clear – see? I arrive *ahead of myself.* He means I will go home a short time earlier, and step onto the path to *find* Rian, and quickly go to Charlecote with the Seven Stones that she hands me. I will simply take them, and not stand in a dither like a child stuck on the pot while the storm gathers. Miranda has already unfolded it to me.'

'Let me say up front, I don't like this,' said David.

'There is more to not like in the world around us,' said Miranda. 'This brave new world.'

'Why do you call it brave?' said David.

Will guffawed. 'Because everything *sticks out*!'

'I did not mean that,' said Miranda, reddening.

'I did.'

David raised his hands. 'Listen. Why not let the stones vanish off into the great beyond, where LeFay, or the UK Government, even the druids, can't touch them?'

'It is right,' said Miranda. 'My father taught me the wisdom of humility before we left the island, saying, see I break my staff, I throw my book into the waters. It was Lord Ceridwen's intent that none should have *use* of the Seven Stones.

'Yet I did use them to make a tempest, but I was too scared of death and the fire from the sky; and so I called forth a power that I should not have. Even Will wishing on the stones for his own life was wrong – though I do not blame him, for I have done much the same. As a result, this world will become more and more one where Derek LeFay ruled England in past times.'

'So the airship we saw was a vision of things to come?'

'It *will* come to pass, unless Will does what is written for us here.'

'Yes, but I'm saying,' said David forcefully, 'let the stones leave this world – tick! But Will stays here, keeps out of danger.'

'I wish to go home!' said Will. 'And is it not so that here is a world where Derek LeFay did last on the throne but an afternoon?'

'I guess it is. Where are you going with this?'

'Then it means that I must have success. Does it not?'

David was about to say, yes, *here* is a world where LeFay never took the kingdom, and ruled for only half a day; but also a world with not a trace of Will Shakespeare. Did that mean that something happened to Will once he had returned? Was it worth saying?

'What does this document say about *you*, Miranda? And the others: Viola, Juliet, Cleo and Flora?'

'It says nothing. But I believe we must, all of us, leave this realm along with Will. I have been looking at some of these books. I do not know if their wisdom is sound, but I think we have no reality apart from Will.'

She looked at Will.

'That's evidently not true,' said David. 'There is truly a historical Queen of Egypt, called Cleopatra, regardless of whether Cleo is her or merely deluded. And you, you're a complex young woman; he's a kid from Stratford.'

'I will bite my thumb at thee,' said Will.

'If Will leaves this world,' continued Miranda, 'taking the stones so they complete their journey from Stonehenge to Charlecote Well... then we melt away. Unless we also leave and enter once more into the realms whence we came.'

'I don't know what to say,' said David. 'But, right now we have none of the stones, and until we get *all* seven, and take them to Charlecote, no one is going anywhere.'

'Then we must get them,' said Will. 'Should we send a message to Juliet through the book of faces, and say what we know?'

'Let me think. It's time for my one cigarette. I'd like to go upstairs. Miranda, do you need to open the way?'

'I do. Follow after me.'

The house above them was old, with low doorways. Miranda opened the passageway by singing a few soft musical notes and they stepped into the walk-in-pantry. David felt an odd distortion of space as he passed under the lintel. He looked back and saw nothing but a wall with shelves laden with jars and large tins.

The large kitchen led out onto an enclosed garden – a red brick wall catching the very last of the day. David stood in the open air and lit his cigarette and then heard a strange engine overhead. Slowly, the dim silver of an airship pushed out of the darkness and drifted to the southwest, picking up a final ray of sunlight.

David pulled out his phone and tapped in the number for Carrie Martinez.

She must have been waiting, for she answered immediately.

'David. Hi. You're not asking me out for drinks, are you?'

'Not today. What time is it in Langley?' he asked.

'Mid-afternoon,' she said. 'I've been up since midnight thinking you might call.'

Part 7

1   Juliet in Mantua

THE SMELL OF BURNING VANISHED. I DRANK IN CLEAN, FRESH AIR, AND heard pleasant voices, and the music of doves. I stood in a piazza, and recognised before me the church where we attended once the baptism of the daughter of Ferdinand Lorenzo.

I was in Mantua. And the buildings were those of my own time – no facades of concrete and glass, no lights or signage. The stones had brought me home. I saw no carriages in the sky; no cars or motorbikes clattering and growling. Instead, donkeys and a goat pulling a small cart and simple sounds. A handsome man on a black horse rode past singing.

It was Mantua. Except I still wore the strange shoes of the future, and a thin, thin cocktail frock of such light material as to be disgraceful. As if I had walked out undressed. Did I think I was St Francis? But no one turned to stare at me; no one stepped forward to accuse me or strike me for a harlot. In fact, people looked past, or through me. The sound of voices was like that heard on a quiet summer's afternoon.

I found myself breathing in short gasps and told myself to be calm. I will hold myself with dignity, I thought, and so set myself a task. A table close by to the church held a display of purses and inlaid boxes. 'I would take one of these purses,' I said to the man who waited there.

He did not answer.

I picked up a purse (real enough); but the man did not move or seem to notice.

I put the stones into the purse and walked off. The man did not follow. No one followed, or cried out stop!

I was invisible, then. Nearby was a fountain and I sat down. I could smell wood smoke from the bonfire on my skin and in my hair. I washed my face and rinsed my hands in the cool water.

I would have entered the church and confessed my sins and misdemeanours, but now something – perhaps the afternoon light on the fountain saying that the day was nearly gone – told me I must seek out Romeo, and quickly. I had left the chateau in the darkness; it was now the afternoon of another day.

A broad roadway led away from the piazza, and I knew this was the path I needed to follow: the road back to Verona. Had not Romeo spoken directions to me only days ago before he slipped away? Here is where I would find him in Mantua.

I walked then ran to where the houses became fewer, to trees and open fields. And here were the gates – open this time – and the tall pines and rolling gardens. And my father's words recollected, *Do not look there. It is the villa belonging to that vile shit Montague'*, as our carriage rolled past that day of the baptism. *Let no one look as if he cares one way or another.*

But I did stare momentarily that day, and so now recognised the gates. And Romeo's instruction that I must follow him to his father's villa in the outskirts of Mantua. *There'll be no one there, Juliet. Just the two of us.*

But now (apart from the servants, and two gardeners dressing the fruit trees, which I would have expected anyway) some gentlemen were waiting at the front of the house, with carriages in the driveway. And the ever-present guards, who, along with everyone else, seemed not to see me as I walked into the grounds.

I heard laughter, murmuring voices. And music. The sounds were coming from the balcony at the far side of the house, which was on an eminence. Why were people here? Had not Romeo said he would hide in the empty villa until I came?

Servants came forth from the kitchen and though I was sure I was transparent to them, I took refuge in a side room of the house.

I sat on a chair (the furniture and floor acknowledged my existence). Time passed. In the room stood a table with beautifully wrapped gifts. A man's voice spoke about the honour of the two houses, his words echoing through the building.

I heard applause, then footsteps, soft slippers.

A man entered the room and walked to the gift-laden table.

Something about him had changed. I said, tentatively, 'Romeo, is it you?'

He seemed confused, and he was about to leave the room, his eyes perhaps having missed me, a shadow in the shadows. I stepped forward.

'Romeo, I have come as we agreed.'

Lifeless words. And then he marked me and his face went pale. Instead of coming near and embracing me, he stepped back and said, 'Begone,' in a dry whisper. Then more boldly, 'Be gone, spirit.'

'Romeo,' I said, 'it is Juliet.'

I spoke in a low voice, urgently, so as to calm him. 'Do you not know me? Please do not look at this overbold dress, it is not one I chose. It's what they wear in the days to come. You see, I have been away in England and in France. And near 500 years away. But so much has happened–'

'You are dead,' he said finally.

'No. I have escaped death. I was... in hiding. I have come back. Will you come away with me, away from this?'

He began to shake.

'I'm shivering, too,' I laughed. 'We do not have to stay in Mantua. It is hard to explain. Magical stones brought me here.'

He looked at me, then glanced furtively out of the room, a look suggestive of the secrecy we shared. I was so relieved and went to him, for now we were together, alone. But – I suppose it was because of my odd transparency – I felt as if I were not in the room. I thought of Viola; I had left her. And Angus.

What was I doing here?

'Juliet? You are alive?'

'Yes!' I said. 'Do I look dead?'

I reached out. My hand passed through his hand as if he were a ghost. He stumbled away from me and knocked into the wall.

'Do not touch me, or come close,' he said. 'I must first...' His eyes looked around the room. A small wood crucifix hung over the unlit fireplace. Without looking at me further he lifted it off the wall and held it up as if it were a paintbrush.

'Why have you come?'

'Because,' I spoke as warmly as I could manage, for he was overcome with fear. 'I did not come sooner because the servants must have discovered us. They must have told my father about our being together. He made Father Laurence tell me a story about how I should pretend to be dead by taking a strong sleeping potion, and that you knew about it, did you not?'

I rambled on. 'I thought he meant to help us, but I heard him confess that it was a poison. Romeo? You see, my father killed me!'

If a ghost can have tears, then I burst into tears. My throat burned. 'I heard that... Someone made a play of what we did. Can you believe it?! There is a play about us, *Romeo and Juliet,* and in this you took your own life on finding me dead. And then I took mine on waking to find you dead.'

He looked everywhere except on me. 'No,' he muttered. '*No.* To do so would be a grave sin.'

I continued. 'I had to come here. I wanted to say to you, Romeo, it should not have gone so far that we both died from it.'

It was odd. I wanted to be away from him. I wanted to be with my friends. I wanted to be alive.

I *should* write that my heart was breaking; but I did not feel that. All I felt was the original loneliness and abandonment of my life welling up. Romeo stood stupidly, holding his cross. His eyes no longer held the light of stars, only the familiar glassy, emotionless demeanour of my family.

My mind ran over each word we had spoken and started to feel outraged anger. 'I thought you said you would wait alone for me, here. Why are so many people in the house? Romeo?'

'My family is here,' said Romeo cautiously. 'For the wedding. The marriage between Rosaline and I took place this morning.'

'You are *married*?' I said weakly. 'Has so much time passed, then, since I last saw you, that this has come to pass? I have been away for perhaps three days.'

I tried to explain Viola's tale of *Petit Ferdinand and the Golden Bottle* driven by sunlight into strange worlds. 'Are we in the following year?'

'A week has passed since I saw you last,' he answered firmly.

'One week? You mean, you have been forced to marry her?'

He looked at the ground.

'I was betrothed to Rosaline these past two years. We always intended to marry on this day. You may as well hear it now.'

'But we are married,' I exclaimed. 'Before God. You and I–'

'No priest declared it. I am sorry, it was my father's bidding.'

'Why do you say these things?' I cried, but it was like a different Juliet speaking. 'You vowed it as we lay together. You were inside me. *Let me fill you, my love*, you said. What has happened, Romeo? What was your father's bidding?'

He did not answer, but backed out of the room, left me alone. He snatched up a necklace from the table as he left.

With as much Capulet as I could find in myself, I strode after him, through the house, and followed him to a balcony. If this was a dream – and it felt like a dream – then I did not want by any means to wake up, as usually happens in dreams, in the middle of unresolved confusion. I wanted to stay in this sleep-state and to get to the very root of the dream before I woke and lost it forever.

2

A LARGE TABLE SEATING THIRTY GUESTS EXTENDED BEFORE ME ON THE wide balcony with its colonnades. I arrived just as the second meats were being served.

The Prince of Verona sat at the head of the table. On one side of him, Romeo's seat was empty and the Montagues were ranged on that side of the table. I knew them by their look and livery. On the other side of the Prince sat a young girl who I knew to be my cousin Rosaline, though, through family estrangement, I had never met her. Her hair was beautiful, her face delicate. She now wore the necklace that Romeo had taken from the room.

Friar Laurence rinsed his fingers in a bowl, talking with one I assumed was Romeo's mother.

Romeo was about to take his seat when he saw me. He began to breathe quickly. His face went pale.

Rosaline gave him a little puzzled look, a caring look that was natural and glad.

'You seem struck with love's arrow,' said the Prince. The dinner guests all laughed.

'At each moment, sire,' answered Romeo, recovering.

'What,' I called across the table, 'was your father's bidding?'

Romeo saw that none but he could see or hear me.

Shouting, for there is such power in being invisible, I said, 'Answer me. What was your father's bidding?'

He said not a word. I found the purse with the stones. As well as carrying me through time, what else might these little things achieve?

'Or answer this,' I declared.

I turned to look at Rosaline. Let her life escape her. In that moment Rosaline began to shake and cough and fell forward, her eyes staring into blackness and her hands clawing at her chest.

The table erupted in a flurry of people standing, with chairs flying backwards.

In a moment, Romeo had Rosaline in his arms and was lifting her to the ground, cradling her head. Through the press of horrified people, his eyes caught mine. 'I beg you!' He pleaded. 'Take my life, not hers. The fault is mine, I will remedy.'

I saw love there but not love for me.

But I was possessed of a horrific anger that held my arm rigid as hatred poured – from the stones or from my heart? – towards Rosaline. She writhed.

Voices inside me were prattling: *And so, a plague on your house! Now, Friar Laurence, churl: his death. The hated Montagues: fill them with the worm. Slay the guards at the door.*

As if I was fighting some wild animal I shouted, 'No', and pulled myself away and crawled and stumbled off the balcony. I fell heavily upon the ground my arms flailing, but wishing now, *Let her live. Let her live. I am sorry. Let her live.*

I threw the purse away and it disappeared soundlessly into long grass and darkness, for I was in a meadow adjacent to the villa and night, blue and mottled, had suddenly come.

All sounds from the villa – the terrified cries, hollow with grief – vanished.

I knelt. What had I done? What would Viola say? What would Angus think of me, that I would strike an innocent person, cause them such suffering? Was I any better than Cleo? Any better than my father?

And then I became convinced in my wretchedness that in taking up the stones, and wishing to *be* in Mantua, I had simply killed myself. I had not *stepped around my death* at all, but become the dead girl I had left behind in Verona. The miracle of my waking alive in England had been squandered. Was it now to be this way forever? Me a restless spirit? Why could I not be *more* dead?

I let out a wail that would do credit to the most desolate ghost.

'What are you?' came a halting voice.

I turned and saw Romeo, alone. He had come out from the house. I could see it now lit with lanterns. Early stars speckled the sky.

'O, Romeo,' I said.

'What are you?' he repeated.

'*What* am I?'

'Are you really Juliet?' There was almost tenderness as he spoke my name, and I clung to it – though I answered him almost hysterically.

'Yes. I am Juliet. Do you not remember? *O my god, my Juliet, yes, yes Juliet,* if you recall. I am *that* Juliet!'

He took some steps back.

'Please, say no more. What must I do?' Romeo asked, 'to make you go from here?'

He deserved nothing of my kindness. I held back my grief and said sharply, 'So, everything we did in each other's arms – it meant nothing?'

But then I remembered Rosaline's tortured face and spoke less sternly. 'How fares Rosaline? Have I killed her?'

'She is shaken. But she sleeps. Naught but a swoon, they say. The heat, the excitement. The priest gave her a draught to increase her vitality, but also to calm the fright.'

'Oh, did he? I'd be very careful of taking *anything* he offers.'

'Do not punish her. Tell me she will be well. I will answer you. Ask what you will! I will answer you–'

'Stop,' I said. 'She will be well.'

He looked away, as if to draw inspiration from the trees.

'My father's bidding was this,' he declared. 'I was importuned by him to look on you and trick you with a semblance of love, to send darting glances, to hold your eyes rudely, and speak flattering words. He also put it out that I was secretly in love with you and had no rest, and wasted away for love of you.'

'I did hear it,' I said, 'and I also contrived to see you if I could – began to yearn for someone called *Romeo*, before I even knew it was you. When *Romeo* was nothing but a name.'

He looked at me and spoke softly.

'I heard of your interest in me, too. Heard that you could not sleep because of me. And I wondered and did begin to dream a little of you thereby. Thus, I began to think much of you. Even though I had not met you.'

I felt as one might feel in a metal cage in the shape of a woman, lined with spikes that are screwed in incrementally.

'What was your father's plan?'

Romeo stared at the ground and kicked the soil with his silk shoe.

'What do you think? The plan was to make you act foolishly, to spurn the protection of your father's house. Thus, I would lure you from your home, with the promise of love, but you would only find, here in Mantua, men who would force your virgin knot. And we would send you back spoiled. A daughter who could not be married. A shamed thing. To shame your family. My love, such as it was, was the trap… *O, Juliet.*'

He said my name tenderly. But I think it was more tenderness for himself and our sad world.

'You say a *trap*; and yet your eyes now tell a different story. You speak my name as if it means something.'

'I spoke *words* of love to you; but love overpowered me instead – for my presumption.'

'You loved me, even though you were long promised to Rosaline?'

'Yes. I did love you. I *wanted* to be in that room with you,' he said, holding himself straight – glad, I suppose, to have found a streak of nobility.

'Was that part of your father's plan?'

He shook his head. 'No, it was not. I don't know what that was. Or do I? It will always be with me. I cannot quite forget how we held each other.'

'Yes,' I said.

'But what were we thinking? In a house so well-guarded. I was fortunate to get away, for your father would surely have killed me.'

'And you did not think to take me with you?'

'No,' said Romeo. 'I could not.'

Whatever hope I had kept for this moment fell apart, like a blown rose.

But at least he lived, and his death at his own hand would not be on my conscience.

3

Angus must have been mistaken in his recollection of the play *Romeo and Juliet*. Romeo (or at least *this* Romeo) did not wish to die for me at all; and now I saw that to die for *him* would have been the stupidest thing. My life was not some famous tragic play as recollected by Angus, but a sick, desperate comedy, and I the Fool.

If I had realised in time that my father planned to poison me, and had instead fled, and found Romeo in Mantua, I suppose I would have wept on discovering his duplicity and begged for him to take me, in honour of the vow of our flesh.

But three days, and Angus, now lay between us, and all my foolishness.

'I am an honourable man,' declared Romeo suddenly. 'When I came to you, I had to offer something of myself. Would you have had me cold in your bed? It was wrong, but also, I could not go against my father. No son should. Though now that I am married, I hope to forge a separate life and be my own man. If *we* were in a fashion "married", then it is – by the will of God – it is over.'

'Is poison the will of God?'

He spoke of it as if it were a curiosity. 'They said you died of fever, is what I heard. They said it was the sweating sickness.'

Voices calling Romeo's name drifted from the villa.

'I am called for. I will go to your tomb,' said Romeo. 'I will pray for the repose of your soul.'

Then my tears returned. I shouted, 'My soul does not need repose!'

He said nothing but looked at me and laughed – half a sigh, half a snarl.

'What?' I said.

As if making a casual remark, he said, 'Well *done*.' He reached for his dagger. 'Your father is here. And I brought myself out here unprotected for *your* sake.'

I turned. There you were, Papa, approaching. And my uncle, and one or two others carrying their crossbows, and men with horses waited by the edge of the meadow. They had come through the long grass silently.

My father looked at me. 'Well done, spirit of my daughter,' he declared. 'Loyal to your father's house, even in death.'

The others crossed themselves on seeing me.

And then I was running away as I heard the whizz of the bolts flying. I ran without looking back, through the long grass and crossed over the small stream. As I fled, I stumbled into a lake, which I knew in a moment to be the very one from my earlier dream. And indeed the same night-blue light flowed around me (and was it not the same dream where Romeo had walked on ahead and left me alone?). And if this were the same dream, or some extension of it then I knew a boat lay moored at the end of a jetty, and that I would, I supposed, find myself drowned in it.

But more horror was to come.

Something whizzed past my head – I thought it was the dart from a crossbow and that my father was pursuing me. But it was a swooping raven. Another flapped past, its wings creaking like a small bellows. Were they the same ravens from that day in the field when I was first abducted? And was I the dead thing that attracted them? I think there were only two, but they felt like a dread flock of birds.

From the shallows of the lake I saw a carriage, with men standing around – one without ears and with blood on his face, one pierced with arrows – waiting for me, calling to me with birdlike voices. One now came forward to offer me a hoop and stick to play with. One held a bag and came towards me to place it over my head.

It was too much. I thought – if you could *call* it thought – to drown myself and bring on oblivion that way. If ghosts could be drowned.

But as I threw myself into the waters someone came up to me and slid their arm through mine and drew me back onto the dry land.

'Don't touch me!' I said despairingly.

It was a woman, a little older than Viola. Her touch was strong and gentle.

'Leave me be,' I shouted. 'I am dead. I would be more dead!'

But she held on to me and said, 'Juliet, you are not dead. This is only a tale that was written about you, and it will be gone with the night. And yet I think you would rather be in the day that is to come.'

I felt I did not deserve such kindness of speech. I clung to her.

She lifted me and I dared to look at her more closely. She had something of Cleo's queenliness, a little of Flora's, but Flora in her more recent equanimity.

'You are Cordelia,' I said.

'I am Cordelia,' she answered. 'Come this way.'

Night now rolled over us like a dark wing. I leant upon her arm as she helped me to my feet and led me from that place of birds rattling in the darkness, away from their rasping voices, away from the lake with its dead forms, away from the man with the cloth bag, and down into a valley, a deep, narrow crevasse, and through silent trees until in the woodland stillness we came to a small cave within the sheltering cliff. The spring moon had risen, dimming the starlight.

In the silver dark I could hear and just see a small stream trickling from the rocks and it formed a pool sheltered with wet leaves. Close by upon a bed of dried ferns lay an old man.

I watched as Cordelia approached him and gently pulled the blanket that covered him more firmly around his shoulders.

She sat by him and stroked his head.

I saw her face looking into a distance – much as Ophelia had looked towards an unseen horizon.

I asked her, 'What happened to you?'

Her expression responded as if it was something she had forgotten.

'O, a man named LeBlanc came and killed me,' she said.

'LeBlanc led me to my death as well,' I answered. 'Or perhaps Cleo did! But I wished on one of the stones and it saved me. Or else I would have burned on the pyre.'

She sighed. 'I'm surprised more of us have not died. I was in a windswept place overlooking the sea, close to Brighton, when it happened, but intent on searching for my father. He was lost. Betrayed by my sisters.'

'You have found him though?' I said, looking at the old man asleep.

'I found him.'

I marvelled at the love that held them – wondered at the kind and gentle man he must be.

'I should, perhaps,' she said, 'have sought out Cleopatra more diligently.'

'Sought out Cleo?'

'And come to a different understanding.'

'An understanding with Cleo?' I was almost put in the mood to laugh. 'How do you mean?'

'She found me through Ophelia's insight. And came. And made demands. But I would not flatter her. And I would not give her the stone.'

'She wanted you to give it to *her*?'

'Yes. But I would not relinquish it; for I did not understand it – and Cleo gave me no insight. I felt I had somehow been given a precious relic to carry and should not give it to just anyone. It seemed to me to be someone's soul, and I should not let it easily leave my protection. And so she went her way. I returned to my task. Then LeBlanc appeared.'

A breeze stirred in the trees.

'It will be sunrise in a little while,' said Cordelia, 'and you have to go before the night here fades and this dream is done.'

'You mean, this is but a dream?' I felt such relief to know it. 'And what I did to Rosaline, likewise a dream? And I am not a dead spirit?'

'No,' said a voice. A young woman came out of the night and joined us.

'Ophelia?' I said. I closed my eyes and reached out to her, hoping that my hands would not pass invisibly through her. They did not.

'May I call you my sister?' I murmured.

'Of course.'

I felt the fabric of her sleeve and her hands, which were warm. And I felt the purse that she pressed back into mine.

'You don't want to lose this,' she said. 'The stones must be taken to Stratford. Try and get them there, to the druid well. There is no other way.' She looked out into the dark forest.

'I did not harm Rosaline, then, only dreamt it?'

'It was a vision. The boy's vision.'

'The boy?' I said, recalling she had spoken of him earlier.

'What you saw was *his* imagination – we are his dreams woven into coarse fabric. You and I, Cordelia, the others – Cleo! – were nothing but visons in the mind of Will Shakespeare, until he wished upon the stones one day. And set all this in motion.'

I looked at her, felt the warmth of her hand (which had once been insubstantial!)

'But we must be more than that,' I said.

'We *are* now,' said Ophelia. 'If and when you come back here to Mantua, if the stones are returned to the druids, then what you did to Rosaline and the vengeance your father brings upon his enemies *will* happen, unless you prevent it. And this I think you may do. Though I might be wrong. The dead don't know everything.'

I kept hold of her hand and began to see my way forward. The question rose up again. How to step around one's death. I prattled. 'Viola has said she will take a lifejacket with her when she returns to Illyria, and so not drown in the waters. And so she will step around her death. And I...'

What must I do? I took a breath. It seemed very simple. I would return to the moment Romeo began to climb to my window. I would lean over the balcony and say: *Mama is within, and I must away and converse with her. And I suggest you climb no more, if you value your silver tongue, or other fine parts of your body*.

The plan grew in my mind, put forth spring buds. If I spurned Romeo, then I would be, firstly, unspoiled, and, more importantly, undeceived. I would then be still my father's obedient daughter (outwardly); and then I would steal away from his house.

Perhaps Alfano could find me a servant's guise. But steal away to where? Flee to a distant nunnery? I did not know; but my days as a fugitive in London would surely help me in the wide world.

'Please, Ophelia,' I said, 'tell me everything I need to know – for I must elude Cleo as much as Malcolm LeFay and his night creatures.'

'There is not much to say. Return Will to his time. Hesitate to use the stones for anything else.'

Then she was gone.

I turned to speak to Cordelia, but the cavern was dark and the only clear thing was the tinkling of water from the spring.

'Cordelia?'

I could see her shadow.

She reached past me into the small fern-covered alcove and brought out a silver cup. She dipped it in the water that was trickling into the pool (heard but not seen) and handed it to me. Two hands appeared in the gloom before me holding what looked like the blueness of the moon, or a circle of sky.

'Here,' she said, 'drink this. The water is from the lake above; but it has passed through the roots of the earth and is pure.'

I drank and found myself sitting outside a café in a warm afternoon.

I was in a piazza. People walked by in the sunlight, taking in the buildings and holding up their phones in adoration of the cathedral. At the table next to me sat two American tourists.

'Which city is this?' I asked the woman nearby.

'Oh, it gets like that, doesn't it?' she said with a laugh. 'It was

Milan yesterday, Genova the day before that. And my goodness, I've almost lost track!'

'Mantua,' said her husband. 'At least I'm pretty sure it's Mantua.'

Then a young man quickly approached me and spoke in a low voice, soft and fearful.

'Juliet? I am Will Shakespeare. Dost thou know me?'

Part 8

1   David and Will in Mousket

IT HAD TAKEN THE REST OF THE DAY TO GET OUT OF ENGLAND AND into the south of France. Carrie Martinez organised a Blackhawk helicopter, to pick up Will and David ten miles from Stratford just before midnight. The driver who turned up at the house gave David a secure mobile phone and passed one or two remarks on the weather.

Will had not wanted to remain in the tunnels; but Miranda said she would stay to read the druid texts, look after the abandoned ponies, and set the way for them to emerge from the secret tunnel at Charlecote Well. From the way she could sing and open invisible doors, he had begun to feel confident in Miranda's druid powers.

The LeFay chateau in Mousket was their destination. Carrie had confirmed – from the American's analysis of the chatter – that Malcolm LeFay was expecting a visit from a woman calling herself Cleo, who seemed willing to hand over certain stones she possessed.

'Why would she do that, David?' Carrie asked. 'These stones are some new kind of superpower element.'

'It's a mystery to me,' said David. 'I think they're just driven by their own confusion. And tell me, do I have support – additional personnel – when I'm over there?'

'Let's just say,' replied Carrie, 'that things are on a knife edge politically. A destabilised UK only helps the Russians. But I *can* provide a helicopter and maybe some personnel. But assume you're on your own – for now.'

They made a good start. But the Blackhawk detoured suddenly to the US airbase at Lakenheath and stayed on the tarmac for hours due to an apparent increase in sunspot activity and the danger to anything electronic. All air traffic in and out of England had been grounded.

'Yes, but it's night,' said David to the pilot. 'Sun is on the other side of the world isn't it?'

In a relatively unlit part of the airfield they waited. The upper sky was strewn with green and pink light. Hours after midnight they were given the all clear. The pilot instructed David and Will to put on lifejackets and told them what to do if they came down in water.

The co-pilot said, 'This is where he tells you to not worry 'cause he used to fly cropdusters.'

'Ready, then, son?' said the pilot to Will.

'Until death it is all life,' said Will.

'Know your Cervantes, then?' said the co-pilot.

'Nothing surprises me anymore,' said David.

Then they were in the air, and the Channel appeared, flat calm – the colour of the moon during an eclipse.

Will, after gazing in rapture at the water and murmuring words about a sea of silver, swung towards David. 'David, thou look'st overstrained. Sleep, and I will watch through this window. I will wake thee if we plunge into the waters.'

David laughed. 'I'm counting on it.' He closed his eyes.

At dawn they landed safely in France, left the Blackhawk with its blades still spinning, and jumped into a rented Renault. They arrived in Mousket at seven in the morning. Fog, as well as smoke haze, lay across the village. Revellers emerged wearily from tents in nearby fields. In the main street people clamoured to buy breakfast from street vendors.

'Who are these travellers?' asked Will. 'Why do they sleep in the open and under canvas?'

'It's a pagan festival where they burn a king made of sticks.'

'They burn the king!? This would not be allowed in England,' said Will.

'I hear they used to sacrifice a pig, until the animal rights people got that banned. It's something the Sons of Mordred like to do. They tried to burn *me* at the stake, once.'

David found Will staring at him. 'Sayest not, David.'

'Not *not*,' said David. 'It was a year ago. I was captured by them on Blanchefleur, an island off Scotland. They tied me up, set bundles of wood around me and set fire to them. They were crying out, *Long live Morgana LeFay!*'

'Oh, David. But the Lord did free thee,' declared Will.

'Well, more or less free,' said David.

'Methinks he spared you so *I* might benefit. For where might I be without you?'

'I hadn't looked at it that way, Will,' said David. 'So, it's not *all* about me after all. That's disappointing. You should meet my psychologist.'

'Thy psychologist?'

'My confessor. A man named Staines.'

'A confessor named Staines is well-named! I would tell him about the stones I lost, and then the stones would be stains. And thus I am shriven.'

'If only it were that simple,' said David, wide-eyed. 'Okay. Breakfast and blending in.'

David pulled into a parking space at the roadside and they walked from the car.

Will tugged on David's sleeve. 'Oh, David! Do you see above us, through the fog? It beareth again the mark of LeFay.'

The silver-grey shape of an airship glided into view, its engines thrumming as it passed overhead.

'This is the third time we have seen it!'

'No,' said David. 'If you look, Will, the serial number on the tail is different. Which is *not* in itself a good sign.'

'It denoteth a fleet?'

'Something like that,' said David. 'Okay, stay calm.'

'I am calm, David.'

David realised that for Will it was just one more strange thing in this world, along with the high towers of London, jet aeroplanes, fast cars, and Netflix.

'Let's keep walking,' said David. 'I don't know why everyone else is acting as if it's the most normal thing in the world.'

He led Will under the awning of a coffee-truck.

'Let's grab a coffee. The American coffee on the Blackhawk, with respect, tasted like arse.'

'They seemed proud of their coffee maker,' answered Will.

'They should be – it's designed to keep on making coffee even after a fireball has incinerated the crew.'

Will began to chuckle and kept on until David thumped him on the back.

'It wasn't that funny.'

'I did see in my mind a dead man pouring coffee from a jug.' Will demonstrated.

'You have a dark talent,' said David. 'Now let's not draw attention.'

The droning airship passed and the grey mass of it dissolved behind grey cloud.

'Does it mean, then' asked Will, 'that Cleo or Juliet have wished upon the stones when they should have not?'

'It could mean *exactly* that, Will. Or maybe even that LeFay has possession of the stones and has done something to screw up time and space.'

'Miranda did speak wisely in saying that wishing on the stones has done more than make a storm, but gives unto these apparitions a local habitation.'

'Oh, maybe we're too late,' sighed David. 'I'm glad, though, that you and Miranda have made up.'

'I should not have dealt unkindly with her,' said Will. 'Perhaps, if more time had passed, I would not have seen her as strange. As thou have done when coming upon things out of place. Thou lookest on the airship and it breathes now a familiarity, David, when once it was enough to make thy hair stand like quills on a porpentine. I should have had patience. If I meet Juliet or Viola, then I will not be harrowed that they live, or that I have dreamed them, as I did dream Miranda.'

'Yes, well, let's make sure that is not the first thing you say if we find them, yeah? Okay, do you see the chateau?'

'I do. It hath a pleasing seat and a sweetness of aspect.'

'Well, Malcolm LeFay hosts a small enclave there of the Sons of Mordred.'

'Oh. You mean, like unto the soldiers we saw in that vision on the airfield?'

'Like unto. But whatever we see, we have to stay calm, okay? Not get too excited if we see bees floating in midair.'

'I am coming with you then?'

'Yes. I'm going to give you this spare mobile, which I'll have recording. Keep it in your pocket, hidden. I'll have mine on too. Don't let it be seen. And if you lose me, or we're separated, come back to the car.'

At the services tent for the festival, David found workers milling. After a minute talking to one of the organisers he came back to Will.

'Okay, put this on – it's a fluoro vest, and hang this lanyard around your neck. We're here to pick up rubbish. That is our disguise. These are rubber gloves, put them on, too. This is a garbage bag, and these pincery things, you use them to pick up paper and stuff as demonstrated, then you find another piece of trash and get a rhythm going.'

'You will have me carry coals hereafter. And thus we go into the demesne of this lord?'

'Yes.'

'I was charged one time,' said Will, 'with poaching on the demesne of Sir Thomas deLuce. I netted trout and took a few hares – but 'twas merely for the sport.'

'I said the same when I got caught smoking pot. But no one's getting caught today, Agent Shakespeare. Let's go.'

2

THEY WALKED DOWN A ROAD AND CROSSED EASILY INTO THE CHATEAU grounds, following the trail of bottles and trash, passing other litter gatherers, and picking up a few objects as they went. They found a path through flattened long grass onto mown lawn, gouged and turned over in places. The rising lawn gave them a view of the circle of ancient stones, from which straw-coloured smoke was rising. The grass around about was burned black. They found enough rubbish on the ground to justify walking anywhere they wanted, even up to the kitchen doors. Broken mobile phones, crushed spectacles, an expensive purse were stamped into the earth. A scythe had been dropped in a flower bed.

'Why is a rope hanging from that window?' asked Will, pointing to the half-open top floor window.

'I don't know. A break-in, or a break-out. Don't stare. Keep picking up rubbish. Stay in character.'

Will proceeded to stab at small objects. 'Aha, have at thee, leg of chicken! Into the sack!'

David was pulling crepe-paper streamers off a wisteria vine near the kitchen when the glass door swung open and Malcolm LeFay hurried out. He looked older and more shrunken than the image Aisha Vani had shown him. He was speaking into a phone and looking at the sky. He did not acknowledge David or Will as he walked into the clear space of the lawns. David edged towards him.

'Is that better?' asked LeFay. He looked up. 'Well, I can't see any blamed sunspots, it's completely overcast ... Well, that little Scottish fucker did something to our phones. I want him hurt. And, oh you've dropped out again ... Estelle, hello, hello?! *There* you are. No, I heard you. ... Well, she disappeared in a split second. Spoilt everything! And this, you know, just shows how powerful these stones are!'

LeFay walked on in a line that took him straight to Will.

David could barely hear what LeFay now said, and he circled closer.

'Bugger, you've dropped out again ... Well, what? Why don't *you* go outside, go up to the roof? I've got plenty of bars.'

LeFay apparently decided to listen, simply saying 'yes, yes' every now and then... until he eyed an empty beer bottle. He picked it up by the neck and waved at Will with it. 'You, boy!'

Will glanced at David, who gestured with theatrical eyebrows for him to respond. Will walked over to LeFay, opened his garbage bag, and LeFay dropped the bottle in.

Strands of conversation came David's way.

'Well, I think you should just keep on wiping out what's left of the druids in Salisbury and Stratford, is what. Use another drone strike. Use as many as you need. I hereby authorise it.'

A voice spoke behind David.

'You. Out of here! Get off these grounds. Geez. Talk about lowering the tone, yeah? I mean at once!'

A tall woman in a blue tracksuit, with her hair in a turban walked past David, her mouth a pout of disgust.

Two security men strode forward and one took his arm. David said in French that he was simply collecting refuse. *'Je suis prêt à continuer.'*

'I don't wanna see him again,' the woman ordered, waving a finger into the sky.

Malcolm LeFay's wife Desiree was everything David's research had revealed.

The security man walked him a few metres and pointed at the main gate. 'Go.' The guard hissed, 'Don't take it hard. She does not like Algerians.' He pressed some money into David's hand.

David walked on. LeFay was now talking excitedly, 'Blow them all to blazes. And also, what's all this talk of a boy? ... That's the one, Will Shakespeare. What's that all about?'

David slowed, feeling the weight of Sir Ambrose's gun in his jacket. Was this the time to use it? Perhaps too drastic a solution.

'Well then, at the earliest opportunity, find and eliminate the boy. Kill him. Kill Will – ha ha!'

David moved on through an open gate and then, taking cover behind the stonework, moved as casually as he could until he found a gap in the wall he could look through.

His insides knotted. Will was still standing close to LeFay, holding the rubbish bag open as LeFay idly dropped in the odd empty bottle.

David was in a sweat, wanting to catch Will's eye, but Will simply stood to attention with eyes averted, making that odd knuckle to the forehead gesture that seemed to indicate servility.

The security guards were now approaching the gate. David finished tying a shoelace and walked on to the services tent. He spent an anguished minute staring back the way he came – where was Will? He walked back along the now empty road.

David stifled a yelp as Will leapt a hedge and joined him.

'David, I am fine, be not anguished.'

'I'm not anguished. Let's get to the car. Will, you should have followed me straight away!'

'But I did hear much that was useful.'

'You did? What was said?'

Will's face took on a look of concentration.

'This LeFay did reveal, in converse, that Juliet has gone to Mantua. Did *vanish* to Mantua. And she has with her all of the stones. He did claim, to prove the merit of his words, that one of their necromancers did sight her in a crystal spherical. But I did stay close so that the words did record.'

Will pulled out the mobile phone, handed it to David and asked, 'Couldst thou give me a letter of commendation to hand to Sir Francis Walsingham?'

'Stay focused, Will. Tell me, why Mantua of all places? Does that mean anything to you?'

''Tis where Juliet's story ends.'

David replayed the voice memo as LeFay spoke to both Will in person, and Estelle on the phone.

Here, get that bottle there, boy ... the others? ... that blasted black woman who says she's Queen of the Nile and her cronies have vanished as well ... No, I don't have a plan for them. They have nothing we need ... They're on their way to Paris, I believe. Oh, here's Desiree, she wants a word.

Desiree spoke: *Estelle, honey, we got LeBlanc and his men chasing after Juliet Cutie Pie ... Yes, he's the real deal; he's former BCRP, he's used to doing his own wet work ... He'll make it look like an accident, but I don't really care ... We'll get the stones back. Malcolm, what's this kid doing?*

LeFay: *Run along, boy, well done, well done ...*

'Okay,' said David, 'that went better than it might have–'

LeFay: *And what's your name, boy?*
Will: *'Tis Will, my lord*
LeFay: *'Good, good*

'You didn't!' said David. He threw down the phone and started the car. 'Don't put on the seatbelt, Will. Lie down.'

Not far off he could see some of LeFay's security guards running fast to the services tent. But what could they do in a quiet French village?

Three bullets shattered the rear window.

'DO THEY HAVE IN THIS CITY THE BOWLS OF HOT MILK AND CHOCOLATE?' asked Will.

'That was yesterday morning, in France,' said David. 'This is Mantua, and it's coffee and sweet pastries now. Or maybe that's all changed along with everything else, and haggis is now the national dish. What would you like that's on the blackboard?'

'I would have the *cioccolato calde e canella* and the *grande colazione.*'

David ordered Will's big breakfast, and a double-strength coffee for himself.

He and Will had left France in the Blackhawk after a dangerous car chase from Mousket back to the airfield. David's many clever manoeuvres included a dangerous overtake that caused an oncoming truck to slam into the side of one of the pursuing cars. He'd also fired Sir Ambrose's gun at a tyre and sent another vehicle careening into a verge.

All the while, Will was chanting through clenched teeth, 'Fast and Furious!'

Even as the Blackhawk ascended with them on board, the last two of LeFay's pursuit cars had reached the airfield.

Not long after the helicopter crossed the border into Italy an electrical problem forced an emergency landing at Milan Bergamo. According to the pilot, the news coming through intermittently over the radio spoke of a Carrington Event – electrical outbursts from the sun strong enough to disrupt communications.

David knew it was far more likely part of the space-time disruption they were stuck in.

They travelled from Milan to Verona in another rental car and, after a three-hour detour on gridlocked roads, finally arrived in Mantua.

The glitchy late news broadcast on a hotel television was still reporting that the ongoing sunspot activity was causing havoc. It was also making the phones unreliable. David had been unable to contact Carrie.

That evening, he and Will walked around the streets going into backpacker lodges, hotels and cafés, looking, observing and listening. They did not find Juliet. Then, while Will slept, David continued to walk. And now, having ordered breakfast, David returned to their *al fresco* table to sit.

Will handed him a flyer that showed a photograph of the Sons of Mordred participating in a military procession.

David's face fell. 'Where did you get this?'

'The man at the table nearby handed it to me.'

David glanced at the two men dressed in red and grey uniforms, enjoying a quick coffee and soda water.

David eyed the leaflet as the waiter delivered food to their table. When the waiter and the two Sons of Mordred officers had gone, he said, 'It's getting to be more than just airships. This is mad!'

'Why say'est?' answered Will over his hot chocolate.

'Because the Sons of Mordred were *never* this visible, or this numerous. Just a few crazies, dotted here and there. Underground. A relic.

'And yet, no one but me notices their now very public existence as something strange Why is that? Is it because I'm with you, who came from a different time? Or is it because I had contact with one of the stones?' He tapped the leaflet. 'It says here they're going to have a parade this morning, here in the piazza.'

'Let us not stay for it.'

'We'll keep our distance.'

Suddenly within and around the café many mobile phones began to chime and buzz, accompanied by relieved laughter and a cheer or two. David pulled out his phone. 'Network's back up.' He scanned the flyer's QR code.

'Okay. There's an office for the Sons of Mordred here in Mantua. We need to really think about this. We can't just walk the streets hoping to bump into her.'

'Which we have done thus far.'

'She does know, doesn't she, that Romeo isn't *here*?' David waved his hand. 'He's only alive in a fictional Mantua. Is it possible that she might have taken the stones – as much as you did in 1580 – and made a wish to be gone from this world? Maybe she was confused about who and what and where she was from, and went to Mantua in 1580? And if so–'

David looked, seemingly distacted by the distant silver airship gliding past, making a bee-like drone. 'Then this is it; this is the end of what we do. There are no stones to be found in our time; they can't be returned at the druid well.'

Will placed his cup on the table. 'Oh. So Lord Ceridwen's plan that we go to the well at Charlecote Manor is naught but a hole in the wind. And so I am pent in this world. And all of this will be my hereafter? And I will not see my father or mother... Is that what thou sayest?'

'I don't know, Will. I'm just thinking aloud.'

'And what will I do?' Will asked, his face furrowed. 'And where will I live?'

'Hey, I was only throwing ideas around,' said David. 'And, um, you come and live with me, Will, if that's what you want. Whatever you need, you just say.'

Half a minute later, Will spoke. 'Thou art the kindest man. We must seek out the others, for Miranda also has no place to go. Or Viola–'

'Finish your breakfast – I'm going to walk around the piazza. You'll be able to see me.'

The day was already warm. Tourists were coming in and out of the Rotonda di San Lorenzo. Town workers were putting up barriers ahead of the parade. David threaded his way around the groups of visitors; some gathered around their guides who held aloft small flags. A flautist played *Ave Maria* in the centre of the piazza. A man dressed as Pierrot juggled three balls, then four, then five.

Nearby, two men in Harlequin costumes made a show of fencing with each other, but instead of swords, they used spray bottles of water. One of the men, on seeing David, angled closer and squirted him in the face as he passed by. David kept on, annoyed the man had targeted him, as he hadn't sprayed any of the white tourists. When David reached the opposite side of the piazza, his rising resentment caused him to look back.

The man who'd sprayed him was now holding a hand to his ear and speaking. His companion, standing idly by, now held two spray bottles. And was also, curiously, wearing blue plastic gloves.

David's skin prickled.

To one side of the piazza, an ambulance came into view from an alleyway. It came no further but sat still, engine idling. The two men turned to it.

David's phone buzzed.

'Carrie?'

'Something's happening, or about to happen, David. Can you hear me? You need to be alert. We've picked up a few radio conversations.'

'What exactly?'

'A man called LeBlanc. I'll try and send you an image.'

The phone gave a burst of static and was silent.

'Carrie?'

David's phone pinged with the arrival of an image, but he didn't need the photo to recognise the man now talking to the ambulance driver. But at least now he had a name for the French man with the comb-over who tried to burn him on the island of Blanchefleur: *Le Blanc*.

David hurried back to Will. The juggler was still juggling and the flautist was now playing *Dancing Queen*. As he neared the cafe he looked back to make sure he had not lost sight of the Harlequin men. One was back to spraying the air and cavorting, but the second was following him, eyes moving furtively. He was also holding his second bottle a little way from himself, as if it contained something dangerous; like a nerve agent.

It was going to be a grab. The Sons of Mordred, perhaps this local Mantuan branch, along with the man called LeBlanc, whom Desiree had praised so highly, obviously knew where Juliet was.

And it looked like their plan was to neutralise her and bundle her into the ambulance.

Back at the cafe, a waiter was wiping down their empty table. David swore and looked around for Will. A crowd of tourists swept around him, and he stepped aside to avoid someone with a walking frame.

David finally saw Will at an adjacent cafe, 50 metres away. He was talking to a woman who could only be Juliet.

Neither of them noticed the two men heading straight for them.

David shouted across the crowd.

Part 9

1

'IT IS YOU, THEN,' I SAID. 'WILL SHAKESPEARE. YOU WHO WROTE THE play, *Romeo and Juliet*?'

'But I have not written it yet!' he said. 'And, besides, 'tis to be called *The Maid's Revenge*.'

I was about to say I thought it a dreadful play, but Will was distressed.

'We must go to my friend, David,' he said, 'for the false king LeFay threatens thee with deadly harm.'

'LeFay?' I said, for my mind lingered in that still darkness with Cordelia. I surveyed the crowd.

A voice shouted our names in warning, Will jumped, and I sprang to my feet.

A man in gaudy silks was dancing nearby, spraying a mist into the air from a bottle.

Will picked up a chair. 'Stay'st thou back!'

An American next to me said, 'Hey, steady there! It's only–'

As a second man, dressed also in coloured silk, barged his way through tables towards me. Will threw his chair at the first man and ran at the second, who also held a spray bottle in his blue-gloved hand. From the bottle came a mist of clear water. Will walked into it, throwing his fists around.

The man dropped the bottle and fled with his companion.

'Oh, 'tis a foul humour,' said Will.

Another man ran up and said, 'Will, lie down, get on the ground now!'

Will did more than lie down. He slid to the ground and convulsed like a poisoned dog.

The man, who I later found out was Will's friend David Cortez, snatched a bottle of water from a table and poured the contents over Will's face.

A young woman from the next table approached with napkins. 'What is it? What was that?'

'Don't touch anything,' said David. 'It's a nerve agent. Some kind of glycophosphate. It dissolves in water.'

People withdrew, except the kind woman who knelt down and would not listen to David warning her to stay back.

Her friend, who sat close-by in a wheeled chair, looked aghast at Will's shaking, and said, 'There's an ambulance over there!'

The American tourists were on their feet. 'What? Shall we call 'em over? Hey!' The man gave a loud whistle and wildy beckoned.

The ambulance of which he spoke – a white vehicle with a snub-nose and the words upon it written as if in a mirror – was already gliding towards us over the piazza.

'The ambulance is not here to help,' David shouted. 'Stay away from it.'

Of greater surprise to me was the sight of Monsieur LeBlanc approaching through the gathering crowd. He pushed a woman to one side and raised a gun – this awful thing that Angus had described.

I heard a loud *crack*! and the American woman at my side fell over.

I still held the stones. It was, after all, only moments since I had been in a dreaming world and the shimmer of it was around me still. Whatever was in my heart, or even beyond knowledge of my heart, in that moment was given shape. And this time it was not my father nor my uncle who let loose the arrows.

From nowhere came a dark hissing and LeBlanc was instantly pierced by the bolts of many crossbows. His astonished face was like that of Saint Sebastian in the picture, though, unlike the blessèd martyr, LeBlanc did not die for Christ's sake.

He did sink down and knelt upon the stones, blood spurting

forth from him. He was soon dead, the gun on the ground at his side. People scattered and made a loud cry.

The ambulance now behaved like a mad thing, like a bull with its head down. Its wheels began spinning quickly, causing smoke to spread, then it drove forwards with increasing speed.

I suppose the driver had no other plan than to crush us to death, as the vehicle swerved to avoid the corpse of LeBlanc but crashed through some empty tables, heading straight for us.

Will and David were before me on the ground, along with the woman cradling Will's head.

Everything moved slowly. Perhaps it was the slowness of the knowledge of impending death. The ambulance knocked a short red cyclinder over and a stream of water launched into the air. It flew up but floated like feathers from a burst cushion, so slow had everything become.

And then the ambulance was gone. Entirely gone. But I felt it – and I know others felt it – moving through us like a shadow. We all cried and groaned. But it was gone.

And gone with it were LeBlanc, and I suppose his accomplices, for I never saw them again. Like my father, I had made people disappear.

Then the water rose high, poised, then crashed down on us, but at the usual speed for falling water.

Someone was gabbling, 'The heck. The heck! Where'd it go?! There must be sinkholes. Everyone! Watch your feet!'

'Omigod,' said the American man, on all fours, sputtering. He reached for his wife, but she sat up and brushed him off saying, 'I slipped, is all. Do you have to make such a racket?'

She bore no wound.

Will sat up, wiping water from his face and pushing his hair back. A quietness descended, as if an angel passed by. The sound of splashing water was loud in the curious stillness.

The woman in the wheeled chair was now standing beside it, her arms held out sideways, her face wearing a look of wonder.

David lifted Will up and stared at him. 'Will, are you all right?'

Will stood without need for further help then he straightened up a chair for David. 'Sit'st thou. David! I am well.'

A waiter stood, staring at the sky and clouds. He began to smoke a cigarette and said words as if in prayer, or else conversing with someone unseen.

David slumped in the chair. 'You should be dead, Will. We should be dead.'

The woman, now with the capacity to walk, came to me.

'You did something,' she said. She took my hands and kissed them. 'I felt it.'

Her friend came up to her and said she should sit down, but she would not return to the wheeled chair. Instead she wrapped arms around Will, and surprised him by kissing him.

'I must be sick the more often,' said Will.

David stood and spoke to me, 'I'm David Cortez, I'm Will's friend, I'm with MI3, though it's probably best to say I'm self-employed.' He gestured at the purse I held in my hand. 'You have the Seven Stones?'

'I do,' I answered.

'You should probably not do that again.'

'Do what?'

'Use the stones to call up a storm, or–'

'I will not be dead again,' I said with a little heat. 'I am done with that.' But I recalled Ophelia's words.

Will expostulated. 'But, David, *I* should be dead. And so would *she* and *thee* if she had not used them.'

Will came up to me and said, as if eager to do penance, 'In the Forest of Arden I was given seven stones by a druid princess in distraught. To escape a horde of ravening creatures I wished on the stones and did come into this... *this*,' he waved his arms. 'And I am heartily sorry.'

'You did wish all this?' I said. 'It was *you* made this world, with everything in it?'

'No, it is far too strange. I cannot claim it. Oh, 'tis a clamouring monstrosity, beyond the wit of a thousand men.'

David interrupted us. 'We have to go *now*.'

Two armoured vehicles, with flags like those flown at Malcolm LeFay's chateau drove into the piazza. The curious silence had passed, and people began chanting; *Vive LeFay*. After them came pipers and drummers, leading soldiers dressed in grey and red. The clamour of the world came back.

I felt a chill that nearly went to vanquish the blessing Cordelia had given me. And then I thought of Angus.

'I need a phone,' I said. 'Please, may I have the use of one?'

Police vehicles began to arrive.

'We have to get away from here first,' said David.

'We go to Stratford,' I said.

'Yes,' said David. 'By tomorrow morning.' His frown suggested this seemed to him then like an insurmountable hill.

'It is very far, then,' I said.

'Very far.'

'We can ride in the Blackhawk?' said Will.

'Let's walk and talk,' said David. 'Stay close – I'm going to try and contact Carrie.'

But the phone did not work.

'The Sun stands amazed,' said Will.

And so we disappeared from the piazza where Romeo and I might once have walked, hand upon hand in a glad, different day. But Romeo – dead in a field, or married to Rosaline, or in withered old age – was more than dead to me now. I was glad to leave.

He had used me for his father's wishes. But had I not used him for mine? To give fuel to the spark of my pride?

2

I DO NOT THINK ANY OF US KNEW WHERE WE WENT, NOW CUTTING AT angles through the more modern parts of the city. Will hastily told me all of his adventures – of how he came into England, and at last was befriended by David. He said how they had met Miranda and I expressed I was glad that she lived. He told me how the Unseelie and traitors aligned with Malcolm LeFay had fallen upon them. And how Ophelia had been struck down. Then he spoke of standing close by to Malcolm and Desiree at Mousket and listening to their plotting. His tale would have cured deafness.

David meanwhile seemed to be having a hopeless broken conversation with his friend Carrie Martinez. When the network expired once more (through the fevered Sun), I was impatient to ask him about Angus.

'I'm sorry, I don't know about Angus,' said David. 'He was the one with you on the train from London?'

'Yes. He was at the chateau with us, when I was nearly burned on a fire.'

David suddenly stopped walking. 'That was the smoke? Damn them!' he shouted. 'They tried to burn you!? And you were unharmed?'

'I escaped. Through the use of a stone, Viola's stone did save me, and after that–'

The sound of a whipping in the air made me pause.

'Helicopter,' said David.

We ran and took shelter in a small church. Our gasping breath echoed in the small dark space that was empty of others.

'Angus has been our good friend,' I said. I told David and Will how Angus and I had first met, how he came with us under Cleo's protection to France. How he was compelled to do so by a memory of a different world.

'So, when he was with you,' said David, 'he remembered living in a world that was not this one?'

I told about how Angus should have been living in Glasgow and yet now lived in London, and how he recalled a play titled *Romeo and Juliet*, in which Romeo died for me. And how *this* was the reason I had gone to Mantua, to forbid him.

David looked at Will. 'That's different.'

'What is different?' I asked.

'The play Angus remembered seems to be a different play – different anyway from the one that Will has thought of.'

He explained to me that Will had written sketches for some plays. But that they had never been performed.

'Except now,' I said, letting them know that I understood – if it could be called understanding – that I was a walking shadow, a player in one of Will's stories, quickened by the magic of the stones.

''Tis all my folly,' said Will sorrowfully.

I assured him (after all, he had saved me from the vile mist moments before) that in Angus's world, William Shakespeare was indeed a renowned playwright, with a theatre built for him.

'Oh,' said David, stirred by this information. 'Will, did you hear that? Do you see what this could mean?'

'I do not,' replied Will.

'It means there's a world where you live and write your plays. And they are still performed, years and years later, and *that* world existed until the moment you came here. And, Juliet, you say that Angus remembered that world when–'

'He remembered it when he held the stone. Or when he took my hand.'

'So, thou meanest, then,' said Will, his eyes wide, 'that I have success?'

'In getting back?' said David. 'Yes – I mean it's all potentially there.'

'And I *do* write plays. And with my very own theatre?'

'It is called *The Globe*,' I said. 'In Southwark.'

'I do like it,' said Will. 'A theatre clept *The Globe*!'

'Well, don't get a big head,' said David, briefly looking out of the church door. 'But it also means that if your friend Angus sensed this other world as somehow his true world, then this one – where we stand right now – could change. Change back. I mean, I imagine it will change anyway once Will goes home.'

David's phone pinged.

'The network doth attend,' declared Will.

'But for how long?' said David.

'Please,' I said, 'may I call Angus?'

David handed me a phone. 'Keep it short if you can.'

I put in Angus's number with trembling hands.

He answered immediately. It was not what I expected.

'Who is this?'

'It is Juliet,' I said, not a little deflated.

I thought he might be pleased, but he answered flatly. 'Yep. Aye. Hold on a moment, thanks. I'll need to grab a pen.' I thought I heard Elke speaking, then I heard a door close, and Angus spoke again in a whisper. 'The fuck, Juliet? Where are you?'

'In Mantua. But I went first to the Mantua of my own time. I had to, well, I went to see Romeo.'

'Aye. You mean back in time?'

'Yes.'

'Okay. And how is he then?'

'He died. I did not see it. I found him married to my cousin Rosaline. He did not want me there at all. Less than a week after I was killed, he was already at his wedding.'

'Well, he sounds like a proper dick. I knew it.'

'And I wandered around as a ghost. I was a ghost, Angus. But I'm not a ghost. You've held my hand. And you know I am real, and living, and warm. Angus?'

Angus said nothing.

'Angus. Where are you?'

'Well, I'm in England. I was just suddenly back in London. And until Viola called and said you were fine, but missing in action, I thought you'd actually been burnt alive.'

'She called you?'

I could hear him breathing. 'Aye. She said you'd disappeared with all the stones, though. Well done, by the way.'

'Why *well done*?'

'Viola said Cleo was pissed off at what you did. I suppose I was a bit pissed off as well. Felt a wee bit discarded.'

'Angus, I want to see you.'

'I'd like to see you, too, but…'

Here I walked to a quiet part of the church, leaving Will and David, and sat down.

'You still have the stones?' he said.

'Yes. I have all of them.'

'And I suppose you could use them to get over here?'

'I would come and see you now,' I whispered, 'but I am told I should not use the stones for anything like travelling, because whenever they are used, it seems they make this world the worse. Ophelia said as much, and—'

'Well, she is right,' said Angus. 'Juliet, I'm in a bit o' trouble.'

'What has happened?'

'Everything's seriously fucked up. Again.'

'I am coming back to England,' I said. 'I'm with a man called David Cortez, and with Will Shakespeare.'

'*The fuck*,' said Angus with a squeak. 'William Shakespeare? You're with William Shakespeare? What's he like?'

'He is like a servant boy that knows little of deference.'

'*Deference*?'

'I meant it in a good way.'

'Well, let's leave that for another day. And who's David Cortez?'

'He is a man from something he named MI3.'

'Wow. Does he have an invisible car?'

'No. We have nothing. David hopes to bring us to Stratford. Will you… will you come and see me?'

'In Stratford? Yes, but I dinnae think we should meet, Juliet.'

I was shocked. 'Why not? Angus!'

'Juliet, it's just… It's … You see, after the bonfire, when I found myself like *bumph* in London, *bumph*, I also found… Well you know how I said that I did nae have a girlfriend? Well, it seems like I do have one. Now'

'Oh,' I responded. 'A girlfriend?'

'I'm dating Elke.'

'*Elke?!*'

'Aye. Apparently, we've been on for a month. Except I cannae recall any of it. Well, bits of it. Right now I'm pretending I've had a bit too much weed, and I have to keep changing the subject when she mentions having had sex because I have nae memory of it. I'm hiding in the bathroom sae I can talk.'

'Together a month?' I said, picking on the least upsetting part of what he had said. 'But how did you meet? You only met a few days ago! When you met *me* for the first time!'

'Apparently it was at a street parade several weeks back. She's a member of the Daughters of Morgana Youth League. And loves to go round in the red and grey, with her blonde hair pulled back in a ponytail.'

'That's impossible. Elke has short hair,' I said.

'Once upon a time in yet another fucking different world. We should nae meet, Juliet, because I need to be responsible to Elke. She's my girlfriend after all.'

'No!' I said.

'And she's in the next room in bed.'

'You were in bed with her?'

'Apparently,' said Angus in a strained voice.

'But I want to see you, Angus,' I said. 'I want to see you in Stratford.'

'But we're going back to our own worlds. Isn't that what all the running about was for? It's what we were all going to do? Viola and Cleo. I'm hopefully going to find myself in Glasgow wie my family.' He sighed. 'Except they've brought in martial law here. There are soldiers on the streets and a curfew. So I'm stuck here in London.'

'I want more days with you, Angus.' I said 'I want you to hold me again like you did.'

The phone signal died.

3

I called Angus's name, shook the phone. The network had
succumbed again to the influence of the Sun.

I wondered if I had made a secret wish for Angus to be in
Stratford for it seemed as if the world changed again. A siren
sounded – erupting like a scream from nowhere – and we heard
cars squealing to a stop outside the church. The large flagstones
within the church began to raise at the edge, and roots squirmed
out from the earth beneath. Was I wishing inadvisedly on the
stones, or else was it just fell creatures drawn as they were at
Yarl's Wood?

'' Tis the Unseelie!' cried Will. He and David ran towards me.

'Out the back,' said David.

We found another exit by going into the vestry and took shelter
a few minutes later and two streets further on in a general store.
We stood by the racks of newspapers and magazines.

David tried to make his phone work, and declared he could no
longer raise Carrie Martinez. 'I was hoping for a helicopter, at
least,' he said. 'But I think the Americans are liking the idea of a
LeFay-style UK.'

'Thou meanest?' said Will.

'That we're on our own.' David turned to me, 'And how is
your friend, Angus?'

'He is alive and unhurt,' I said.

'Where?'

'In London, but *his* world has changed again.'

David must have seen something not so buried in my face.

'Don't do anything rash. Please, Juliet.'

I held out the purse in my hand, calmly, though it felt as if an
axe had gone through me, and said, 'Should Will take possession
of these?'

'I do not want them,' said Will firmly.

'No,' said David. 'Not Will. The next person we give them to will be Miranda.'

He bought a satchel from the shopkeeper and told me to put the purse in it. 'Put it round your shoulder, there's a strap that'll keep it tight.'

I did as he said. Though did a mere piece of rough fabric offer any protection? Protection from my desire, as much as from the Unseelie? The stones could sense my yearning – perhaps formed it – and all I needed to do was "fall into the stones" and I would be with Angus. I felt I was walking along a high ledge.

A television hung from the ceiling played the news, though the images seemed to come from behind falling snow. There was no sound, but pictured were Malcolm LeFay and Desiree driving in an open car through the streets of London, with crowds on either side waving flags and bannerets of LeFay.

Will looked at the pictures. 'David? See'st thou? Is it England?'

'Something like it,' he replied, his brow deeply lined. He was looking in his wallet.

'What troubles thee?' said Will.

'Do you see these banknotes?' He held one up. 'A few days ago they showed the faces of Queen Elizabeth, or King Charles, but now, look.'

We stared closely. The image on the banknote was none other than Malcolm LeFay, wearing a regal jacket, with the haughty Desiree in the shadows behind him. David searched his pocket for coins. These too bore the head of LeFay.

'I haven't the vaguest idea how it happens,' said David, 'but if we use the stones, then England gets further away. You went to Mantua, and suddenly LeFay owns a complete set of airships, and has militia groups across Europe. And the Windsors have fled England. You,' he raised helpless hands, 'you saved us from death, but now LeFay is virtually the King.'

'But,' I protested, 'if we do not use the stones, how else do we get to Stratford by tomorrow?'

David looked at the waving flags. 'If we use the stones again, we might get to England and find no druid well in Charlecote.

And perhaps Miranda will no longer be safe where she is hidden. She's the only one among us who knows the right druid spells, if that's the word. Her father is a druid lord. She is waiting for us near Stratford. She can send the stones back to where they belong, and at the same time create a gateway so Will can step back into the day in 1580 where he came from. And you–'

'And I will return to my time.'

I must have looked as if I hated the idea, for Will burst out, 'I'm heartily sorry for the ill that I brought unto thee. I did imagine dreadful things to mark the seasons of thy life. Perhaps you could stay in this world where 'tis safe?'

With his words, Will opened a floodgate.

'Can it happen?' I exclaimed. 'Cordelia said that what I saw in Mantua – what I *did* in Mantua – was but a dream. Perhaps a premonition? And if I do not go back there, then it might not happen. Without me to step into the dream it would be no more than music on a page: unplayed so unheard.'

'But *staying*?' David said. 'I don't think that can happen, Juliet. When Will leaves this world, the rest have to go as well, or else you stop existing in this place.'

'What does that mean?' I asked weakly. 'Do I become a spirit in this world if I remain? Appearing and disappearing and saying odd things to no end?'

And looking in on Angus from a distance. Calling out to him, but never to be heard.

David answered in an anguished voice. 'Miranda said it. She said she read about it in one of the books at the druid hideout. But, I don't know, I don't know. They might be wrong; she might be wrong.'

It seemed as if my path was set, and I must return to Mantua. Those who are taken out to be hanged must feel this way. And I had not even Angus to see my pain.

A dark metallic vehicle with heavy wheels drove past the shop. It bore flags and pennants, showing it to be filled with men loyal to LeFay. But they were too busy blowing vuvuzelas to see us where we stood behind the sliding glass door. Still, we shrank back.

As soon as they passed, the sky darkened, and something struck the window. A black bird with lizard eyes had flown into it. I let out a cry as more birds began to strike the glass. The Unseelies had found us.

'The stones do draw them,' said Will.

'Turn your coats inside out!' I said. Will was quick to do just this.

The door slid open and a couple ran in seeking shelter. Small batlike creatures came in with them. The woman's face was streaked with blood. Viola had once said these demons came only for us; but now many shared in the torment.

Will immediately ran outside, his hands around his head. David and I fled the shop, into a swirling grey fog as David called to Will to stay with us. As we ran down the street, a tree suddenly bent its limbs to snatch at us, but we evaded it. Will in his out-turned coat ran past untouched – the branches seemed to find him not to their taste.

I believed that we had only minutes of life left to us.

We turned down a narrow alleyway between an old church and a new concrete and glass building. Several small men with goat's heads, dressed in leather armour, barred the way, and one immediately ran at us with a spear, its hooves clopping on the cobblestones. David grabbed the spear off it and swung it wide to sweep these grotesques to one side. The bleating was horrific to hear. A crossbow bolt slapped the pavement. David spun round and fired his gun. A mailed creature fell heavily to the ground. But as we ran on to the end, a police car came to a halt in front of us, with its lights flashing. David cast aside his gun. Policemen leapt from the car and began to shout and point at us.

I had the satchel with the stones. Should I make the police car disappear? What was there to lose if I did something that might save us? It would be for Viola, and Flora, and Angus. The air shivered, and I thought: let it come. Let us go from here and be in Stratford, with Angus.

The world became diffuse.

In the building next to me – the walls were floor-to-ceiling glass – I saw a flickering, or a darkening, as if the light within had been eaten up. Standing inside was a woman, very queenly, beautiful but very pale, dressed in green and black. The silk she wore was glossy as a raven's wing. Her look of scorn, quite distinct through the green-blue glass, made me think of Cleo. Had I summoned her? She was the last person I wished for. I put my thoughts to one side.

''Tis her!' said Will gripping my sleeve. 'Morgana!'

'Juliet,' said David, his head shaking, 'maybe now is the time…'

The policemen came towards us, guns drawn and motioning for us to kneel.

I heard running feet on the stones behind and then a figure in black launched between Will and I, straight into a policeman, who flew backwards into the car and lost his gun as he fell.

Viola, for it was she, landed with sure feet and then performed a cartwheel and kicked away the rifle the next policeman was holding. He reached for another weapon inside his jacket, but the holster was empty. Viola held up his gun, as if plucked from the air in a magic trick.

'*Stai cercando questo*?' she said.

I looked back, and the woman in the window had gone. Gone also were the flying creatures, and the sky was brightening.

4

THE DRIVER OF THE POLICE CAR NOW STEPPED OUT AND SAID MILDLY, '*Tutto bene?*'

'*Si, va tutto bene,*' said Viola. 'I see a bar at the end of the street. Why not take your friends, enjoy a drink.'

'*Si, si,*' said the man with growing comprehension. 'Hey! Giovanni!'

'Are we on strike again?' asked the other policeman, rising and dusting himself off.

I looked back down the narrow lane and saw a simple herd of goats milling beside the church. The creatures that had possessed them were gone. With what magic?

Viola wore a backpack and from it pulled out a few last horseshoes and threw them down the lane.

'There, to make sure. Come, we will go in their car,' said Viola; then to the driver, 'Do you mind if we take your car?'

'A car is for driving,' said the officer.

Viola embraced me and gasped. 'Juliet! Where did you go?'

'I went home. I went to Mantua. To the past.'

'To Mantua? Did you find Romeo?'

'I found him, and he did not want me. Not in the least.'

She stroked my cheek. 'I suppose you have the stones?'

I patted the satchel I was wearing. 'I have them here.'

'And have you had news of Angus?'

'We spoke on the phone only minutes ago. He is well, and he is in London. But now he has a girlfriend of several weeks standing that he did not have before.'

A siren sounded.

'It is time to go,' said Viola.

We all climbed into the police car, I in the front seat, Will and David in the back. I was concerned that Viola took the driving seat.

'I am Viola,' she said to Will and David.

'I've seen your picture,' said David.

'And I have seen yours, and Will's.' She handed over a sheet of paper that was resting on the dashboard beneath a spare pistol and a half-eaten apple. The paper had all our photos printed on it, underneath the heading *Terroriste*.

'I am Will Shakespeare,' said Will. ''Twas I brought thee here into this world.'

'Yes,' said Viola, 'I hear you are the *author* of all our troubles. And we, nothing but your idle thoughts.'

'Please do not hit me.'

'I'm David Cortez,' offered David. 'So you know about–'

'What? Know that I am airy nothingness, shaped into this moment; that I am an imagining, even though I have a heart that beats?' She touched her breast then gave her hand to David. 'And is not my hand as warm as yours?'

'I've been running,' said David.

Viola reversed the car and dented the side panel against a bollard. She was dressed in her close-fitting ski suit, and her favourite jacket (turned inside out again), now accompanied by a matching gold patterned scarf that drew the eye.

The car crashed into the wing-mirrors of several cars.

'Why dost thou keep in reverse?' said Will.

'It is a one-way street, and if I reverse, then perhaps I will not stand accused, for the car faces in the right direction still.'

'I will remember it,' said Will.

'You should keep both hands on the wheel,' said David, returning Viola's hand.

We shot out into a main street and miraculously missed a number of passing cars and a small child on a bicycle.

'I'm guessing you have one of the stones, then?' said David to Viola. 'To help you do all this?'

'What?' she said. 'Are you saying I only rescued you with magic?'

'I think you have magic enough,' said David.

'A bucket, make haste,' said Will.

'But where are we going, Viola? If I might ask?'

'The place where the airships keep harbour,' said Viola. 'It is outside Mantua. For we must return to England, yes?'

'That's right,' said David. 'The stones must be at Charlecote Manor tomorrow morning.'

Viola and David seemed to be unsuccessfully avoiding each other's gaze. But I was struck by David's question. How *had* Viola bewitched the policemen? I had taken all seven of the stones at the chateau.

'Viola, is it that you have a stone?'

Viola smiled. 'Tch, Juliet!'

Of course! When I saw her throw the false blue stone away while we stood in the herb garden of the chateau, she had done no such thing!

'You took six of the stones, Juliet, and one that is an innocent pebble painted blue. I retained mine, of course.'

'Is that how you found us?' said David.

'It helped a little,' said Viola. We roared up a ramp and onto a raised road. 'Juliet, after you vanished from the garden, Cleo insisted we go to Paris.'

'Why Paris?' asked David.

'It is the city of love.'

I answered the question. 'They went because Cleo wished to visit the *Musée du Monde Égyptien* that holds her treasures.'

'That is right,' said Viola. 'And we broke into it, in daylight. I confess I did use the power of the stone to open doors and unlock locked display cases. *And* to elude capture.'

'That needs to stop,' said David.

'I understand. Miranda has told me of the dangers.'

'You spoke with Miranda?' asked David.

'I spoke with her. But Cleo has all her finery now. And she did mostly use her queenly powers of persuasion. Which are not inconsiderable. The Director of the *Musée*, poor man, knelt and placed the ring that Marc Antony once gave her back upon her finger. I do not think though he expected her to walk out wearing it, and the necklace, and other treasures of hers–'

'But why?' said David. 'She's getting dressed up in Egyptian bling for what reason?'

'She hath need of no reason,' remarked Will. 'She is the queen.'

'Will, be serious,' said David.

'*You* have not met her,' said Viola. 'She cares for nothing that you hold precious. She wishes to go back to Egypt and embrace her destiny. I think she holds no more ambition for this world. She died in Egypt from the bite of the asp and has no plan to avoid this on her return. But she wants all her triumphs, the signs of her greatness, on her person, so that she can board the sacred boat of her gods, and travel to the afterlife in royal fashion. She woke in this world a beggar. She goes home to become a goddess.'

'Look not at *me*,' said Will.

Viola continued. 'Then Cleo weakened. Her illness from the snake came on with force and she had no Ophelia to aid her. So I was caught in Paris avoiding the gendarmerie, with a sick woman dressed in cloth of gold, still as arrogant and demanding, and I not knowing where *you* were, Juliet.

'But I had Cleo's phone– she had spoken at times with the Lord Ceridwen – and Miranda had found *this* phone's number in his papers. She called and spoke to me, told me about Will and David, and our insubstantial nature, and she relayed a message from you, David, that you had gone to Mantua seeking Juliet–'

'I texted her.'

'And so I took an airship to bring us here. We are now going to that airship. And I am glad that I am meeting you, Will. For I would know…' She paused a moment. 'What, Will, did you contrive in your imagination for my brother?'

'I did conceive,' said Will, 'I did *imagine* that you do find your brother. He does not drown, you are both washed ashore in Illyria, and after some harmless diversion, there is a glad reunion.'

Will spoke no more, for Viola held up her hand. Tears began to pour down her face. She turned on the windscreen wiper.

'That is good news,' I said.

'It is,' said Viola. 'It is very good.'

I was quiet for too long. She took my hand.

'Juliet?'

'I do not know if I have the strength to do everything I must. I would first reject Romeo. But what if we could not resist each other, for that is how it was. And perhaps my father was, in any case, long-planning to kill me to make some wound in the heart of his enemy? Is that beyond him, Will?'

Will shook his head. ''Tis within his compass.'

'And so even if I stepped around my poisoning death, I would not last a day in my father's house.'

'Then,' said David, 'as soon as you return, you immediately flee the house, go undercover somewhere.'

'No,' said Viola. She slowed the car to a halt in the emergency lane and held my gaze. 'You don't go back to Verona. You come instead with me. I will have an extra lifejacket. Sebastian surely now does not need one. He will wash up on a beach with some brag about how he slipped the hand of death. He is my brother after all. But you are my sister. And so let us go, leave this fading world together.'

Except for separation from Angus, it was almost a complete relief.

'And it is allowed?' I said.

No-one spoke.

'I suppose we might hold hands and stay very close,' said Viola. 'Like needles upon a magnet that cling to each other. We will ask Miranda.'

Then she took both my hands in hers. 'Yes?'

'Why does everything have to hurt so much?' I said. 'I will not see Angus again.'

'No,' said Viola. 'But if we succeed then Angus will be returned to his true world. You would wish that for him?'

'Yes,' I said, though everything inside me said No.

A police siren was coming closer. Viola accelerated back into the traffic.

5

Viola brought our vehicle to a stop at a small airport. She *parked* at a steep angle in a ditch, thus jamming closed some of the doors. We climbed from the car through the doors that could open. In a field beyond a low fence sat three large airships with grey and red markings. They seemed all sail and no vessel.

We climbed over the fence and Viola walked purposefully towards the nearest airship.

A set of stairs was built up against the gondola suspended from the sails.

'There are no metal aeroplanes that will fly,' said Viola. 'They say it is because of the intemperate Sun. England has sealed its skies. But the paths of the air are open to an airship owned by Monsieur LeFay. We will fly to Stratford with Pendragon Air.'

'You're going to steal this?' said David.

'It is stolen already,' said Viola with some assurance. 'That wish and the pilot's agreement is in place from yesterday.'

'Okay,' said David, not very convinced. 'Then things will not get worse?'

'I hope not. I will make no new demands of the blue stone.'

Guards dressed in a livery of the House of LeFay stood around the vessel, seemingly unconcerned about us, and in their manner almost lost in a daydream. I had time now to look at the galleon hung beneath the smooth grey sails with windows the shape of lozenges. We climbed the stairs and walked into the passenger area. The sunlight came in through more large windows at the stern.

But I had not time to think around this, for in a semi-circle of cushioned seats within a bay window, Cleo sat like a statue of a queen upon her throne. She wore many jewels, and a dress like leaves of gold, overlain like the feathers of an eagle. She wore a tiara, and earrings. Her face was heavily powdered, like the glaze of an unfinished vase. She was unwell; her mouth was set like one who holds in pain. She did not acknowledge me, and no one spoke to her, so separate from us was she in her finery. From a break in the clouds a shaft of gold sunlight poured into the cabin.

Two blonde air stewards came forward. 'Welcome aboard,' said one, and gestured for us to take a seat close to Cleo. I stood in a different area at the opposite end.

Viola came to me.

'I could have died in that fire,' I said.

'Yes. But she *did* tell me to lend you my stone in case you were in a pinch. She would say, I'm sure, that everything has gone according to *her* plan.'

'Of course she would,' I said. 'Ophelia died following her commands. And I fear that Cordelia died because Cleo spurned her.'

'Really?'

'I cannot be sure. Ophelia said Cleo would have taken Cordelia's stone by force.'

'We have come a long way because of Cleo,' said Viola. 'And, yes, we could all be dead, but not because of her. She rescued us from Yarl's Wood. She did not abandon us. But now she cannot speak. And it is up to us to carry things to their end. Sit with me. They are preparing for this ship to rise. Tell me what happened with Romeo.'

We sat down, she took my hand, and I told her there was nothing in it; that my love for Romeo was but a fetching servant, a play of love, a trinket. I was ashamed of my folly. And the best that I could do for Romeo would be to check him at the start. Send him back to his father, and then there would be no possibility of a visitation by my spirit, bringing death to the whole house of Montague.

'I wish I could stay here in this world,' I said, 'everything that held me to Verona is dust. I wish I could have met Angus in that better world of his. I would have met him as a traveller, not as a fugitive. Viola, are you angry with me for taking the stones?'

She gave a little shrug. 'Hardly. You were brave. You defied the Queen of the Nile. That was something to be seen.'

Ropes fell away from the airship; the engine blades slashed at the calm air.

'We set sail,' said Viola.

'So here is Cleo,' I said. 'But where then is Flora?'

'Come,' said Viola. She led me to a different section of the gondola.

Curled up on one of the bench seats, asleep beneath a blanket, lay Flora, with her hair tossed over her face. I would have spoken, but Viola pressed fingers to her lips

'Shhh, she is sleeping. I have never known such a one for sleep. Not even my brother. I think she is making up for lost nights. She wakes for food, eats and drinks heartily, then sleeps again.'

'She is very changed,' I said, for her face was serene.

'Yes. The only violence I have heard her speak of late was when she said *I could murder that pillow* before plunging her face into it.'

Will, who had been wandering around the cabin, came close and simply stared at Flora.

I turned to Viola. 'What brought about this change in her?'

'I think she has found a purpose,' said Viola. 'She found a way to, shall we say, make friendly with Malcolm LeFay.'

'With LeFay?! To what end?' I said naively.

'To have a child,' said Viola. 'To have a child that might someday claim the throne of Scotland.'

'But she knows,' I protested, 'we cannot stay in this time. How might she step around the death waiting for her? Was she not hurled from battlements? And what of Cleo? She seems close to death. Will she know enough to avoid the bite of the asp?'

'We had to carry her on board when we fled Paris. Her breathing is faint and low. She does not speak. I don't know how we will manage her when we come into Stratford. Perhaps we take extra lifejackets, and Flora and Cleo can both come with us. Cleo might recover and become the Queen of Illyria.'

Viola sat beside David. There was happiness in their glances. Perhaps because we seemed to be safe under the influence of the blue stone, at least for the coming night, they could forget our predicament.

The air stewards asked us to find seats and one gave a speech about the unlikely event of landing on water and demonstrated how a lifejacket was to be fitted. Useful knowledge.

The airship left the earth. I saw the land become like the embroidered coverlet of a bed, and my heart – though it was not in a state for such things – burst with joy.

'Didst ever think,' said Will beside me, pressing his face to the window, 'that we could be like unto eagles and drifting hawks?'

'I did not,' I answered. 'And you did not dream this?'

'I did not. It is beyond *my* dream,' said Will. ''Tis the felicity of man's mind.'

I could see a silver expanse afar, and the voice of the pilot told us that we would presently cross the Ligurian Sea.

Viola came over and asked me for the satchel. She took from her jacket the blue stone and dropped it in the purse with the remaining six.

'I hereby relinquish the stone,' she said.

She bowed her head, prayed, then made the sign of the Cross.

She returned the satchel to me and said, 'There, we have the Seven Stones. And now we rest.'

I placed the satchel on the chair next to me.

The air stewards brought us wine and cheese and roasted nuts, laying them on the low table. I saw that Will held the little packets in his hand and seemed disinclined to eat. Viola meanwhile went to sit with Cleo. I watched her take the queen's hand in hers and bent her head to her face. But Cleo only sat upright, said nothing. Viola then conversed with David about remedies.

For a moment I was reminded of my mother, who often sat in a frozen attitude while physicians walked and talked around her inexplicable frailty.

I said to Will, 'Can you tell me what becomes of my mother?'

I saw the same stricken look in his eyes as when we previously talked.

'I do not know,' he replied. 'I did not even think it. I hardly thought.'

'My father took his revenge on Romeo, even though it was *he* who had me poisoned. Though I did not look but turned and ran. Is there more to this unhappy tale of mine that you can tell me?'

'I had thee kill Rosaline, and then Friar Laurence, and then several guards met with a witty end at thy hand. There was more death,' said Will, 'as I did arrange it. In my thought, after Romeo lies slain, Rosaline's father kills thy uncle, and so back and forth. Not many survive the wedding feast. 'Tis not as many though as die in *John Wick*, but if I had given to the Montagues and Capulets the devices of these times, I could have surpassed even that.'

'And that is the end of the tale?'

'No,' said Will. 'I did make it that thy father embraces holy poverty, and, twice ten years after, he dies a leper at the shrine of St Juliet, grieving what he did to thee.'

I could not speak for moments.

'He does that?' I asked. 'I would not have foreseen that. O, that I must die at his hand to break his heart. Was it an afterthought?'

'I did not think so deep,' said Will sorrowfully. 'I only felt proud to be such a grocer of death, handing it out like sweetmeats when I had my first thoughts on the matter. But when I go back... When I go back, I will write thee differently. From now, I will be not so glib. I will be more stinting of death; or else make the watcher feel it the more. See the heart, not just the play.'

'You don't want to see my heart,' I said.

But as he spoke, I thought about Cordelia and the cavern where her father lay, the cup of water, and the ravens gone. I saw Viola sitting with David. My heart melted. I thought of Ophelia, my 'sister', and even of Cleo, and I felt a strange joy. I wondered what might have been had Will not seized the stones on a stormy day in 1580. I would not be with him, looking as it were from a height across the various parts of my life, much as we had seen the fields below us in the rising airship.

The air stewards now brought us warm food, and I bade Will eat. We travelled and the lights in the gondola came on. The world beyond faded to black, though the sky was marbled as though with streamers of green and violet in the very highest parts.

The network was active again. I tried to call Angus but received no reply. Will fell asleep. Weariness poured through me like a stream of poppy. I had not slept since Lille, and when I lay down on the seat, sleep came instantly.

I dreamt that I had left Verona, successfully abandoned my father's house, and now rode in a small ship to Illyria. And upon a jetty, Viola stood waiting for me. This then was the answer to what might happen if she and I could not travel *together*. Even in the dream I felt a thrill of excitement.

Then a monkey played a small concertina in celebration. The sound of it woke me up.

I sat up gasping, the music still playing. Then the music stopped.

A few hours must have passed and the airship flew on with its interior lights dimmed. Will was asleep. The sky rippled with the light of the sun-flares. The music began again. I could not see Viola or David. I approached Cleo, who was as motionless as before. The music came from her suitcase. I took out her mobile phone and stepped back to my seat.

A message appeared.

    Kindly answer your phone!

It was from Malcolm LeFay.

6

I woke up Will.

'It is Malcolm LeFay,' I told him. 'He is sending messages to Cleo. He is calling her!'

'Pray that I might look? Can'st open it? Send back that he is a faithless, notable coward, a bottle-carrying dotard with a face that would sour milk.'

'Where are Viola and David?'

He looked around and clasped his hands together. 'I think they rest in restless fashion.'

I looked around and surmised that Viola and David had availed themselves of one of the private lounges.

Another message came through.

> We hold Angus McTeague here in Stratford. Return the stones immediately or he dies.

I swore. 'What do I do?'

'Do not wish on the stones,' answered Will.

I groaned. For what if it were our delay and our timidity that had wrought the changes? These stones had brought life to the sick. All I had heard of their use so far indicated escape and freedom.

'O, 'tis easy for me to say!' cried Will. 'But Angus will benefit, will he not? If we come to the end, and I have success in aiding the princess Rian, then he is returned to his world! Did you not say it was his sweetest hope?'

'I did. I did. And so you'd have me do nothing?'

'Perhaps,' said Will, 'we can send some dissembling words to LeFay – make it seem that we are hastening to him; that Cleo simply diverted to Paris to, to purchase fineries for his coronation? And that we will surely bring him the stones at midday tomorrow! Yes?'

'Yes?'

'But, by then, I and thou willst be gone, melted to airy nothing; the stones will be gone; and he will be left holding naught but his own stones.'

The phone in my hand buzzed again. Now it was an incoming call from LeFay.

Spurred by the threat to Angus, I pressed to listen and LeFay's voice gushed out.

'Cleo. At last. It's Malcolm here. We need to talk.'

I said nothing.

'I want those stones back. Now. You have no right to them. The druids come under the laws of England, and therefore, as the King of England…'

His voice was low and furtive. Almost as if he was speaking behind someone's back. This made me bold.

'It is not Cleo. It is I, Juliet.'

There was a pause.

'Put Cleo on, please, my dear. I want to speak with Cleo.'

'But she is resting,'

I had tried one of my father's tricks of calm amusement.

'Wake her!'

'For you, *sir*? I think not. She is the Queen of the Nile. She is not to be woken for an upstart, a faithless coward and a murderer.'

All I could hear then was muffled voices. Will stood looking at me with his hands touching together in prayer. I heard Desiree's voice. LeFay spoke once again.

'We have your friend Angus here upstairs, in a locked room. And we have gathered up others. O, yes! We have–'

I heard him scrabbling around, then he seemed to read aloud:

'We have Daisy and Damian. Deliver those stones to me, or there will be *consequences*! I would wake Cleo now!'

'She does not have the stones. I have them.'

LeFay paused, then said in the steely voice I well remembered:

'Well, if you like, we can take your little friend Angus outside and put him in one of our bonfire baskets, and there won't be much left for you to weep over–'

I didn't need Will's words.

'Would you like it that I do to you right now what I did to your Monsieur LeBlanc? Or shall I transport your wife to one of your bonfires and put her in its cage and let her burn? Shall I conjure it now? Do you wish for that? Because I will do it if you so much as lay a finger on my friends.'

I took up the satchel and removed the purse.

'I will find David,' said Will and he stumbled away, calling back in a parched voice, 'Juliet, there will be a new world, but we must get to Stratford–'

'No,' I said. I made a wish that whatever was the poison in Cleo's weakened frame, it should pass into Desiree. And I heard shouts and cries at the other end of the phone.

Immediately there came a loud *smack* as a bird flew into the window of our gondola. And then a man-faced crow was clinging to the rigging outside. I dropped the purse in fright. Another bird hit the engine. Other winged creatures circled the airship. Another crack and a small batlike thing entered the craft. I still held the phone and heard LeFay shouting.

'No, no, I'll, whatever it is… I'll do what you say, I'll…'

Will was knocking on the doors of the private cabins and calling out, 'Juliet, turn thy coat!'

I twisted myself in a knot putting my coat on backwards. My mind returned to Angus. I knew I could wish for him to be removed from Stratford and to a safe place (in bed with Elke? Anything, anywhere!). Or could I send him beyond worlds, back to his true home? But as I turned to retrieve the purse, I saw Cleo standing there, no longer sick, with the purse in her hand.

'You willed,' she said, 'that my suffering be relieved.' It was clear that she had regained vitality.

Smack went another bird into the window, but Cleo stood her ground.

'Thank you, Juliet, for your words, *The Queen of the Nile is not to be woken for an upstart.*' She spoke in her warm, compelling voice. 'I think we are friends again.'

She said other words about how I was proving my love for her. 'But, Juliet, you need to be bolder still. So that the forces of Morgana and her vassals do indeed not increase because of our actions. See and learn from what I would do in this circumstance.'

I did not grab the stones from her, for who was my enemy?

Cleo now made a wish, and in an instant, time was annihilated.

7

In the space of a breath, it was the morning of the next day. And I stood angrily asking myself why I could not be strong like Cordelia and have resisted Cleo. But such thoughts were the business of the past. For now I stood with Viola in the gardens at Charlecote Manor, she and I somehow wearing yellow lifejackets. And if the world of LeFay had indeed strengthened, we had somehow overleapt it in a breath.

The grounds were familiar. The red-brick buildings of the Manor rose up before me. Cleo stood in her golden robes with her arms raised. Close by, the old fountain in the gardens had been shattered to reveal the ancient druid well. Above the well, a gateway of blue light.

We did not really know in that moment what had happened, or what precisely had gone before. If anything had gone before. But here we were, with Charlecote Manor before us. And though we had stepped into a kind of nightmare – smoke-filled turbulent skies; demons flying thick as crows above us – in that instant it was like waking from a dream.

I recalled, as if it were a memory, the first light of this sudden morning, and the airship falling from the sky, brought down by an air defence system set up around Stratford. I suppose LeFay must have known somehow that Stratford was our destination. One engine had fallen away as I looked – cut by the cable of a barrage balloon – and the silver fabric nearby caught fire. The earth rose up and I put my head on my knees as I was told to by the air steward. We had careened across a field of stubble with the ribs and spars of the airship falling around us. And then all forward motion stopped. Viola and David supported Cleo between them and carried her from the airship, for she was still not strong enough to make long distances.

I recall we slid down inflated pathways to the ground. Flora held me steady as we crossed the smoky field, crying, 'We'll no' fail now, bonnie lassie'. Viola had given her a lifejacket and said to her, if she did not mind a little water, she should come with the two of us.

Will, a servant of his own creation, was carrying Cleo's suitcase and running along behind her.

Did this *happen*? Or was it what *might* have happened?

I recall at the edge of the field, a man with a blue van signalled us with a torch. He drove us away, down a long narrow lane overhung with branches. The sun rose red through blackened skies.

I recall an ancient oak tree in a clearing, hollow, as if it held a room within, and a rough bark door for an entrance; and a woman in a pink puffer coat standing guard saying, 'You're in time. Go down there! Go, quick as you can!'

Smoke drifted through the wood. We stepped into the tree – the resinous aroma filled my nostrils. We descended steps leading to the druid tunnels that weave underneath England. Roadblocks and barriers had been placed around Stratford and Charlecote Manor, but we simply went under them, travelling through low tunnels in little carts drawn by miniature ponies.

In a cavernous chamber beneath Charlecote Manor a man stood by a staircase calling out a measure of time: 'Five minutes and counting…' There were around fifteen other men and women.

A young woman wearing an elegant white gown stepped forward. It was Miranda. She came and held each of our hands and she and Will bowed to each other.

David had somehow taken the purse with the Seven Stones from Cleo and he handed it over to Miranda.

I do not recall much of what was said. Was anything really said in that strange no-time?

But I remember Will saying to Miranda, 'I am ready, but I must carry one of those crystal squares, so as to blast the Unseelies.'

'There will be no need,' said Miranda. 'The battle will be here. Besides, you would likely take off your own head.'

I recall David taking Will aside, holding him by the shoulders, looking in his eyes and speaking words of encouragement. Will kept dashing away tears.

And where was Angus? Was he safe? Would I ever know what happened to him?

Viola told me to put on a lifejacket. She was already wearing the one she had brought from the airship.

'It is just you and I and Flora will need these. Cleo returns to Egypt.'

And the world slowly came clear. But the recollection of what came next is like the voices in the last threads of a dream.

Miranda held the Seven Stones in her hand and a rainbow light began to fill the chamber. She addressed the gathered druids.

'I have told each of you what you must do.'

She held out her hand and seven men and women, plainly dressed, stepped forward and each took a stone.

Miranda then took up some pieces of clear crystal – the weapons that Will seemed to require.

'I will go first,' she said. 'Up the stairs, into the garden. I will free the waters from the fountain; and then I will make a shield of floating crystal. Let me go first, and when the blast is done, you seven must come out.'

She looked at Will and the rest of us, 'Follow the seven, stay close to them. When the door of blue light over the well is seen, walk in. Will, go in first. Wish for where you want to be: though my words to the stones will set things so you need only walk forward. Farewell.' She smiled. 'My foot, my tutor.'

'It's time! Go now!' cried the person at the foot of the stair.

The pain of farewell was so great I was almost thankful we had passed though it before it truly sank in.

David caught at Viola's arm, drew her to him, and kissed her.

Miranda vanished up the steps. The seven druids raced after her. We set in behind them and moved together up the dark stairs.

A loud rumble and a crackling from above gave us pause, but we kept on up a narrow spiral stair that wound through the roots of a tree. Viola gripped my arm and held me close. A tremor shook the stairwell. Above us, daylight flared.

Then we stepped through a door into the gardens at Charlecote Manor.

Perhaps it was here that we re-entered time, and the morning of the Equinox was around us.

Cleo had somehow managed to take the foremost position and she stepped out before us, a sublime smile on her face.

8

Over the garden, protecting us, was a dome of some ethereal substance, conjured by Miranda as she had said. The manor house and the gardens beyond, the dirty sky and brown streaked sunlight, and the Unseelies beating against the glass, were colourless and strange behind it.

Still, the gold of Cleo's gown flashed in the morning light. She took off the cloak she had been wearing and passed it back without looking, as if to a waiting servant; but, of course, there was no servant, and the garment of inestimable value fell to the dirt.

In the centre of the garden, a spring gushed from the ground. Miranda had broken the old fountain that constrained the waters of the well. The Seven Carriers formed a circle around it. As they did, Miranda began to sing. The druids opened the palms of their hands and the stones of their own accord floated in the air and circled towards the well, now a dark eye of water pulsing in the lawn. The seven druids stood back with hands raised. The stones darted away, outwards and around us, flitting like dragonflies here and there.

I was concerned; were they under Miranda's control? For she did not stand with the druids but walked away to stand at the edge of the crystal wall, stretching out her hand. She was only a few steps from a dark fire that had erupted beyond the wall, out of which strange forms leapt, striking at the barrier.

But the Seven Stones knew their work. They drew closer to the water and formed a turning circle over it, guided I suppose by the upraised hands of the druids. As they settled into their turning, a shape of blue light began to form. The way for us from this world.

'Wait on my word!' cried one of the druids.

I saw Desiree on the other side of the barrier, sitting in a wheelchair, shrieking with anger. Malcolm LeFay was jumping around, shouting and pointing his finger and hitting the wall with a garden rake.

From the dark fire beyond our place of safety, a figure rose. It was the woman I had seen briefly in Mantua. The sky darkened with cloud, and the sun became like a moon.

Will cried out, ''Tis Morgana!'

'Will,' said David. 'She can't get in. You're fine.'

But Morgana began to attack the wall. Her hand, holding a red fire, broke through the crystal shield, and whiteish cracks spread outwards. Morgana looked in at Miranda with scorn and hatred, mouthing words. Morgana's hand, now her arm, intruded.

Miranda instantly stepped forward and seized Morgana's hand in hers.

I wanted to cry out, *No, she will take you!* but they stood with hands locked, and neither seemed able to let go of the other.

I realised then Miranda had no plans to leave this world along with the rest of us.

One of the druids shouted, 'Will Shakespeare! Step through!'

Will approached the edge of the blue opening. But as he did the crystal wall shattered and faded like the sparks of a firework. Will was struck in the arm by a crossbow bolt. Crying out, he sprawled into the light of the gateway and vanished. David, shouting Will's name, leapt after him, and was gone also.

An armoured, winged shape flew towards us, but some druids, holding crystal weapons called forth lightning and repelled it.

'Before it closes! The rest of you, go! Viola!' shouted the druids, their arms still raised.

But Cleo stepped towards the portal ahead of us, brushing Flora and Viola aside. She faced us and declared to the gardens, 'At last, Egypt is mine once more.'

I realised she had no intention of simply dying as Viola had believed.

'Viola, Juliet, Flora, come with me. For I would have you attend–'

'Go!' shouted the druids.

'Do not be simple vagabonds in Illyria, but stay close to my bosom, look on the world from my high throne–'

'Go!'

'You will look on emperors and empresses, and the lords of the world as they prostrate themselves before me.'

I was dancing with frustration; but at the same time was shaken by a growing realisation: Will had *gone*, yet we had not faded away. Had Miranda guessed wrongly? Could I remain here after all? And somehow meet Angus?

'We can stay!' I shouted. 'We are yet living.'

But the choice was taken from us. From the corner of my eye, I saw something flash – it came from one of the towers of Charlecote Manor. A *crack* like a bullet sounded. One of the seven druids who held open the gateway was struck and fell backwards. *Crack*. Another druid clutched her leg and hopped away. Their concentration failed.

Cleo did not pass through the portal.

The stones flew together to form a bright blue point, and the opening was gone.

9

I was once again in the shipping container with the odour of rags and paint. The stink said I was not in Verona. But this time the door of my tomb was ajar and, as a breeze stirred and caught hold of it, it swung open. But no light poured in. I pushed the door open further and fell out into darkness.

'Viola?' I called. 'Viola?!'

No one replied.

I was alone.

I found the original path as a grey light touched the trees. Further on I climbed through the gap in the wire mesh fence and stood once more on the lawns of Charlecote Manor. I saw no sign of any of the violence of the previous moments. The grounds were empty. The air was clear of smoke. No creatures, no druids, no King Malcolm, no Desiree, no Morgana LeFay.

And no Viola, or Flora; no Cleo.

I could see the outline of the buildings, but they were unlit and silhouetted against the slight colour of the sky.

The grass was silver-grey with dew. My feet felt the wet and the cold seeping through and I whispered, 'O, God, let it be that I am living flesh, and not a dead spirit somewhere.'

I called out for Ophelia, but she did not come. Perhaps a good sign. A wind rose, the first breath of day. Birds began to call in the hushed air.

I recall how once the sound of the morning lark came to my ears as I lay with Romeo (him eager to steal away); but this time, the birdsong brought no fear or disillusion.

The morning light was stronger now. The oak tree from which we had emerged showed no sign of a door. But the druid well had changed. It was no longer a pretty Empire-style fountain – a saucer filled with lilies supporting a nymph; nor was it lying shattered as I had only moments before seen it. It was now an old carved stone from which a small spring of water gurgled.

An ancient thorn tree arched over it. The tinkling of water embroidered the stillness.

I walked towards the main house and the lightless Education Resource Centre. A grinding sound turned into an approaching car that skirred to a stop in the carpark.

An older man I had never seen before stepped out.

'Juliet Capulet?'

'It is I, sir.'

'We haven't met. I'm Sir Ambrose. I am David Cortez's commanding officer. He sent me to find you.'

'You have seen David?'

'He's somewhere. I don't exactly know where. Tell me, are there others here in the grounds – you know, the *rest* of you?'

'I have seen no one, sir,' I answered. 'But I heard that you were killed?'

'That's for another day. I'm on my way into Stratford, Ms Capulet. You should come with me.'

I hesitated.

'It's either come with me, or Border Force *will* pick you up again. I'm sorry to be so blunt. The world has transformed; but some things never change.'

I climbed into the car and we drove away.

'What is in Stratford, sir?'

'Seatbelt. I am hoping your friends. Angus?'

'Angus!' I exclaimed. 'LeFay threatened to hurt him.'

'And a young woman, Daisy, and another friend, Damian.'

'But they are not harmed? Tell me they are not hurt!'

'I can't say. Information's been scarce, and England was burning a short while ago.'

I was glad Sir Ambrose drove faster than even Viola. I was not able to ask any questions for he had to take a phone call, and the only words then were, 'Yes … go on … go on … understood … God, *really*?'

We came swiftly to the centre of Stratford, and I knew immediately something about the wider world had changed, not just the shape of the druid well. The large sculpture called *Standing Man*, which the bus driver had spoken of with affection, was no longer there. Instead, life-sized bronze statues of people in old-style or else modern costume, stood on the bridge. Players, performers, jugglers, soldiers, kings, and queens. Along the bridge were banners hung from lamp posts. The town seemed now a more festive place.

Sir Ambrose finished his call.

'Where in Stratford are we going, sir?'

His answer surprised me not a little.

'The street is Warwick Court – here it comes. And it's a place called the Mantua Apartments.'

'Mantua?!' I said. 'We go to Mantua?'

'It's just the name of some flats,' he said. 'These flats have been taken over by Malcolm LeFay and his Merry Men and turned into a kind of operations centre. This is where the Sons of Mordred have been holding your friends and others, who they labelled dissidents.'

I saw the smoke even before we turned into the street. Out of one upper window, flames were pouring. A fire engine drove past us with sirens blaring. Sir Ambrose pulled aside to let it pass.

Several police cars and vans were already gathered. Men dressed in black stood holding weapons. I worried they were Border Force.

'They're ours,' said Sir Ambrose. 'Don't worry. You're safe with me.'

'And Angus is within?' I pleaded.

We exited the car and were escorted to one side of the building by a woman named Aisha.

'Sir Ambrose,' she said, 'we're bringing them out now. Better move back for the fire service, sir.'

The policemen brought two figures from the building. The first was Desiree, capable of walking, followed by Malcolm LeFay. They were haggard and dazed, dressed very ordinarily, and they said nothing as they were led to a police car. Malcolm briefly stared at me as they went by.

Aisha looked troubled.

'There's a woman who stayed inside, sir,' she said. 'She's been identified as – it's Estelle, Ms. Peltier, sir.'

'And?' said Sir Ambrose.

'I'm afraid she's gone, sir. Some petrol bombs went off.'

Sir Ambrose stood to one side, his face a shadow.

I understood later that Estelle Peltier was David and Sir Ambrose's former Lady, the Director of MI3, a kind of baroness who had been loyal to Malcolm LeFay, and who perished in the fire rather than give herself up.

'Sir, two other LeFay men have been taken out the back. But there aren't as many in the building as you suggested.'

'Thank you, Aisha. Well, it's better to over-cater than not, yes?' said Sir Ambrose, looking at the heavily armed SWAT team. 'What about the teenagers? I'm looking for two males, one female. Aged about sixteen. Angus, Daisy, Damian.'

Aisha Vani pressed her finger to her ear and listened.

'There's no one else in the building, sir.'

The fire engines were spraying the buildings, and we had to move back.

'Alright, Aisha, get this lot to stand down. Gentlemen, thank you.'

'What has happened?' I asked as the armoured men dispersed.

'Well, the Sons of Mordred *were* here,' said Sir Ambrose. 'I know it. In fact, the whole place was occupied by LeFay loyalists. Angus McTeague was definitely held here.

'But, do you understand, Ms Capulet, when I say that, *all that was in a different world*? They simply aren't here anymore. It *might* be the case that, if I understand things correctly, these friends of yours may not know you, not recognise you. This is going to be a bit like remembering a dream. You've got to fix it in your head when you wake, or it'll be gone forever.'

'Then Angus has returned to Glasgow?'

'To Glasgow?'

'Angus once lived there. That is his true home. Sir, can you help me to go there?'

But Sir Ambrose was looking elsewhere. 'Just a moment, Ms Capulet.'

A man was trying to get out of a newly arrived car and a policeman was telling him to drive on.

'David?' I exclaimed.

David wore a modern suit and shoulder length hair. He wore a golden earring I had not seen before.

'Juliet,' he said, and he seemed overcome.

'Come on, let him through,' said Sir Ambrose.

The policeman stepped back.

The passenger door of the car opened, and Viola stepped out. Together she and David came to me. Viola flung her arms around me.

'You are alive!' said Viola. '*We* are alive. And I have news! Juliet! I have just spoken with Flora. She is in a hospital in Paris.'

'In hospital? She is hurt?'

'No. She is well and sitting with Cleo. Apparently, Cleo fainted at the Egyptian Museum two days ago.' She raised uncomprehending hands. 'She has been in the hospital since; but they have, I hear, cured the snakebite, or the effects of it. She is well, but under guard of the *gendarmerie*.'

'I was in the place where I first came to this world. Close to the Manor. But where were you?' I asked.

'The field where the airship fell from the sky. I found myself there, by the side of the road. As if I were *Petit Ferdinand* fallen out of his glass bottle. But no airship. And then David drove up.

'And Juliet! It was said we could not stay in this world, without ceasing to exist; but here we are! I remember, I think, you guessed it in those last moments.'

Her face saddened and she shook her head. 'And we are here. Here. And not in Illyria.' I had never seen her so sad.

I knew then her dream of being reunited with Sebastian was finished. And I felt we had been cast up on a shore, eyes searching the sea for wreckage, counting our blessings and counting our losses.

David left us to speak with Sir Ambrose. As he walked away, I saw even his manner of walking was different, as if he had spent much time astride horses.

'And what has happened here?' said Viola.

'Angus was in there,' I answered, 'in these buildings, but he is gone.'

'He is then back in his true home?'

'I think thou speak'st right,' said David, approaching again.

'David,' I said, 'is it truly you?'

'It is,' he replied. 'I didn't have time to do anything about the beard. I'm sorry about that.'

He cast his eyes over to the police car where Malcolm and Desiree sat like effigies. Then he gave a long sigh. 'Juliet, it's been one year since I saw thee. A year since I saw that man LeFay over there, and mark how Desiree looks not as she did before?'

'It is still her,' I said.

Sir Ambrose now approached, having given attention to his phone. 'I can report, Ms Capulet, that your friends Daisy and Damian are at their schools. As they should be. And I've found Angus McTeague living in Glasgow.'

'In Glasgow. With his sister, Maggie?' I asked.

'What else about him can you tell me?'

'His father is a detective?'

Sir Ambrose nodded. 'I have an address here.'

'But will Angus know who I am?' I asked. 'Will he remember what has happened? Or will this world seem as vague, now, as his true home once did to him?'

'My feeling,' said David, 'is that he might remember. Anyone who has had contact with the Seven Stones, or been struck by druid crystals recently, maintains a sense of disjunction. But as this world settles into being itself, well, there's a likelihood that everything we did together will fade. Sir Ambrose, can'st thou organise for Juliet to go to Glasgow in the next hour?'

'David, since you saved my life, I'd organise you a holiday in the bloody Bahamas.'

We drove a short way to the main streets of Stratford and parked outside a *taqueria* on Greenhill Street.

'It is so changed!' said David. 'I was walking along this street only three days ago – in 1581 – and I recognise only one or two buildings. That tree yonder is much grown.'

We went in and David ordered burritos and a coffee. Viola ordered a big breakfast and said I must share it with her. David inhaled the aromas of the room and groaned.

'They have not coffee in Stratford in Will's time. The best I could manage was elder tea sweetened with burnt sugar from Cyprus. I spent a year experimenting with ground hazelnuts in hot water.'

When his burrito came, David exclaimed. 'Ah, English food!' After eating, he began to explain what had happened to him.

'I saw you follow after Will,' I said. 'Did you go back into his time?'

'We both did.'

'1580,' I said and for a half moment I missed it deeply.

'And were you a spirit?' said Viola.

'No. I was very flesh and blood. When Will got the crossbow dart in his arm, I leapt, unthinking. But Miranda had set everything up. She *meant* to draw Morgana to her. And she was ready with a very neat plan. Because Morgana LeFay is a *faerie daemon*, it means she can move between realms, but she can't be everywhere at once. So, if she were being gripped in this time, and this world – and Miranda had no intention of letting her go – then she could not be back in 1580 attacking Will or the Princess Rian. So that was the moment Will was to go back. Except he was struck by a bolt and I went with him.

'We did find ourselves in the Forest of Arden, in a dark storm withal. I stumbled onto Will – I actually trod on his hand – but he was not so badly wounded. He had already pulled out the dart and I tied something around his wounds. Then we heard galloping. That was Will's horse, coming back along the path towards us, through the rain.'

'Did you meet another Will Shakespeare?' said Viola.

'No. There was no second Will. It's to do with settled past versus emergent reality and something called the essential standpoint. Or so the druids of that time told me. Anyway, we hurried forward and found Rian, wounded and with a lot of dead faeries and goatish people lying around. I said we'd come from the future and gave her such tokens that eased her mind – one of the crystal squares that I picked up when no one was looking.'

'Your manner of speech has changed,' said Viola.

'Thinkest thou? Anyway, Rian handed the Seven Stones to Will and he set off apace, on small hidden tracks and over the meads. So, there I was. Rian had the square of crystal and knew how to work it and made for us our own sphere of protection. Like that which Miranda crafted for us here, only smaller. A few things came at us, but they were ghostlike, and no longer a danger. Then we came by the common path safe to Charlecote Manor.

'Sir Thomas deLuce, a friend of the druids, was waiting there, and some druids who had survived. And they did what we saw them do here: they made the stones orbit over the spring of water, and the stones vanished. It went very calm. King Derek lasted after that about a half day, powerless without the presence of Morgana, or the stones, and it became Elizabethan England once more.

'The druids did weep when they saw Rian. They said one of their people had had a vision that the Queen Angharad and her consort, and their lords and houses, were all dead; and they thought the girl dead also. Her father, though, did survive, with one or two others. The druids at Charlecote did dress Will's wound and he was given some foul-tasting herbs and recovered within a day or so. I stayed around Stratford for one year.'

'I did not expect to see you again,' said Viola. 'Perhaps I might have acted in a less brazen way.'

'Too late now. You can't send me back,' said David. 'And I have thought of thee long hours since.'

'Why did you stay away for one year?' I asked, 'even though it is but moments to us?'

'The chief druid said they could open a doorway for me to return, if I desired; but it had to be at the well and at the same time of the year: at the equinox, when the stones become *available.* Don't ask. And especially if I wanted to come back earlier than I had left. And I did. I came back three days before any of this began. So, while I was gallivanting with Will across Europe, *I* was also here in England, keeping my head down, and letting everything run on so I didn't overturn the established sequence. I did small things, however, such as saving Sir Ambrose. I got him out of the druid house before the Sons of Mordred hit it with drones.'

'He should be very grateful,' said Viola.

'I think he is. I plan to have much goodness of it. And, so here I am. And the books that Miranda was reading, or her assumptions about your survival, were wrong in one respect.'

'Wrong? In what manner?'

'You are both alive in this world, though the stones – and Will – are gone. Yes? The druids in Arden know a lot more about all of this.

'All that stuff about you and Viola and Cleo and Miranda and Flora having to leave this world, or else you'd melt away? That option, to leave, was not actually available to you; only to Will. And I suppose to me as well. The druids did explain it to me this way: because you came from nothing into the real, if you had passed through the gateway, you would have returned to being abstract ideas somewhere in Will's imagination.'

'Do you mean,' I said, 'that if Viola and I *had* stepped through, we would be no more?'

'That's right. You have shape in this world, but nowhere else.'

I felt an unpleasant chill. 'So, we were fortunate the doorway closed before we could step through.'

'Not fortunate,' said David. 'After rescuing Sir Ambrose, I

made sure he was in hiding in the tower at the Manor with a rifle and telescopic sights from about midnight, so as not to be caught by the time jump that Cleo set off. Sir Ambrose is an expert shot. I told him that the moment he saw Will and myself pass into 1580, he had very few seconds to spare. He fired some rubber rounds and knocked over some of the druids. The stones slipped from their control, and the portal closed before you could go through it into annihilation.'

'You are saying,' said Viola, 'that you came back to *stop us* from going through?'

'I did.'

'To save our lives?'

'Yes. And, well, also, I came back because I didn't like 1580. There's no toilet paper for starters. They didn't get any of my jokes. I could barely stomach the rabbit and pigeon pies. And I will not stand to see bullbaiting for a kingdom. I felt like an outsider – people stared. They wanted to take me to Queen Elizabeth and show me off at the Court. They said she kept a few black children in her entourage for amusement.

'So I spent more time with the druids, because they're outsiders on the whole. I saw Princess Rian crowned at Stonehenge. And I suppose there are more druids now than–'

Viola leant over the table and kissed David before he could say much more.

'And how fares Will?' I asked finally.

'Oh, Will fares very well,' said David. 'He has *started* writing out his plays.'

'And improving on them?' I said.

'Let's hope. And also, I was given the house of John o' the Water by the druids, as a thank you for saving the world, and they did also give me a gift of coin, and from that I paid for Will to spread his wings a little. Paid out his apprenticeship. Helped him get to London. He's doing very well.'

David pointed at the walls of the room. 'In fact, mark this, he has done very well.'

The framed posters on the wall of the *taqueria* were all bills for plays performed in Stratford – and all written by William Shakespeare. When we realised this, we drew close to the posters and read with keen interest.

There were so many of them – *As You Wish, A Midsummer Night's Dream, The Twelfth of Night, Faste and Furious, A Hamlet Somewhere, Macbeth*, and a comedy, *Angus and Juliet*.

11

Glasgow shone in the sunlight as the helicopter came to land, hardly an hour after sitting in the café. Sir Ambrose accompanied me on the journey into the city from the helipad, but after giving me a charged phone, it was, he said, up to me. He said to call him if I had a serious problem, though he planned to shadow me for security reasons. The car let me out at the place where a blue elephant sat on the pavement. The *Ganesh Spices and Grocery Store*.

I walked into the shop and found many people inside – some buying hot food or carrying out boxes of frozen samosas and sacks of lentils. I stood behind an older woman who was being served. She counted out small coins from a purse, paying for the tins and jars that filled a large cardboard box on the counter. A second assistant came up and asked what I needed, and I asked if they knew of Angus McTeague.

The older woman turned to me, 'Angus,' she said, 'he is here with me – he came to carry my groceries. He's a good boy.'

'Mrs Chandra?'

'That's right, dear. Are you looking for him? He's over in the aisle by the spices.'

I stepped around some customers and found Angus standing by himself.

'There is a camera on the saffron,' I said.

'I was puttin' it back,' he replied, dropping a packet. Then he looked at me as if he *might* know me.

'Angus, say that you know who I am.'

'Juliet? That's sae weird,' he said. 'You, you were in my dream last night, and here you are. In the dream we talked about saffron, that's freaky; and you're from Verona. Hang on, what am I saying?'

'Do you remember when we first met – in England?' I said.

'And when you took my hand, you remembered things about Glasgow, and this shop with the tripping hazard out the front.'

'Something like that was in the dream as well. Holy fuck. You know, I came here to pinch the saffron, because I had this mad idea that if I stole it and got shopped, then it would put me on a path tae my real life.'

'If you took my hand now, you might then remember everything we did?'

I reached out and took Angus's hand.

'This is nice o' you,' said Angus uncertainly. I think he might have said something else equally stupid, but then his eyes changed and took on a deep clarity and he looked at me, as if seeing me for the first time – which is how you would always wish it to be – but also knowing it was me.

'Juliet,' he said, as tenderly as when we kissed in the city of Lille. 'I remember now. That's right! And it's mad! We did lots o' things together and, and I love you, Juliet, and we got through, an' this is my home, and you're here! And you know, I was pissed off because you had a boyfriend.'

I said quickly, 'I don't have a boyfriend anymore – or even a fiancé.'

'Well, let's no' get carried away.'

I kissed him.

'Does that help to make it clearer?'

'Try again.'

A young girl came into the aisle.

'Angus, what are you up to? Ooo, kissing.'

'Shut-up, Maggie,' said Angus. 'This is my friend, Juliet.'

'Ooo. *Angus and Juliet*?' said the girl. 'Like the play!'

Epilogue

DAVID AND VIOLA MARRIED IN THE SUMMER. THEY HAVE BECOME my guardians and we live now in the house named 'John of the Waters'.

I attend the nearby druid school in Stratford, majoring in English, and my favourite writer is Angel Hemingway.

Daisy remembered meeting me at Charlecote, but her boyfriend Damian could recall nothing of it, or of Angus; though once we all met up, Angus and Damian became good friends through a shared interest in Joy Division. I had to get used to calling Elke by her name Sonya. Now that she is home in Austria, we write to each other. She has a vague memory of liking Angus and says I made a good choice.

Flora and her baby Fyfe live with us also in Stratford after some time spent in France. The baby bears more than a passing resemblance to Malcolm LeFay.

Malcolm LeFay and Desiree returned to the chateau in Mousket and have made no more claims to the throne.

Cleo, freed from French custody by Sir Ambrose, moved into a penthouse in London, a gift from another new admirer, but then fled to New York with many of the ancient treasures she had stolen from the *Musée du Monde Égyptien*. The matter is in the courts, but one does not hear about it due to suppression orders.

A few weeks after the events I have written down, David drove Viola and me to a house in York. There, accompanied by Sir Ambrose, we met Miranda, Cordelia, and Ophelia. But I am not allowed to say much about this. Perhaps Cordelia's tale will be told.

The Comedie of Angus and Juliet – an early play that Will must have written for me as a kind of apology for his first attempt – is fine as far as it goes. In it, Juliet of Verona meets a traveller from Scotland, falls in love, and goes to live in England where they have many humorous misadventures. But I could never read it or watch to the end. I am happy to be living it: certainly happier in this than in the very first version that gave birth to me.

Angus is a little awestruck that *The Comedie of Angus and Juliet* – a play from 400 years ago – is about him as well as me, and that he inspired a play by *William Fucking Shakespeare*.

I have also seen Will's *Romeo and Juliet* – the play that Angus remembers. It was only discovered a few short years ago and some doubt its authenticity. Angus and I went to see it at The Globe in Southwark. I prefer this dark, tragic *Romeo and Juliet* to the light-hearted *Angus and Juliet*. For even though it gives me nothing to live for, except love and a sense of bleak and tragic immortality, I make my own choices from a pure heart and have most of the good lines.

About the Author

Gordon Thompson is a writer, publisher, artist, and musician. He is also the author of *Scheherazade and the Amber Necklace*.

'Gordon Thompson has a lovely control of language and an eye for description, with the writing and atmosphere reminiscent of ... *The Neverending Story*.'

The Age / Sydney Morning Herald

Gordon is the founding publisher of the independent Clouds of Magellan Press, supporting many emerging writers since 2005.

Acknowledgements

Our revels now are ended.

A very big thankyou to Ashley Sievwright – we co-wrote an early iteration of the 'William Shakespeare Extended Universe'.

Thanks to Petrina Barson, Helen Bell, Colin Batrouney, and Matija Sraj, who provided generous feedback on various drafts.

Thanks to Narrelle Harris for brilliant editorial – my lines now move trippingly; and to Lindy Cameron, Publisher at Clan Destine Press.

www.ingramcontent.com/pod-product-compliance
Lightning Source LLC
Chambersburg PA
CBHW021041310726
48969CB00006B/1753